The Minotaur's Maze

THE WORLD BELOW BOOK TWO

VIVIENNE LEE FRASER

For Sam and Jim who allow me time to escape into my fantasy worlds.

CHAPTER 1

The Morning After the Night Before

E arly morning sun casts a giant shadow over the common of the ancient oak resting at its centre. It is a brother to the two magnificent specimens that wizards encouraged to entwine their limbs to frame the entrance to the council chambers millennia ago. The tree sings his song to me as I shelter under his branches, waiting for Eleanora to appear.

I will his song to soothe me, but I remain agitated. I could lie to myself. Tell myself that my unease is because this is my last chance to escape back to my bed beside the fire in the World Above. Honesty forces me to admit that is only part of it.

Unease creeps through my bones because of this place and the memories it brings of a time in my life of great misery and change. No, I will not go there. Better to focus on the present. Better to work out how to avoid joining Snake and that blasted elf in their foolish quest to save their parents from being banished.

If only they'd had the skill to sidestep Bernais's machi-

1

nations last night. If only they allowed their parents to go through the judgement process, all would have been well.

No, I am lying to myself again. All would have been well for the elf's parents. Their connections would ensure that. Snake's mother, however, being only a gnome, and with Bernais intent on her downfall… who can say what will happen to her.

I pace a little under the arms of my friend the tree, and I only stop when two council members enter the great hall. It is almost time. I take a steadying breath. Ginth fo Drefin, Snake's mother, is still in captivity, albeit in the castle under guard. Through no fault of her own, she is caught up in some political scheme beyond my understanding. If I can do anything to help her, I should just do it and stop dithering.

I release a frustrated sigh. That elf, Priscilla, is so very ill-equipped to help her parents. They kept who she was from her, so she really has no idea how to even be an elf, let alone how to live in a magical realm. I should not hold who she is against her. I should be the better creature and support her more.

My resolve wavers as I catch Bernais, one of the Queen's cousins, and his cronies entering the common area through one of the surrounding archways. There is something of his father about him, and it sends shafts of fear to the very pit of my stomach. Once I had not believed him to be as evil and bitter as his father, but the events of the last few days have caused me to change my mind—the acorn has not fallen far from the tree.

'Ah, there you are, Percival. Shall we go in?'

Eleanora's voice comes from behind me, and I wait until she and her sister, Eugenia, join me before saying my hellos. Elias Crown is with them, as are two wizards I have not met before. I can only assume they are the rest of witchkind's representatives on the Great Council.

I suspect this group spent last night plotting and scheming for some particular outcome today. It is, after all, what the greater creatures do whether they are forced into it like this group, or by choice like Bernais and his followers.

Elias smiles at my greeting. 'Are you ready to do this, Percival? The Queen will consider it a great service, and—'

'Yes, I am ready,' I say, cutting him short. I do not want him to voice what such a debt of gratitude may mean for me, or what I may or may not request from the Queen for helping out. I have a nice life now, and I am no longer sure I am ready to start down that path again.

Besides, that is not why I will help the two children from the World Above. I will help them because I should, and also because Bernais is up to something. He may call himself Crown, but he is a Baarenson through and through. And, like his father, his plans will no doubt end up causing harm to others, and I will do everything in my power to prevent that from happening.

As if summoned by my thoughts, Bernais walks close by as he enters the hall. I am positive this is so we will overhear his words.

'This charade of Elias ruling our kind stops here and now, and I will return to my rightful place at the Queen's side.'

'She must name you heir soon. I am surprised she hasn't already,' a superior-looking elf turns to say.

They are too far away from me to make out Bernais's response, but from the corner of my eye, I catch Elias stiffen.

With all thoughts of my warm bed at home driven

from my mind, I wonder why the Queen does not just attend the Seelie Court and put an end to this infighting.

As I walk beside Eleanora into the chambers, I straighten my shoulders, determined to thwart Bernais's schemes at any cost. The song of my friend the oak follows me in, strengthening my resolve.

···✦···

The gentle press of his lips on mine melts my legs, and I lean my body against his as I reach up to twine my fingers through his hair. My heart beats a tempo in time with his, and he draws me closer as he murmurs, 'Pris.' His voice is deep with longing. I part my lips and…

Crash!

The covers fall to the ground as I sit bolt upright in bed, staring at the open door bouncing against the wall.

'Oops. Ever so sorry, Your Highness.' A young girl—a gnome, judging by the rounding of her ears—colours a deep shade of crimson as she makes her way across the room and places a tray on the table by the window.

'No worries,' I say. 'I was awake anyway.'

My hope that the small lie will make the girl more comfortable as well as cover my own embarrassment at having been woken from such a dream fall on deaf ears. She mumbles something unintelligible and rushes from the room, slamming the door behind her as she leaves.

'Good one, Pris,' I mumble. 'How to make friends and influence people.'

I reach my arms above my head and stretch, a yawn escaping my lips, then rub the sleep from my eyes. It is hard to believe only a little over a week ago, all I had to worry about was how to fill the time between finishing my A-Levels and starting university. In the short time since then, my parents were kidnapped and I had been persuaded by a guy who thought he was a gnome to go on a wild goose chase to rescue them—only to find he really is a gnome, and I am an elf; and not just any old elf, but a goddamn elven princess.

Now I am in a magical world, about to go on some sort of quest, and the only person I have spoken to rushed from my room like a banshee was chasing her. Hold on, are banshees even real? I should ask Snake.

At the mention of Snake, my thoughts rush back to the dream, and my heart starts to race all over again. Unfortunately, the dance at the World Below's Midnight Ball had not gone quite like the scene in my head.

Most of the night had been spent watching our parent's trial, falling into a trap set by one of my newly found cousins, and ended with us committing to a quest to ensure our parents' freedom. Hardly the perfect build up to a romantic kiss.

Only after all of that had we danced. And Snake had indeed lowered his head as if to kiss me—something I would have more than welcomed—only to stop when he became aware people were staring at us.

If the covers had still been on the bed, I would have thrown them off in agitation. All right, people were watching us, but he knows I do not hold with the stupid notion that creature races should not intermingle. If Snake cared for me even a little, he wouldn't worry so much about it either.

I wander across the room to pour some tea. Catching sight of myself in the mirror, I do a double-take. My white corkscrew hair is a fright, making a fizzy halo around my head, which manages to accentuate my now pointed ears

—just one of the changes my body underwent when I entered the portal into the World Below last night.

Frowning, I spend a moment trying to calm my hair, then give up in disgust before really studying the strange reflection staring back at me. It's a little alien, but I guess it is still me. I mean, I don't think I'll ever get used to seeing my hair white instead of its usual brownish black. Although my blue eyes are a little more almond shaped, they're definitely mine. And my skin is still its normal light brown.

Mmm, that was something else that bothered me last night. Dad and I were the only elves in the room with dark skin, which made us both stand out in the crowd. I'm used to being in a minority because of my colour, but there's something more to it than that, I'm sure. What's more, I suspect that something is why people won't tell me about my family history.

When I ask questions, they act cagey. At best, they'd tell me it's something for my parents to explain. It is more than frustrating and means I still know very little about where I fit in down here.

I shake my head and move to the table and pour myself a cup of tea. There are so many questions my parents need to answer, I barely know where to begin. Then again, they can't say much while they are locked up, accused of profiting from their work in the World Above.

So, I guess finding out who I am and why they kept our magical origins from me will have to wait. In the meantime, I need to concentrate on figuring out why that elf Bernais was so intent on railroading Snake and me into going on a fantastical quest—the first one to be undertaken in hundreds of years.

He wants me and Snake out of the way for some reason, I'm sure of that. I wish I knew why. And I don't trust him to wait for us to return before he makes another move against my parents or Snake's mother. If I want them to be safe, this quest needs to be wrapped up in a few days, giving him little time to plot anything new.

I take a sip of tea and glance towards my backpack sitting by the door. Should I get dressed? Will my clothes even fit me? When I walked through the portal, I didn't just get pointy ears, I grew about half a foot. Fortunately, my dress grew with me or that would have been embarrassing. But what about my other clothes?

An unknown someone had placed the pack in the carriage as we left the ball last night. I was so excited to be riding in a horse-drawn carriage and then to arrive at a gnome house, I had not even checked the contents.

Because it was late, I hadn't been able to see much of the World Below last night, but now…. I spring to my feet and fling the window open. I'm instantly disappointed. This is one time when expectation does not meet reality. My window opens onto a walled garden that can be found in almost any English village.

Sighing my disappointment, I sit back down and content myself with an in-depth study of my room. By candlelight last night, it was all shadows. Perhaps in daylight I will find something different in the magical realm. The bedding and furniture are all made of wood and natural fibres, but they look and feel very little different from anything in the World Above. My study of the bedding is interrupted by a knock at the door.

'Come in,' I say before looking down at the ankle-length embroidered white cotton nightgown left on my bed last night, wondering if it was the done thing to invite people in when still in my nightclothes.

All worry about my attire disappears as a familiar figure enters the room. I jump from my chair and rush over to Snake's aunt. 'Glisth, I am so happy to see you again,' I say as she envelopes me in a one-armed hug.

'And I you, my dear Princess.'

I slip from her embrace, a little embarrassed by the intimacy, as we had only met the day before.

'Glisth, please, I have already asked that you call me Pris.'

The gnome nods almost shyly. 'As you wish, Pr… Pris. I hope you slept well.'

Smiling, I respond, 'Like a log. I was just about to get dressed, but I'm not sure….' I gesture to my pack.

'My visit is timely, then. I have brought you some clothing.' She holds out one of her arms which is draped in cloth.

I make no move to take the clothing. 'I have my clothes here, and I think I would feel better in my own things.'

Glisth places the clothes on the bed before returning to the hallway to retrieve a pair of boots.

'I know, but where you are going, anything not of this world may not be admitted.'

'What would happen if I wore my own things? I won't find myself naked, will I?' I laugh at the thought.

Glisth frowns as if actually considering this as a possibility. 'Well, I am not quite sure, I must say. I think… um….'

She is saved from providing an answer by a girl entering with a bowl of warm water and towels. Glisth uses the interruption as an opportunity to place the boots by the bed and change the subject. 'I am sorry there is no time to visit the baths.' She waits until the girl leaves before adding, 'I will wait outside while you wash and dress. Then I will take you down to meet the family.'

The water is a perfect temperature, and I let out a sigh as I scoop up the warm water and splash my face. After washing the sleep from my eyes and taking a quick bowl bath, I pull on the fine cotton underthings. Why had I ever thought man-made fibres were so luxurious?

I hold up the green, almost black, moleskin trousers and laugh. Surely they can't mean me to wear these. A twelve-year-old would have trouble fitting into them. Still, they must mean them for me.

I sit on the bed and try to force a foot down one leg. The material is slightly stretchy, and they behave more like leggings than trousers, and they expand to fit—perfectly. I stare down in wonder. Is that a result of the material, or is the clothing here magical?

The knee-length black leather boots I pull on over top are also a perfect fit, reinforcing my theory about magical clothing. The boots would be quite stylish except that there is no dainty heel. The soles are flat and ridged, suitable for walking long distances, but not for setting off an outfit.

Finally, I pull on a loose white linen shirt before taming my hair into a plait, using the linen ribbon provided to tie the end. Washed and dressed, I am ready to face anything.

Glisth nods approvingly as I enter the hall before turning on her heel and leading the way through a maze of corridors. The house's internal walls appear to be made from a whole tree, and I resist the urge to reach out and feel if it is real.

Finally, we emerge onto a landing encircling a large room. I can see at least three other entrances at our level as well as a beautiful carved wooden staircase circling down to the living area below.

My eyes are drawn to the roaring fire surrounded by an array of armchairs and couches, but a quick scan of the area below also reveals the largest wooden table I have ever seen. As someone is already seated there, I am pretty sure I will be denied a relaxing breakfast by the flames.

As we descend, Glisth explains the dwelling houses of the extended Fieth family. She tells me that each branch has their own quarters for relaxing and sleeping. However, in a gnomen dwelling, mealtime is generally a communal affair, and this room is where everyone congregates to eat.

'Most of the family broke their fast an hour or so ago and are gone about their business. We thought it best to let you sleep so as not to overwhelm you with their questions,' Glisth says with a chuckle. 'They can be a bit much when they are all together.'

Sitting at the head of the table is a male who, if he was human, would be about sixty or seventy years old. He is definitely related to Glisth's husband, Earth, as he has the same round face and bright eyes. There the resemblance stops. His eyes hold merriment, and there is no sign of welcome as gaze meets mine.

'Good morning,' I say in my politest voice. 'I'm—'

My words are drowned out when a woman around the same age as the man bustles through a swing door, carrying two plates piled high with bacon, eggs, sausages, mushrooms, and tomatoes.

I don't realise I am hungry until the smell of food wafts by. My stomach grumbles. Loudly.

'Excuse me,' I say, colouring a little in embarrassment.

'You should never apologise for a healthy appetite, my dear,' the older woman says, indicating a chair at the table. 'Come. Sit. Eat. I will get some coffee. I understand my grandson prefers it with his breakfast.' The woman heads back into what I suspect is the kitchen.

As she disappears behind the swing door, I shuffle awkwardly towards the table, conscious of the scrutiny of the man seated at the table.

'Come on, then, lass. Let's be having yeh. Don't let the

food go cold or Chríona will not be pleased. Where is that boy?' His voice is gruff, but not unkind.

I pull out a chair as Glisth says, 'Fieth, may I introduce you to Princess Priscilla Crown. Pris, this is Fieth, the head of our clan.'

'I am pleased to meet you, sir. And, please, call me Pris.'

The man guffaws in response. Not quite what I was expecting.

The door behind me bangs, followed by an admonishing voice. 'Fieth, do not be so rude, staring at our guest like that. It is not like elven royalty are strangers to our home. Leave the girl alone and let her eat.'

She pats me on the arm. 'Don't mind him. He is not at his best in the mornings. I am Máthair Chríona, but you can call me Chríona. Everyone does.'

The woman, who must be Snake's grandmother, pours coffee for everyone before sitting down and saying something quietly to Glisth. Under instructions to leave his guest alone, Fieth joins their conversation, allowing me to enjoy my meal.

Although the food is amazing, I am so tense, I can't force much of it down. Finally, I admit defeat and take a mouthful of coffee before asking, 'Where are Earth and Snake this morning?'

'That young lad is still in bed. No doubt my son will bring him along soon. Earth is due at the council any time now, so I expect he is getting ready.'

'The council?' I repeated.

'Yes, the council are meeting this morning to finalise plans for your little adventure.' Fieth smirks.

My appetite disappears completely at the reminder that this is not some pleasant visit to the Fieth house, but simply a night's stay before Snake and I must undertake some sort of epic, and very probably life threatening, quest to free our parents.

..·ᴗ.··

'Come on, young Sneak Thief. My father awaits us downstairs, and I must head away to the final council meeting soon.'

It takes me a moment to realise Uncle Earth is speaking to me. I'm not accustomed to anyone but my mother calling me by my secret name, but we're in the family stronghold, so of course they would not call me Snake.

'You go on. I'll be ready soon,' I say as I finish making my bed.

I slept last night in the room given to me as a baby before we left the World Below. Someone at least updated the decor to be age-appropriate. The centre of the room is taken up with a double-sized four-poster bed, yet there is still room for a couple of chairs around the fire, a desk in one corner, and a heavy oak wardrobe in the other.

In between the fire and the desk is a window, and I stare out it now while I finish doing up the buttons of a dark green linen shirt. The street below would not be out of place in a Jane Austen novel. The English village scene, however quaint, is a reminder that I know so little about my family home—I'm as much a stranger here as Pris.

There is a brief knock at the door, and my father enters. A young boy follows him in. The boy is wide-eyed and can't take his eyes off me. I smile, but the boy ducks behind my father before daring to peek out again. Behind him, Earth moves into the doorway and taps his foot impatiently.

'See, I told you your cousin was here.' Agret, my father, ruffles the boy's hair. 'Go say hello. He won't bite.'

'You are the son of the Oidhre?' the boy squeaks, not moving an inch from his hiding place.

'What?' The word escapes before I can stop it.

'Oidhre—the heir,' Agret explains.

My mind whirrs. 'I... I thought as grandfather's brother, Earth would be….'

'When my father leaves this land, which I do not believe will be any time soon, as his eldest son I shall be The Fieth. He named me his successor at a family gathering last month.'

'But…. What…?' My mind freezes, unable to process this news. What will that mean for Mum? And for me? Will we be able to return aboveground once dad is outed as heir?

My father places a hand on my shoulder. 'It has not been formalised yet because I am still under censure, so no one outside the family knows.'

I turn to stare out the window, mulling things over. Will my father ever rejoin Mum and me in the World Above? Just when I'm getting over his having abandoned us in the first place, will we lose him again? 'So, this means you won't come back with us to the World Above?'

There are footsteps as my father follows me. 'Your grandfather is still young, and none of the details are set in stone.'

Still, I don't move because another thought has crept into my head. Dad is the heir because he is the oldest son. I am my father's only son, so is there an expectation that someday I will become the head of our family?

As if my father senses the change in my thoughts, he

leans in closer and whispers, 'As I said, nothing is set in stone, and there is plenty of time to worry about the future later.' So the rest of the room can hear, he says, 'Come, it is time for you to pay your respects to the head of our clan. He is waiting.'

I nod and turn in time to see Earth leave, taking the awestruck cousin with him. Agret waits while I tuck the shirt into black moleskin trousers and pull on the black leather boots someone left by the bed. They, like the clothes, are a perfect fit.

I am in no hurry to meet the rest of the family. Knowing how uneasy Mum felt in their company makes me wary. Still, I can't put it off any longer. Following my father through what appear to be corridors made from the trunk of a tree, I smile as I realise all those traditional English cottages I saw through the window were likely built around a tree like this one.

I keep an eye out for Pris. I know she stayed in Earth's dwelling last night, but I had thought she would meet me for breakfast.

A smile pulls at my mouth when I remember how beautiful she was, dressed for the Midnight Ball. So beautiful that she sent my senses into a frenzy. So beautiful that as I had bent my head to kiss her, I'd almost forgotten who was watching us.

I might have had a memory lapse, but the disapproving gazes focussed on us reminded me that most of the creature races in the World Below don't allow mixed relationships. So, while Pris might be okay with us being together, there are many here who are not. I had drawn back at the last minute, aware that, at the very least, we should not flaunt our attachment.

'Snake, are you all right?'

Dad's voice brings me out of my reverie.

'What?'

'For a moment there, you looked all… well, all gooey-eyed.'

'I didn't,' I reply, automatically defending myself. 'I was just thinking.' My relationship with my father is still too new for me to share my feelings about Pris. For a starter, I have no idea if he would approve.

Seconds later we arrive at the central family room, and my heart races. I remember this. But surely I can't really. I was only three when we left. My eyes fix on Pris, who is picking at the food on her plate and looking decidedly uneasy.

She glances up, and her eyes meet mine. There is uncertainty there, but also defiance, and—is that worry? Is all that directed at me?

Okay. We haven't had a chance to talk since last night. So we haven't spoken about the almost kiss, or the fact that Bernais's cronies were watching us like hawks. Which means I haven't explained that I hadn't wanted to make our situation worse by such a public declaration of our friendship—especially when I had no idea how the laws currently stand on mixed race liaisons. Hell—I don't even know how my family would feel about it.

When we reach the bottom of the stairs, I move to sit beside Pris, but my father places his hands firmly on the chair back. I am left standing awkwardly by the table. The move does not go unnoticed by the older woman sitting beside my aunt, Earth's wife—Glisth. I get the impression that maybe my grandparents are amongst those who would not appreciate a close friendship between a gnome and an elf.

My father formally introduces me. 'Fieth, Chríona, may I present my son, your grandson, Snake Fieth—Sneak Thief.'

There is silence for a moment, and my stomach clenches into a knot. Finally, my grandmother stands up and rushes towards me.

'Welcome home, youngling. It has been too long.' She pulls me into a hug. I hide my embarrassment at being embraced by a stranger by bending down to allow her to better wrap her arms around me.

When my grandmother finally lets go, she stares up at me almost as if she can't believe I am here as tears trail down her cheeks.

'You have grown into a fine gnome, as I knew you would. You do your mother credit. Although it is grand to see you, you should have returned to us way before now.'

She turns to her son and opens her mouth as if to say something. Agret starts to speak, but the old man at the end of the table holds up his hand.

'We know, son. You had a disagreement with the lad's mother, one you should have sorted out years ago, but they were always welcome here. You could have made yourself scarce while they visited.'

'Ginth never felt right about…'

'We know,' Chriona said. 'She lived with us, grew up with you all, and she always thought your love story was trite: the wealthy son falling for the ward. She never could believe it was real.'

Chriona's gnarled fingers clasp mine. 'Your mother was not a child of my body, but Ginth is a child of my heart. It was I who discovered her talent for finding lost things, and I who trained her and gave her a family name.' She lets go of my hand, pulls out a handkerchief, and dabs at the tears on her cheeks. 'I do so miss my girl.'

My father looks at his feet, shuffles a little, and sits before gratefully accepting the coffee cup Glisth pushes his way. The words he speaks next are flat and lifeless.

'I did not treat her well, Chríona. I was young and foolish. I never saw her as a person, only as my love and my wife. I never made her feel valued for who she is.'

This is the second time my father has admitted his responsibility for the split in our family, and it's one of the reasons why I let him back into my life years after he deserted Mum and me.

'Yes, there is much for you to atone for, Agret. And now, because of something you caught us all up in, she is suffering again. She is being held prisoner, and your son must go on a quest to free her.' My grandmother shakes her head. 'Here, Snake, sit down. Eat before it gets cold.'

As I sit, Pris turns to look at my father. 'What does Chríona mean? Were our parents… are we about to go on this stupid quest because of something you are caught up in?' she demands.

My father stares into his coffee cup.

'Why didn't you say something when we met with you in Mawnan, or even last night?' Pris presses him.

'Ah… um….' My father cannot seem to find the words to answer.

'What is going on is that the men of this family are a part of something. Political business, Chríona means,' my grandfather starts to explain.

My father sits taller in his chair. 'No, Father, let me. Snake has a right to hear it from *his* father.'

I pick at the eggs and toast in front of me, waiting for Dad to explain.

'For a long time, our family has been friends with Elias Crown, especially my uncle, Drow. Since my return to the World Below, I have been working for Elias. Not just to get this spurious sentence commuted, but also because something odd was going on at the palace. The Queen was worried, and he felt our family's particular skills might be useful.'

Why is my father working with the Queen's people?

'What is going on with the Queen?' Pris demands before I can gather my thoughts into a question.

Agret doesn't respond. The silence lengthens, and I realise this is a good time to add my piece. I raise my head and ask, 'I thought Grandfather was the Queen's right-hand man? Why did Elias need you in the castle?'

Did my father's eyes just widen? Is he impressed I know this much about our family alliance with the crown?

Fieth's hand crashes down on the table, causing the dishes to clatter. I twist in my seat and find obsidian eyes glaring at me. 'We do not speak of palace business out here where anyone can scry our conversation.'

While my mind contemplates the possibility of someone spying on us in the family home, Pris clenches her fists.

'If you didn't want us to know about any of this, why did you bring it up?' Her words are clipped, a tell-tale sign she is reining in her anger.

The Fieth half stands and leans his own fists on the table, making an imposing figure. 'Being of royal blood will buy you much, but it does not allow you to question me in my own house. I said it has to do with why Snake is here. Your reason for being pulled into this is something very different.'

'You know what—'

'Enough, Princess. Eat your food and let Agret finish.'

Pris locks eyes with my grandfather, and for a moment, I think she is going to challenge him. I don't remember much about Grandfather, but what I do remember is that he doesn't like to be crossed. She holds his gaze for a moment, then folds her hands in her lap. Her voice is contrite as she says, 'My apologies. I know so little about your world. I did not mean to offend you.'

'Our world. This is your world too, my dear,' Chríona said. 'Fieth, sit down and stop frightening the girl. You men are making a real hash of this, aren't you just.'

Under the stern gaze of his wife, the head of the clan sits down, snorting his displeasure, but not daring to disobey. In the royal castle, he might be a man to be reckoned with, but here there is no doubt who is in charge.

Satisfied everyone is calmer, Chríona continues. 'What Agret and Fieth are trying to tell you is, something has been going on at the palace for some time now. Bernais is obviously involved. Elias has been trying to figure things out and protect the Queen's interests. Great Thief—Agret —has been using his skills to help out.'

'We noticed they were involved in some sort of power struggle last night,' I tell them.

'It is more than just a simple power struggle,' my grandmother says. 'None of us common folk have seen the Queen for some time, and many fear she is ill. Bernais has been making the most of the power vacuum to shore up his position.'

'Hush, you talk too much, Chríona,' Fieth interrupts.

'It is no more than they would hear in the markets,' Glisth says, defending her sister-in-law.

Agret wraps his hands round his mug and does not meet Grandfather's eyes as he speaks in support of his mother. 'She is right, Father. It is no secret. Nor is it a secret that Bernais has taken the opportunity her absence provides to sideline everyone else of royal blood—all except Elias, who was appointed Chancellor and so sits above him on the council.'

'Are you suggesting my parents are caught up in all of

this because my mother has royal blood?' Pris asks, glancing round the table.

Fieth nods, and Pris's fingers drum a beat on the polished wood. I can almost hear the cogs of her mind moving.

'But why attack my mother? We live in the World Above. My parents distanced themselves from everything to do with your world,' Pris ponders as her fingers continue moving.

'And what do Mum and I have to do with any of this?' I ask. 'We were also far away from The Court. Can it be as simple as Bernais not wanting the Fieths to be elevated to Elvenkind?'

I found out last night that Elias petitioned the Council on the Fieth clan's behalf to have them raised to the status of elves. He believes we have paid our debt to society by faithfully serving the crown for hundreds of years.

'Not that I can fully understand why the gnomes rebelled centuries ago, nor why they had their powers limited and were indentured to elves, but your mother being charged with benefitting from her work in the World Above would not wipe out all those years of good deeds,' Pris points out.

'Oh, Fieth, there is so much these younglings should know before they head off today. So many strands of the past are coming into play, pulling their lives this way and that. Can we not delay their departure by even a single day?' Chríona asks.

Fieth opens his mouth to speak, but my father speaks first. 'I am afraid not, Mother.' Dad takes Chríona's hand across the table. 'I would hold no hope of convincing the majority of the members to delay their departure for anything that may help them in their quest. In fact, the time for these two to meet the council is almost upon us.'

My mouth is suddenly dry. It can't be time already. I am not ready to find out what Pris and I let ourselves in for when we agreed to go on a quest last night. I stand on unsteady legs and allow myself to be hugged by everyone.

Pris moves to my side, and I try to meet her eyes over my grandmother's head, but her eyes are glazed over as if her mind is elsewhere. She is only brought back to us by Glisth wrapping her arms around her and wishing her all the best.

Finally, the goodbyes are done. Dad leads us towards the door, and Glisth follows. My stomach grinds, and I take some deep breaths to settle myself. My family reunion has left me more unsettled than I have been for some time. With all the revelations, and hints about World Below politics, I have more questions than answers. And I still need to talk to Pris about what happened last night and try to make things right with her.

As Dad opens the door, Pris asks, 'Where are our packs?'

'Remember, dear, I told you that where you're going, you can only take things from this world.' Glisth squeezes her hand.

There is such a forlorn air to Pris as we step through the door. I drop in behind my father and slip my arm through hers. If I'm feeling so out of place here, it must be even worse for her. A week ago, she didn't even know this world existed. Now to be told she can't have anything familiar with her on this quest to provide comfort…. The least I can do is remind her I am still here.

'Come on.' I grin at her in what I hope comes across as encouragement. 'Chin up. I mean, what is the worse that could happen?'

···◡···

'Snake, why would you tempt fate like that?' I ask, unable to stop myself from smiling as a horse-drawn carriage pulls up and Agret helps me inside. I take a moment to marvel at the fact I am going to be riding in a carriage, like the Queen does through the streets of London.

Snake grins back as he sits beside me. 'Do you think it would be odd if we did a royal wave?' he asks.

The knot in my stomach loosens a little as I chuckle. Relaxing back into the bench seat, I finally admit to myself that the conversation during breakfast disturbed me more than a little. All the talk about political machinations and how Snake and I were being used—well, anyone with half a brain could have guessed that. It was everything they weren't telling us that bothered me.

Agret takes the seat opposite and pulls down the blinds. Closing his eyes as if to doze, I realise he is attempting to give Snake and me a little privacy.

Snake leans closer me, and I notice the tension around his eyes and mouth. 'I said it because I'm scared out of my mind, but I don't want anyone to know. I'm worried they might do something foolish if they find out.'

His breath ruffles my hair as he speaks, and butterflies do a little dance in my stomach. This morning's dream is still forefront in my mind. I am moments away from one of the scariest meetings of my life, and my body reacts like this? Really? And after he wouldn't kiss me last night?

My eyes close for just a moment, and I draw in a calming breath to get a grip on my emotions and my traitorous body. I turn to Snake. 'I'm scared too, but I can't believe they'll send us to do something that will place our lives in danger. I mean, they're not barbarians.'

Agret clears his throat. 'I could not help but overhear, and… um… while the council will not do anything like throw you into an exploding volcano, much as Bernais might want to, this quest must be a real test of both mind and body for it to be meaningful.' He shrugs, a rueful smile crossing his face. 'I am afraid it will not be some easy task they set you.'

Snake's laugh is hollow. 'Thanks, Dad. We were trying to calm our nerves, not stoke our fears.'

Agret's eyes widen, and his tone is stricken as he splutters, 'Oh, um. Sorry, I didn't….'

'It's okay, Mr Fieth. I don't think there's anything you could say to make me feel worse than I already do this morning,' I assure him, and his embarrassment and discomfort appear to ease a little.

Before any of us can say anything to make the morning more awkward, the carriage pulls up. Too full of nervous energy to wait for someone to open the door, I jump out and stumble as I try to find my footing on the cobbled road.

Having steadied myself, I turn around to take in my surroundings. If I didn't know I was in the World Below, I would believe myself to be in a hall at Cambridge University, only on a grander scale. There are four several-storied buildings with a green-grassed common at the centre. Along the longer two sides of the green stand ancient oak trees. An arched stone entrance stands opposite us, cut into the first storey of a building topped with a clock tower. A smaller, older dwelling can just be made out through the other side.

Our transport pulls away, revealing an imposing entranceway made entirely of the entwined branches of two massive oak trees. My jaw drops. The space between the enormous tree trunks is easily two stories high and, surprisingly, has no door.

I peer into the shadows, and my jaw almost unhinges when a centaur makes his way down the stone steps towards us. He appears as if conjured by magic and, as he comes closer, I realise he is the creature who enforced peace at the ball last night.

The head of the Queen's Guard, Captain Fairburn, is a tall, imposing creature with the most amazing muscled torso I ever seen. The lightly bronzed skin of his abs ripples as he moves, and it is difficult to pull my gaze away. I force my eyes upwards as he draws to a stop in front of us. The sardonic smile he throws my way tells me he is well aware of the reaction he causes.

'Well, don't I just feel inadequate,' Snake says from close by, and my cheeks burn.

'Fairburn,' Agret acknowledges the Guard Captain.

'Good morning, Agret,' Fairburn responds, his smile changing to one of welcome, and I actually swoon. I mean, the creature must be older than my mother, but when he smiles, something happens to my insides... something I can't control.

Agret leans down. 'It's perfectly normal, Princess. Something about the centaur's magic means few can resist their charms.'

The words don't help much. I hate not being in control. It is hard enough trying to sort out things with Snake without a magical creature playing havoc with my hormones.

'Princess, Snake. I would welcome you to our council chambers, but I am sure that for you two, this does not feel like a social occasion. Agret, I am afraid we must leave you here.' Fairburn gestures to the carriage now waiting on the other side of the common.

'But….'

'Some of our friends are inside, Agret, and you know we will do our best by the younglings.' He gives Agret a reassuring smile, and my belly does that swoony thing again. I really need to work on that.

I resent being called young by this creature who stirs such a physical response in me, even if he is probably hundreds of years old. Unfortunately, I am too nervous to think of a suitable quip, so I make do with sending a glare his way.

Agret hugs Snake and tells us both to take care of each other. As Fairburn ushers us in through the entrance, I am sure I catch Snake's father wiping a tear from his eye, and my stomach tightens in response.

Standing under the branches of the magnificent oaks, Fairburn asks us to wait a moment. 'We may not get a chance to speak again. This is a brave thing you two undertake, and I must say, I regret having ever been a part of it.'

I catch Snake's eye, and the look he sends me tells me he is also unsettled by this admission. For a moment I consider ignoring the remark—after all, we have more to worry about than the centaur's conscience. That moment soon passes, and my pent-up emotions flow forth.

I dislike being forced into anything, and I am tired of creatures telling me how sorry they are that Snake and I were manoeuvred into doing this, yet they've done nothing to prevent it.

'If you're so unhappy, why didn't you stop that farce of a trial last night? Why didn't you stop Bernais from rail-roading us into this?'

After letting the first words out, I can't stop the rest from following. 'You're all sorry we're paying for something you did or failed to do, yet none of you will explain what's going on. And none of you will tell us why you involved Snake and me.'

Snake's arm drops around my shoulders, and he pulls me close as he too addresses the centaur. 'If anyone can stop this madness, then it is you or the Queen's cousin, Elias. Can't you speak to the Queen and ask her to intercede—to put a stop to this?'

Fairburn's eyes cloud with some emotion I can't name. It looks like fear, but that can't be right. What could he possibly be afraid of?

He takes a deep breath and shakes his head. 'Rest assured, Princess, we have done all we can for you. Now it is up to you to show those who wish to belittle you and your families and yourselves how brave and resolute you are—to show them you will not be cowed by their petty games.'

As far as pep talks go, it isn't a bad one. Then he goes and spoils it when he adds, 'Use your heads as well as your brawn. Trust in who you are. You are more special than both of you believe, and for different reasons. We have put our faith in you. Don't let us down.'

I tense as my anger threatens to bubble over again. I did not ask for this. I don't care about their faith. I just want my parents back and to get as far away from their stupid games as I can. Snake gives me a squeeze, and I remember this is not just about me. I force my anger to a slow simmer.

'Fairburn, I think you need to understand that Pris and I are doing this for her parents and my mother, not for some greater good.' In that calm manner he has, Snake articulates my thoughts exactly.

'Don't get me wrong. Bringing Bernais down a peg or

two would be nice, but it's only the icing on the cake,' I add, unable to stop myself from smirking.

The centaur sighs, and I almost lose my focus as his muscles ripple. 'I have had my say. You can do with my words what you will.'

I close my eyes to clear my head. When I am again centred, I turn to Snake and square my shoulders. 'Are you ready?'

He nods, and I face the centaur. 'Captain Fairburn, please lead the way.'

He doesn't move. He stares pointedly at Snake's arm still draped over my shoulders. I glare back defiantly.

Snake removes the offending limb, although he doesn't move away. 'No use aggravating them more than we need to,' he whispers.

'They do not appear to be concerned about how we see them, so I don't see why we should extend them that courtesy.'

Snake stares straight ahead. It is almost as if he hasn't heard me. I seethe. I have dealt with racism all my life, and if you don't stand up to it, other people's expectations will limit your choices. At some point, Snake will need to choose to stand up to them, or he will lose me.

Unfortunately, now is not the time to have that discussion, as there is too much else we must deal with today. Still, I find it hard to let go of my disappointment as we walk in to meet our fate.

CHAPTER 2

The Trial of the Minotaur

T he butterflies in my stomach multiply exponentially as we enter the council chambers. I instinctively reach for Pris's hand. Our fingers lightly brush, and I quickly draw back, then check myself. Her words in the entranceway struck a nerve, even if I did not want to show it.

My butterflies settle as I entwine my fingers through hers. We may not be able to be together as a couple, but that doesn't mean we can't face our fate as friends. In spite of my resolve, my stomach does a somersault when Bernais emerges from the shadows. The scowl on his face intended just for me deepens when he catches sight of our clasped hands.

I have no idea why he hates me. He glares pointedly at our hands, and I resist the urge to let go. Instead, I raise my chin and defiantly meet his eyes. I or my mother will pay for that later, but I enjoy a brief moment of triumph.

My glory is short-lived. Elias walks to the centre of the room, and his movement draws my attention to the other creatures already there. Seated in a semi-circle in front of us, all the higher creatures are represented: elves, witches, wizards, gnomes, and dwarves. The glow around them tells me they are powerful magical practitioners, each and every one of them.

Their display of magical ability reminds me that Pris and I are starting out on our quest relying solely on my meagre magic. Pris only recently learned to create a flame, and she hasn't even had a chance to explore what she is capable of. Will that be a problem? I can't help but think it will be. Mum always talked of how commonplace using magic is in the World Below, so I am sure we will have to cast spells at some stage.

Still, Pris can fight. I mean, I can throw a punch, but she can really fight. She is almost unstoppable when she goes all ninja. That has to be to our advantage—maybe Pris offers more on this quest than I do.

I mean, I've studied the theory of magic and physics, but I've only used my talent to pick a few locks. Living in the World Above, we tend to avoid magical displays in case people notice.

Apart from knowing about magic, there is little else to recommend me. I can fight in a pub brawl and probably survive. I play a pretty mean guitar, but I really don't think that is something that will help us out of the situations we will face.

By the time Elias speaks, I'm breaking out in a cold sweat, and I know I made a mistake committing to do this stupid quest.

'Princess Priscilla, Snake Fieth, welcome to the Creature Council.' Elias's formal words of welcome stop me from bolting from the hall and halt my dwelling on how unprepared I am for what lies ahead. Pris gives my hand a brief squeeze, and I stand straighter. For better or worse, we are here, and we pledged to this quest to save our parents. Whatever my failings, I will give it my best... for my mother's sake.

Elias continues, ignorant of the fact that I'm spinning through a range of emotions and trying to talk myself back into this game.

'Ginth fo Drefin, Princess Cecily, and Prince Malachi—'

'That upstart is not—'

Elias stops the other elf short. 'Whether you like it or not, Bernais, Malachi is entitled to be called Prince.'

I barely have time to wonder why the interchange between the cousins seems so significant before Elias starts again.

'Ginth fo Drefin, Princess Cecily, and Prince Malachi have all been charged with personally profiting from their magic in the World Above. This crime is punishable by banishment from that place. In the most severe cases, the convicted are also banished from the World Below.'

Elias stops and waits for the import of his pronouncement to sink in. Beside me, Pris stiffens, almost as if she had not realised the severity of the crimes her parents were charged with.

'Although it appeared that these cases would be successfully defended—'

'I must object here,' Bernais interrupts. 'I do not believe we can definitively say anything of the sort.'

Elias closes his eyes for a moment, whether because Bernais is stretching his patience or to gather his thoughts, I have no way of knowing for sure. I suspect the former.

After taking yet another deep breath, the Chancellor carries on. 'Although there seemed to be a good chance that the defendants may have been judged not guilty, Snake and Priscilla have decided to undertake a quest so that they could petition the Queen to absolve their parents of all charges.'

Pausing again, Elias makes sure there are no objections to this statement before continuing.

'Last night and early this morning, the council sat and agreed upon the details of the quest.' Elias pauses for effect.

I bite back a sigh. This guy should have become an actor. He really knows how to milk the moment. Unfortunately, at this rate, we'll be starting out tomorrow, not today. I wish he would speed things up and get it over and done with. Not just because my nerves have my stomach doing somersaults, but also because each minute spent here is a minute more my mother has to spend in captivity.

'Because neither Priscilla nor Snake has spent much time, if any, in our world, the council agreed to send a guide with them in the form of a creature of limited magical ability. Percival, please step forward.'

A funny-looking man about the size of a ten-year-old child steps out of the shadows. It takes a minute for me to place him. Then I recognise him—he was Eleanora's companion at the ball last night. Today he is dressed totally in black. His pencil moustache and slicked-back black hair are groomed immaculately. In his pale face, his catlike emerald eyes are disconcerting as they flick over us disdainfully. Dismissing us, he turns his attention to Elias.

Again, like I did last night, I can't help thinking I know him from somewhere, but I don't know where. I also can't figure out which creature race he belongs to. What I can see is that he is not at all happy to be going with us.

'Percival's role is to help the two of you understand the limits of what you can and cannot do while in the World Below. He can explain our customs and practices and let you know whether something you want to do will break any of our laws,' Elias explains.

Pris leans around me and smiles cheerfully at Percival. 'Welcome to the team.'

He glares back. 'I am not, nor will I ever be, part of your team.' He manages to make the word 'team' sound like something nasty he trod in.

'Well, this is going to be fun,' she adds, winking at me.

She is trying for levity, but my stomach is clenching, and I'm regretting the small amount of breakfast I ate. The longer this audience drags out, the more my sense of dread increases. It's almost like they are putting off telling us about the quest. Why don't they just get on with it and put us out of our misery?

Then, as if Elias reads my mind, he takes a deep breath and announces, 'Your quest is to retrieve what is at the centre of the minotaur's maze.'

My jaw drops, and the buzzing in my ears blocks everything out. Sometimes you should be careful what you wish for. We're going to face a minotaur! This is way worse than anything I could ever have imagined.

.·•◗·.·

I shake my head, trying to clear my ears, because I am sure I did not correctly hear what Elias said. A minotaur. He can't be serious! I look over at Snake for support, but he gives me nothing. His face is sort of blank, and he's staring straight ahead like he's gone into shock.

'But minotaurs are mythical creatures,' I blurt, my mouth moving into action before my brain kicks in.

Elias's smile is condescending, which sets my teeth on

edge. 'Many myths are based in truth. The minotaur has lived in our world for millennia. He is a solitary beast, and only those who can successfully traverse the maze are deemed worthy to enter his domain.'

Beside me, Snake relaxes. 'Oh, so you don't want us to fight him, then?' He tenses. 'Or do you?' It seems saying what comes into your head before thinking it through is catching.

Again, Elias smiles. 'I cannot say either way, Snake. Whether or not you must fight him to gain entry to the centre of the maze will depend entirely on how your quest progresses.'

I'm numb. I've read myths and legends in the same way all school kids do, but I'm a realist. All those fanciful tales weren't my thing, so I paid very little attention. If I'd known that at some time in the future, I would face something from those legends, I would have studied harder— prepared better.

I realise I am gripping Snake's hand tightly when he reaches over and pries his fingers loose before shaking his hand to revive his circulation. My eyes slip sideways, trying to work out how Snake is taking Elias's revelation. I'm concentrating so hard on him, it takes a moment for me to register that Eleanora, the Witch of Wimbledon, is speaking to us.

'…so you would be fools to concentrate on the end of the quest,' she finishes up.

'Sorry, what was that again?' I ask.

Bernais sneers and I ignore him. I like that man a little less every time I meet him.

Eleanora catches my eye and offers me a patient, sad smile. 'I was saying you would be fools to concentrate on what happens when you reach the centre of the maze, when the maze itself will pose its own challenges,' she repeats.

I stare at the glamorous woman, allowing her words to sink in. She's warning us that this quest will be dangerous from the moment we begin. I'm speechless. I mean, part of me realised I had committed to going on a quest with Snake. Part of me also realised it would be no stroll in the park. Still, traversing a dangerous maze to confront a half man, half beast to retrieve what he is guarding—that is next-level crazy.

'Is there another option?' I ask.

Everyone, and I mean everyone, including Snake, stares at me in amazement. I resist the urge to squirm under their scrutiny. I want to tell them all that I refuse to go. This is madness. We're in the twenty-first century, and these sorts of barbaric practices went out of favour years ago. The set of the faces around me tells me this is not an option. Eleanora's next words simply confirm my guess.

'I am sorry, my dear. You committed to the quest last night. Since then, the council has formulated the most appropriate challenge for you two to undertake. There is no turning back now.'

My mind is racing, and it's hard to grasp hold of any one thought. Her words replay in my head. I stop them and play them through once more, probing for a hidden meaning. I believe she chose her words carefully—very carefully. I think she might be trying to tell us that some of them have worked out a way to try and help us through this ordeal.

No. I mustn't think that way. To rely on anything but ourselves will be too dangerous. My martial arts training taught me to assess each situation as it presents itself, iden-tify the dangers, and act accordingly. That training is what will get me through this, not waiting to be helped by complete strangers.

I turn to Snake. His face is a little pale, and there is a sheen of sweat on his brow. I don't think he expected anything this dangerous either. I give his hand a squeeze and smile at him in what I hope is an encouraging way. 'We got here by ourselves. We can do this too,' I assure him with perhaps more conviction than I actually feel.

His face is blank with not even a hint of a smile. 'This is a whole new level of hard,' he whispers.

'But I have a whole new body with an even greater reach,' I say with a laugh, but it comes out a little strangled.

Snake turns a stricken face to me. 'I never thought of that. Will your, um different, er… dimensions affect your ability to fight?'

It's like he just threw a bucket of cold water over me. 'You know, I haven't even considered that possibility.'

My heart beats a little faster as my mind identifies this as a real cause for concern and starts to turn it into a worry. I gnaw my lip and catch Bernais smirking as if he has overheard our conversation and finds our fear amusing.

I will not let him see I am anything other than confident. I will not give that slimy elf the satisfaction of knowing I am scared. So my body is a bit bigger. So our guide doesn't want to be with us. So Snake is freaking out. I *will* find a way around all of this—for my parents' sake.

Two servants carrying packs enter the room, and a third enters hidden behind a towering array of weapons. Fairburn appears from nowhere and ambles over to them. How does a cloven-hooved creature move that quietly?

'Each of these packs contains a jacket, wet weather gear, a sleeping roll, and travel food,' he tells us.

I look in horror. 'What about a change of clothes?' I ask. On top of everything else, I am not going to be able to change my clothes for goodness knows how long. It's a step too far.

The centaur frowns. 'Why would you need to change your clothes in the middle of a dangerous quest? Surely there will be more important things to worry about.'

'Ah, I guess,' I mumble, embarrassed I hadn't considered that. Then again, it's not like I go out on dangerous missions every day. If I am going to be in these clothes indefinitely, then that means there are unlikely to be any bathrooms…. Hold on. What about toilet paper? Was that on the list of things we're carrying?

I open my mouth to ask, and Fairburn grins. Can he read my mind?

'Everything else you need can be found in the forest, Princess. Moss especially can be quite useful, I think you will find.' I am immediately grateful to the rather forbidding-looking head of the Queen's Guard for pointing out this piece of information.

I take my pack, and Fairburn waits until it is in place before saying, 'Now you will need to choose your weapons.' He motions the weapon carriers forward.

'What?' Snake looks doubtful. 'I think giving us weapons may put us more in danger than it will any enemies we might come across.'

Fairburn frowns. 'Of course, you missed out on military training…. Still, you cannot go completely unarmed.'

He rummages through the metallic array. 'Here, each of you should carry a decent knife.' He hands over two sheathed blades about the size of a decent kitchen knife and two leather belts. 'Carry these at all times. You never know what they might come in handy for.'

As we attach the sheaths to the belts and secure them

around our hips, Fairburn studies the remaining weapons. He hands a bow and arrow to Snake, saying, 'I seem to remember Percival being a decent shot. If you get time, perhaps he can teach you to use it.'

Behind me, Percival snorts, and I resist sending him a glare. If he isn't going to be helpful, the least he can do is be quiet.

'Take the rest of these away,' Fairburn orders the servants before retreating to the back of the room.

Eleanora takes his place behind us as Elias says, 'We are all set, then. The council appointed Eleanora as adjudicator of this quest, and she will take you to the start point. We wish you good luck in your endeavours.'

Before I can say anything in response, my stomach lurches, and the room spins around me.

CHAPTER 3

The Maze Entrance

The wind whips around us, chilling me to the bone. I had forgotten how cold the mountain air can be —then again, it's been a while since I have been this high in the mountains. I distance myself from Pris and Snake as I turn slowly to survey the scene below.

A central tower peaks above stone walls that are so tall, they block out the ground on the other side, even from our elevated vantage point—the home of the legendary minotaur.

My stomach clenches, but not because the minotaur or the maze are so imposing, but because of where it is situated. Reluctantly, I walk past Eleanor to stare at the source of my unease. Below us, on the other side of the mountain, is a hamlet almost encircled by a great forest—the Wyld Woods—my home.

Eleanora's hand rests on my shoulder. She is the only one who understands what being so close to home means to me and why I rarely ever return. A heavy sigh escapes my lips. Wishing for what might never be is a waste of time. I must focus on the job in front of me—of us.

'Are you ready?' she asks quietly.

I nod and we turn back to the maze. I join Snake and the elf while Eleanora moves to our left.

'Below, you should be able to make out the door you must go through to enter the maze. Once you are beyond the walls, the quest begins. The minotaur only allows those who are worthy into the inner sanctum to face him. Whatever tests you face while traversing his realm are designed by him, and they are unique to each individual or team.'

Snake and the princess tell her they understand. I am sure they think they do, but they are woefully unprepared for the games our minotaur likes to play with those who enter his domain.

'As Elias said, Percival is here to support you and help you understand the laws of the World Below. He may not assist you directly or he will become part of the quest.'

'I don't understand what this means,' the princess says, her brows drawing together. 'Can he help us or not?'

'He can give you information. He can answer a question or tell you how things behave differently here than in the World Above. The moment he physically or magically helps you to complete a task, he will be a part of the quest, not a helper. Is that clear?' Eleanora finishes and waits for a response.

Snake nods, but the princess shakes her head. 'Surely by choosing what information we need and when, he will be helping us.'

Eleanora catches my eye. *This one is going to be trouble,* her look tells me. She rubs her forehead. She has been up all night, and no doubt the princess's questions are taxing her, especially as she still has so much to do to make sure this quest turns out as they have planned. She squares her shoulders and says, 'He will tell you when he is unable to do something.'

'Oh, okay.' The princess's shoulders relax fractionally, and guilt twists my stomach as I realise that I am not the only one nervous about what the next few days will bring.

Eleanora's voice jolts me from my thoughts before I become lost in them. 'Right, moving on. If you decide you no longer wish to proceed with the quest, simply say 'soars' and you will be brought back to this point.'

'Will you meet us here?' At least Snake is asking practical questions—questions that will not lead me back into my head.

'Yes. I will await your return in the village below and will come and meet you should you decide to give up. Are there any further questions?'

Yes, why am I here? I think but do not say because I am distracted, and also because I am actually asking myself, not Eleanora. I may behave like I am merely following Eleanora's direction as a true familiar should. However, all I would have to do is voice my fears and tell her I do not want to do this, and she would find another helper.

Why do I not say the words? It would be so easy. After all these years and even from this distance, I sense the trees and plants of my home calling to me. I can no longer commune with them as I once did, so their song brings melancholy, not joy. To be so close yet so far away from them is a kind of torture.

I could go back to the village with Eleanora. But would that really be easier? My family is down there. They would welcome me, but they would also have so many questions, and I still have no answers… even after all this time.

I shake my head, as if that will dislodge the fears and memories that have haunted me all these years and force my attention back to the others. The princess is saying, 'What happens to our parents should we decide we cannot continue?'

'A good question. Their fate will be in the hands of the council. Given its current makeup….'

'I'm guessing that would not be a good thing,' the princess finishes.

'Is there any advice you can give us?' Snake takes a step forward as he speaks and now stands beside the princess. In spite of last night's closeness, they are so far apart today, as if they now dance to different songs. The mean part of me, the part that cannot abide elves, says thank goodness Snake has come to his senses.

Unfortunately, I suspect the closeness the two developed getting to the World Below will be needed in their quest to retrieve the item from the centre of the maze. I arch my back to release my tension. This is not so effective when I am standing upright. I adjust my clothes and make sure I am presentable.

'I would suggest we try not to get killed,' I say, hoping to alleviate the tension.

The princess blanches, which serves to make her dark skin almost as pale as the other elves in the World Below.

Eleanora frowns at me. 'I suggest you keep an open mind, use your brains, and play to your strengths. Now, we can put this off no longer. It is time to go.'

She points to a path on the right that winds down to the valley below. Snake adjusts his pack and heads off.

As he leaves, Pris gestures at me. 'Where is *your* pack?'

I glare at her. 'I am able to access everything I need.'

'Percival keeps all he needs in his pockets.' Eleanor lips turn up playfully as she adds, 'He would never let his appearance be marred by something as inelegant as a backpack.'

Pris glares at her own pack with distaste. The one thing she and I have in common is our attention to appearance, and I feel some sympathy for her having to carry that monstrosity.

Eleanora smiles. 'I understand.' She waves her hand, and Pris's pack turns her favourite colour—purple. 'No need for everything to blend in on this quest.'

Pris smiles, a hint of a tear glistening in her eyes. 'Thank you. That was very kind.'

She walks past me and waits at the top of the path while I say my goodbyes.

'Take care of them, Percival.' Eleanora bends to hug me, and for that moment, she ceases to be the Witch of Wimbledon and becomes my friend Ellie. 'Take care of yourself as well. I am aware being this close to the forest will test you, but perhaps you may decide to do a little more than give advice, and gain something more than the Queen's gratitude for yourself for taking part in this nonsense.'

'Such as being granted peace to sit by the fire at last?' This is not what she means, but I am trying to deflect. My emotions are still too raw to bear discussion.

Her smile is sad. 'You know what I mean, Percival.'

I do know, only too well. While I gave up hope of that a long time ago, tired of the hurt that longing brought, my friend, Ellie, still dreams it is possible.

··◗··

Fear and anger give wings to my feet, and I am almost running as the mountain begins to flatten out. I keep expecting to hear footsteps behind me, but I am surrounded by silence.

What is Pris up to? Why hasn't she caught up? Neither

of us want to do this, but putting it off isn't going to achieve anything. The sooner we start this, the sooner it will be over and our parents will be safe.

I keep repeating, '*Will be safe*' in my head in time with my steps. I picture my mum sitting on the stage in the Underground Ballroom last night, her eyes expressing trust that I would do the right thing. A vision of Bernais sneering as the others do his dirty work eclipses it. My stomach flips, threatening to dislodge my breakfast as I remember the moment I realised he would do whatever it took to convict my mother. Remembering it also recalled the moment when I studied the faces in the room and saw that everyone hated my mother and wished to do her harm.

The path is twisty, and I almost wrench my ankle on one of the numerous rocks jutting out from the dirt. I stop and suck in gulps of air. I need to calm down. It will not do me any good to dwell on last night—to wonder what my mother could have done for so many creatures to hate her so much. I need to keep a calm head.

No matter how much I tell myself to stop replaying last night, I can't help it. The vision of Pris dressed and ready for the ball and bemoaning how plain her dress was makes me smile and softens my anger. I couldn't understand her concern, as she was easily the most beautiful creature I had ever seen.

I fast forward to her fixing my hair, then to our kiss and the way it lit a fire inside me. Then later, when we danced, how she fitted so perfectly in my arms as we moved in time with the music. We were so in tune that everything was perfect, then I bent my head and almost kissed her.

The visions disappear, and all I am left with is my regret at not finishing the second kiss. Not just because it would have been amazing—because it would have been—

but mostly because of the hurt on her face when I drew back.

Pris is against racism in any form, but withholding my kiss was not just a reaction to the class and race lines my mother drilled into me as a child. It was the pure hate Bernais and others displayed towards my mother and towards me that made me reconsider my actions. The set of their faces as I danced with Pris was not common old prejudice. There was more to it, and whatever that is still chills me to the bone.

What frustrates me about this is that I can't work out why they are that way. Although I know a lot more than Pris about the culture and history of the World Below, I know little more about my family than she does her own.

My mother never talked about them, or why she was brought up a part of the Fieth clan, or why she always felt less than them. Apart from Earth and Glisth, the Fieth clan are strangers to me, even my own father.

If I put that together with all the things hinted at this morning but not said, I am more confused and feeling more alone than I was when I arrived.

I walk a while longer, wrapped in my thoughts, trying to unpick what my grandfather and father's work at the palace has to do with why I am here today. I'm sure it's something more than a preoccupation with our clan being returned to the status of elves. There is a bigger mystery behind what is going on.

As I reach the bottom of the path, a rock clatters behind me, and I slow a little for the others to catch up. I expected the walk would clear my head, but I am more agitated than I was when I started off, and it is mixed with guilt at taking off alone when we should be working together.

Percival appears first. Who is he? Who does he remind

me of? *A cat.* The thought pops into my head, and I almost laugh out loud. It's absurd, but he really does remind me of the cat who is always sitting in front of Eleanora's fire in the World Above. His eyes and his mannerisms… they're just so… feline.

Pris follows close to Percival, and soon our small group is standing silently in front of the wooden gates that break up the stone wall. From here the wall is so high, I can't see the top. The gates themselves appear to be made of a single massive plank of wood. There is no opening, no hinges, and no lock. There isn't even a knocker to summon a gatekeeper.

I take a step closer, studying the ancient wooden surface, hoping to find a spark of inspiration. I had thought getting us through the doors would be something I could contribute, but there actually has to be a lock for me to pick or manipulate before I can be of any use. I'm stumped.

'Over here.' I wander over to where Pris is tracing some writing carved into the stone with an index finger.

'Do you know what it says?' she asks.

I shake my head. 'No, I can't even guess.'

We both turn to Percival. He sighs heavily, as if we're asking him to do some impossible task. He ambles over, reads the words, and translates for us. 'Questers Must Force Entry.'

'What? Are you sure you are translating it correctly?' I snap.

Until that moment I would not have believed anyone so short could look down their nose at someone my height, but that is exactly what Percival did.

I resist the urge to take a step away from him. 'Okay, if that is what it says, what does it mean?'

He shrugs. 'That is for you to work out.' He turns, finds a rock close by in the shade, and sits.

I turn to Pris. 'Any ideas?'

She frowns, and for a moment I think she is puzzling an answer. Then I realise she is frowning *at me*.

I am immediately defensive. 'What?'

'So *now* you want to work together?'

Heat flushes my cheeks. I know she deserves an apology for my taking off, but it is actually difficult to form the right words. I mean, the almost kiss from last night is forming a wall between us I can't seem to get past—I can't explain to her the hatred in the creatures' eyes. And I can't explain my need to rescue Mum from their clutches as quickly as I can.

'This morning's been strange. I just needed a little time to myself to get my head in order,' I tell her.

'This situation is hard for all of us,' she points out, rather unnecessarily, I think.

There's another long silence, and still the right words don't come. If I simply say I'm sorry, what am I apologising for? Walking ahead? Not kissing her? For not knowing enough about what is going on to plot a way through this? For dragging her into this in the first place?

In the end it is easier not to speak at all, so I shrug. 'Well, we're here now; we had best get on with it.'

Her sigh is a touch overdramatic. 'I guess so.'

Silence falls again as we hold each other's gaze. So many unspoken words hang between us, and I can almost feel Pris willing me to explain what is going on in my head. I am first to break away. 'Let's see if we can find something that might help us.'

I follow the line of the gate while Pris walks in the opposite direction, checking the stones. I examine every part of the door, every crack in the stones at the edges. I even use my toes to dig a little around the base. There's nothing. Frustration gets the better of me, and I bang my fists on the wood. The door creaks, and I freeze. Am I imagining things, or did it shift a little? I plant my feet and push as hard as I can. Next thing I know, I am standing in the open and the gate is behind me. Was it really that easy all along?

'Hey, guys. You just need to push really hard, and the door will open,' I yell.

My voice echoes around me. Did my voice carry over the wall? I turn and press on the wood, meaning to go back through and tell them what I found. Nothing happens.

I'm sorting through possible options for a way to communicate with the others when Pris and Percival stumble through the gate, almost falling at my feet. Relief washes over me as I steady Pris. Her smile at working out the solution fades as she meets my eyes.

'Did you hear me call?' I ask, surprised at how hopeful I sound.

'No.' Pris's response is terse. 'Fortunately, Percival saw how you managed to get through.'

'Oh, that's good,' I say, fully aware of her subtext—that I shouldn't have gone all the way through without making sure we all knew what was happening. I want to tell her that hindsight is a wonderful thing, but I'm sensing now is not the time to be flippant. Besides, she has stepped away and is looking at something imbedded in the wall.

I walk a few short paces to her side. 'What's that?'

'Some sort of stone marker.' She moves to allow me to get a better look, then gestures at the scene in front of us. 'It shows the destination of the potential paths we can take through the maze.'

I follow her gaze and see five paths leading into darkness, showing five possible ways we can go.

'What are our options?' I ask, leaning over her shoulder to read with her. I'm distracted by the faint smell of lavender that still lingers in her hair, but I force myself to concentrate on the words, which are fortunately in English.

Engraved inside each of the arrows pointing to the paths are the following options: Heart's Desire, A Desirable End, Heart of the Matter, Journey's End, and Centre of Life.

'Could they be more oblique?' I mutter.

'Perhaps we're meant to choose what resonates most with why we are on this quest.' Pris's voice wavers as if she is a little uncertain.

It's so obvious these are quest choices when she puts it like that. I stare at them, trying to work out which one will get us to the centre of the maze and back to our parents the quickest.

'We are here because we desire to set our parents free, so we should follow the arrow of Heart's Desire,' Pris says as I am still thinking.

'If only I could,' I say under my breath.

Pris cocks her head to the side. 'What was that?'

I can't tell her I am unable to follow my heart, because it will not lead to our parents, but to her, and that is not why we are here.

·· ·◗·· ·

Snake is staring at me in confusion. Then his face hardens as if something has hit him, and he doesn't like it. I wait impatiently for him to speak.

'We need to get to the centre of the maze as quickly as possible. The longer we're out of the picture, the more scheming Bernais and his cronies can do. That means taking the most direct route, so I think we should follow the Centre of Life path.'

Now it is my turn to stare, and I hope my annoyance is clear to Snake. On top of his being distant since we almost kissed again last night, he is now arguing about why we are here; arguing about which statement resonates with us. And why can't he see his path will not lead to the centre of the maze?

The maze isn't life, the maze is a test. What does the Centre of Life mean anyway? Air could be the centre of life. It could also be water, family, love. It's too airy fairy and is clearly the wrong path—both for our quest and if we want to move as quickly as possible.

'Why not the Journey's End, then?' I counter.

'What if the end is the other side of the maze, the way out, instead of the centre?' Snake asks. 'Then we wouldn't be able to retrieve the object, and we would fail. We are looking for something with centre in it.'

'Oh.' So he is actually thinking this through. I didn't consider what end we might be led to. 'What is wrong with following your heart? I believe it would take us to the centre of the maze too, given that is where we want to go.'

'It's an emotional response, and both Eleanora and Fairburn counselled us to use our heads,' he states matter-of-factly.

Okay, he has a point, but my gut tells me he is approaching this the wrong way. We both chose to be here because we love our families.

I place my hands on my hips, ready to challenge him. 'So we should just disregard our feelings?'

He nods. 'For the duration of this quest, yes, I believe so.'

I get the impression he is talking about more than choosing our path. Although my heart sinks a little at the thought, I am not ready to let this go yet.

I keep my voice controlled as I point out, 'Wasn't it love for your mother that sent you to find my parents? It was love for my parents that helped me overcome the shock of finding out magical creatures were real. I don't think following our hearts again will do us any harm.'

Snake will not meet my gaze. What is going on with him? Why is he being so obstinate?

'Getting to the World Below was a piece of cake compared to this.' He sweeps his hand out, indicating the five paths in front of us. 'And when we're finished here, Bernais will still be waiting for us, ready to cause more havoc. I'm just saying that although our hearts brought us this far, perhaps it is time to start using our heads.'

Okay, that is hard to disagree with. There is definitely something bigger than the both of us going on here, but surely trusting your heart is the best way to move forward when there aren't enough facts to base a decision on. I am about to suggest this when a voice comes from behind us. Percival. I had forgotten he was there.

'Can you not compromise?'

I consider this for a moment before asking, 'Which path would you choose?'

He shakes his head. 'It is not for me to decide. I simply observe you are at an impasse, and if we want to move on from here before it gets dark, you need to work together to find a third way.'

I resist the urge to throttle the smug look from his face. But he is right.

'Do you like any of the other options?' I ask Snake, ready to compromise if he will.

Snake shuffles his feet and stares at the pattern they make on the ground. 'I still think we should go with the Centre of Life.'

Is he not even prepared to try and meet me halfway?

'Can you at least take some time to consider one of the other options? What about A Desirable End. Surely that would also take us to the centre of the maze given that is where we want to go?'

Snake continues to look at the ground. My anger is beginning to bubble. He's not even trying to work together. 'Look at me,' I demand. When he doesn't, I decide I've had enough of all this beating around the bush. 'What's going on with you? Can't you even consider an option with heart or desire in the wording?'

He raises his head, and his green eyes are blazing. I have never seen Snake angry before, and the sight shocks me into silence.

'My heart leads me to you. My desires lead me to you. As I can't be with you in this world or the other, I can't trust my heart, and I can't have what I desire. I am left with trusting my head, and it is telling me to go to the centre.'

As he holds my gaze, challenging me to respond, his fists clench and unclench. Anger and frustration radiate from him.

I'm so stunned by the ferocity of his emotion, I can barely breathe. The depth of his feelings blows me away. I mean, I knew something was growing between us, and I for one want to see where it goes…. But hold on—is he saying we are not worth fighting for? Even after all we've been through together?

'We can work something out—' I start to say, but his look of stony resolve silences me.

He shakes his head. 'Haven't you seen the looks on the faces of the greater creatures when they see us together? They would rather see me dead than with you.'

He is so certain of the animosity directed towards us. Did I miss something last night? I start to doubt myself. I shake my head, certain I would notice that type of disapproval. I always have done in the past.

'Your father, Earth, and Elias are friends,' I say. 'Maybe things aren't as impossible as you make out.'

'Whatever their friendship is, my family are servants to the crown, and we always will be, whether we are called gnome or elf. But this is more than that. Surely you saw something?' Snake begs me to confirm his assessment of the situation, but I can't.

I'm sure Snake isn't lying, but perhaps his own upbringing and heightened emotions are affecting his perception. I turn to Percival to inject some sanity into the situation.

'Percival, tell him he is mistaken, that we can be friends… close friends.'

'There are many forms of friendship, Princess. What type are you referring to?'

Ooh, I want to shake him. 'For instance, would anyone object if I were to date Snake?' I almost spit the words out.

'Date?' Percival rolls the word around in his mouth, and I clench my fists in frustration. 'I am not sure the concept has an equal here. Would you be able to court him? No, given who you are and who he is, it would not be acceptable.'

I am so shocked, my mouth falls open. He speaks so

matter-of-factly with no concept that this is not acceptable in a modern world. I straighten my spine and glare down at him. I have fought racism all my life, and I will fight this —but only if Snake wants to as well.

I lift my chin. 'I will not accept this.'

Snake's shoulders droop. 'I don't think it is up to us.' It's almost as if Percival's confirmation of his fears has dispelled his anger and left him defeated.

His acceptance of the situation irks me more than his despair. 'Are you just going to give—'

I stop mid-sentence as Snake hoists his pack over his shoulder and strides off down the path leading towards the Centre of Life.

CHAPTER 4

A Path Once Chosen

T he crunch of gravel under my feet fills the late morning air as my boots briskly pound the path heading towards the Centre of Life. I resist the urge to turn and make sure Pris and Percival are following me, not wanting to confirm what my heart already knows —that they are not there… yet.

My stomach churns as I contemplate the enormity of choosing our path through the maze without getting Pris to agree. I am pulled between wanting to help my mother, becoming a part of my family below, and sorting out some way of keeping Pris in my life without losing the other two things.

I'm a mass of worry and fears, and I am fighting to keep my head in amongst the emotional confusion clouding my senses.

Can't she see it's not that I don't care, but that I care too much? All this talk about fighting to be together is tearing me apart inside. I'm fighting my attraction to her with every fibre of my being, then one whiff of the shampoo in her hair almost does me in.

I stomp on, keeping an ear out for the sound of foot-steps telling me Pris is following. As time passes, I have to admit she has chosen her own path to the centre of the maze. I am alone, with no one to blame but myself. I've pushed her so far away, she would rather not be with me. She will probably be better off without me anyway.

My plodding feet eat up the miles as I fight the urge to turn back and reunite with Pris. I follow the twists and turn of the hedge-lined path leading me through the shadows until they spit me out through a gateway into a clearing.

This isn't how a maze is supposed to work. This isn't the centre of anything. In fact, it looks like the beginning of a path through a forest. I turn to find I am now in the shadow of the hedge, and the opening I came through is nowhere to be found. There is no way back. I am on my own.

At around midday, I stop by a stream to eat some trail bread and drink some water. I fill the water skin I find in my pack, then lean back against a tree and close my eyes for a moment. The bubbling of the stream as it flows over rocks takes me back to when Pris and I went to the White Lady Falls to meet the White Witch.

I miss her jokes and how she teased me as we walked. Hell, I even miss her quirky clothes. I wonder which path she took? Is she okay? At least she has Percival with her. I will do perfectly well by myself, but the magical world is new to her, and she hasn't fully gotten used to her powers.

Deciding I can't stop here all day, I pick up my pack and carry on walking. The path winds through the woods, and just when I think I will turn a corner and arrive at my destination, I find more trees lining more paths. I have long since stopped wondering about which route to take because each choice leads me exactly nowhere.

I continue to walk on until the sun begins its descent.

My limbs are weary and I'm sick of trees and rutted paths and, most off all, I'm sick and tired of walking. I wish I had someone to complain to. I really miss Pris.

Venting my frustration, I kick a loose rock, sending it flying. It bounces off a tree trunk and back onto the path. Why did I have to go and fall for the one person I can never have? A bitter laugh escapes my lips.

'Okay, I am falling in love with her, and I can't do anything about it.' My voice echoes.

Let it go. Concentrate on freeing your mother, and worry about the rest later.

My peptalk lifts a weight from my shoulders. I am certain Pris and I will meet up at some point and get through this—together. With a lighter heart and renewed determination, I follow the path through towering green trees.

Appreciating walking through such a beautiful forest, I start to hum a tune, and my fingers make the chord forms as if they were playing guitar. The song I write in my head is melancholy—a love song of sorts for a love that can never be. It is one of my best yet, and I wish I had some paper to write to it down. Instead, I repeat it over and over so it will stay in my head.

So intent on remembering the tune, I let myself get lost in the melody. I don't notice the forest thinning until I turn a corner to find the path carries on through some fields towards a village. The hamlet is close to the forest edge and nestled by a stream—probably the same stream I drank from earlier.

To the other side of the village are fields and a smattering of farm buildings. I make out more trees on the horizon. There is only one way for me to go, and that is through the village. I pick up the pace. Perhaps I can camp the night in a field on the other side, then start out early in the morning.

Shrugging my pack more squarely in place, I continue on, humming under my breath. As I draw closer to the dwellings, I begin to pass creatures. Most of them have rounded ears peeking through their hair, telling me this is a predominantly gnome village; although some of the inhabitants are squarer in shape, indicating some dwarf heritage too. Most of them ignore me, but some raise their eyes from their work to follow my progress.

As I enter the market square, I am surprised when many of the stall holders stop what they are doing and stare at me. My skin prickles with discomfort. Perhaps they don't get many travellers through here.

Murmurs follow my progress, and I walk a little faster, sensing I am not welcome here. I catch the words of one female when she speaks more loudly than the others. 'It's Breaker of Hearts returned to us.'

I frown. I don't know who they think I am, but I'm certainly no heartbreaker. I almost laugh at the thought, considering the state of my love life.

A small crowd is gathering outside one of the shops on the edge of the marketplace, and I slow as I approach, wondering if they will allow me to pass. They make way for an elderly gnome who steps directly into my path, halting my progress.

The gnome looks me up and down before leaning on his stick. 'Well, you have the look of him, but your eyes are green, and you are slighter in build. The tune your mind is holding on to could be one of his, but you are the age he was when he left—he would be much older now.'

What the…? I sense everyone is waiting for some sort of response, but what do you say to that?

Nonetheless, the words spill out. 'I'm sorry? Who

would be older? And where did he leave? I mean, where am I exactly?'

The gnome chuckles. 'This is Elder Grove, in the Western Edge of the Wyld Woods'

I frown. That can't be right. The Wyld Woods? Weren't they on the other side of the mountain Eleanora took us to?

'But I'm meant to be in the maze.'

Everyone laughs.

'The maze can send you anywhere it wills, and you were sent here,' the gnome explains.

'Why would the minotaur want that?' I ponder out loud.

'My guess is your quest is to find that out.' The gnome's tone tells me he is quite serious.

More people are joining the group, and I shuffle in discomfort. Why am I here? Because I remind the locals of someone? There is only one way to find out.

'Who is this, um, Breaker of Hearts you think I resemble?'

'He is my son.'

Okay. What else might I need to know?

'Why did he leave?'

The gnome closes his eyes, but not quickly enough to hide his pain. When he opens them, he answers in a steady voice. 'He was tempted away by an elven princess to join her court when he was about your age. We have not seen him since.'

His pain permeates the air as the gnome beside him places a comforting hand on his arm. My next question sticks in my throat as his words tug at my heart. I was going to ask if they know any of the Fieth clan, but now I wonder if the minotaur sent me in the wrong direction.

Pris is the only elven princess I have met. Perhaps the minotaur has mixed up our quests.

'I answered your questions, now I have one for you,' the gnome continues, oblivious to my inner turmoil. 'Did you bring an instrument with you? I am sure we would all enjoy listening to your song.'

I didn't expect that. I shake my head, operating on autopilot. 'I didn't think I would need one in the maze.'

The man nods. 'Quite sensible. If I loan you one, will you play your song for us? I sense its beauty, and I would be grateful if you would share it.'

'Do you have a guitar?' I ask

The gnome stares blankly at me.

'It's a stringed instrument. You strum it,' I explain.

He nods. 'A lute might work. How many strings do you need?'

'Six,' I answer, still trying to get my head around the bizarre turn this encounter has taken.

He disappears inside the shop and returns with an honest-to-god lute, like something out of a history book, and hands it to me. People move aside, revealing a bench outside the store. I sit on the seat, placing my pack at my feet.

I run my fingers over the strings, turning the pegs to tune it as close to a guitar as I can. Strumming produces an unusual sound, but with finger picking, the sound is closer to what is in my head.

It takes me a little while to get the tune exactly right, and I hum along to the notes as the song comes together. A little while later, I am adding the lyrics I played with as I walked. When I stop, a loud applause echoes through the crowd.

Feeling like myself for the first time today, I pick out some

Irish ballads from my childhood. When I run out of them, I play Ed Sheeran's "Galway Girl," which gets everyone's feet tapping. As I finish up, the elderly gnome steps forward.

'The lad must be tired.' I start to object, but the gnome shakes his head. 'It is almost dark. That is enough for now.'

The crowd grumbles, but starts to disperse, muttering their thanks as they depart.

Handing me a supple leather case for the lute, the gnome helps me put it away. I hold the lute out, but the gnome waves his hand as if to brush it away. 'No, lad—that instrument has claimed you. It would be a sin for me to take it back.'

It is a beautiful instrument, but I can't take it. 'I haven't any money…. I can't—'

'Please—your performance was thanks enough. We have not had music of that quality in the village for quite some time. Now, my wife will flay me alive if I do not offer you a meal and a bed for the night.'

Now I'm even more embarrassed. 'You're too kind, I really—'

'Should accept. You may sleep under the stars for many nights before the maze has done with you. Sleep in a bed while you can.'

I believe my host will be quite upset if I refuse and, to be honest, I would prefer to eat a hot meal and sleep in a bed. So I agree to stay. I follow the gnome into his shop and wait while he closes up, resisting the urge to touch the amazing instruments on display. He then leads me through a workroom and into a dwelling at the back.

As I step through the door into a large family room, the smell of food cooking hits me, and my stomach grumbles. I chuckle as I spy a well-used wooden table set for three. Seems like my host would have been in trouble had I decided not to join him.

I resist the urge to drop into one of the armchairs placed either side of the roaring fire as the elderly gnome shuts the door behind us. 'I am so sorry, my manners escaped me. I must introduce myself. I am Mender of Hearts.'

I gasp. He used his true named even though we are all but strangers. To offer such intimacy on first meeting is not common. Not comfortable with returning the favour, I introduce myself using my public name. 'Pleased to meet you, Mender. I am Snake Fieth.'

The gnome's expression freezes when he hears my name, then he catches himself so quickly, I wonder if I imagined it. 'Ah, a city gnome. I thought as much. In our hamlet, the new fashion of using formal and informal names has been slow to catch on.'

I bite back a snort. The convention of public and private names has been around since the rebellion, which was hundreds of years ago.

Unsure what to do now, I wait for the gnome to give me some direction. He stares at me long and hard with a face that is difficult to read. The silence is becoming awkward, and I feel the urge to blurt out something to break the tension. Before I can make a fool of myself, an elderly female gnome enters from what can only be a kitchen, carrying a steaming bowl of stew.

'Ah, Snake Fieth, please allow me to introduce my wife, Keeper of Hearts.'

'Pleased to meet you, ma'am.' I hold out my hand, and she beams as she shakes it firmly.

'Put your things over by the door and come and eat,' she orders. 'I stayed a while listening to you, so I am running a little late. I will just fetch the bread from the oven.'

I lean my pack against the wall by the back door where

she indicated, and as I straighten, my eyes linger on the portrait of a full-grown gnome and a female gnome about my own age. The girl looks familiar. I look closer, but her name doesn't spring to mind.

'That is Breaker of Hearts and his daughter. Her mother died in childbirth, and her father moved to the World Above soon after,' Mender tells me when he finds me in front of the picture.

I get the sense he is waiting for me to comment or react in some way. I'm starting to find this all a little odd, but the moment is gone when he says, 'Come, we do not want the food to go cold.'

···👁···

I take a seat at the table where I can sneak another look at the portrait while we eat. I'm sure I know that girl. I wonder if she is one of the gnomes I met in the World Above.

The meal is delicious, and the conversation mostly revolves around music. They enjoyed my songs from the World Above, and Mender is interested to hear about the instruments we use. He explains that he makes and sells a wide variety of instruments, and as we speak, I'm sure he is working out how he could produce something new.

At his request, I draw a rough sketch of a guitar, and I swear if Keeper had not sent a warning look his way, he would have headed into his workshop right away to begin making one of his own. Trying to distract him, I ask Mender if he himself plays at all.

He smiles shyly. 'My gift is for making instruments, not playing them.'

'You play the pipe for dances,' his wife interjects, 'and a very pretty sound you make too.'

Mender demurs. 'The true musical talent in the family went to our son, Breaker. Much like you, he plays the lute and sings. He could draw deep emotions from even the coldest of hearts.'

'You obviously miss him a great deal,' I say. 'You said he's in the World Above?' A small touch of guilt flashes through me because I am only encouraging him to talk about his son in the hopes of finding out who the girl in the picture is.

'Yes, he is, or I hope he still is. It was an odd business for sure. Princess Petunia, heard him play and invited him to join her household. He was not ready to leave home, but then he saw the princess's companion, and we lost him,' Mender reminisces.

'More than taken with,' Keeper adds. 'It was love at first sight for both of them.'

The elderly couple's eyes meet across the table as they share the memory.

'So, Breaker joined the princess's household and moved to the Capitol. He made many friends and gathered quite a following of fans of his music. I could say he got in with the wrong crowd, but—'

'His friends were right thinking, and you know it,' Keeper of Hearts says. She turns to me. 'You will not remember the time of the blight when all the passages to the World Above were closed. Now we all understand that keeping the two worlds apart caused disease in our land, but back then, it was considered to be blasphemy to speak of such things.'

I knew about the blight. My mother had spoken of it a few times, but in the same way she spoke of any other period of history. It is obvious that for these gnomes, the events were very real. I want to ask them more.

'What Keeper is trying to explain is, our son was part of the group trying to convince the Creature Council to open the gates and allow movement between the worlds as a way to cure the blight. His Patron, Princess Petunia, was the group's leader.'

'He must have been very brave to support such an idea,' I say simply because there was a pause in the conversation, and I was sure they expected me to say something. They nod, and I am relieved I hit the right note with my praise.

'He was also perhaps a little foolish.' Mender said. 'The group was full of creatures from all races, and they mingled without considering how much they challenged the established way of doing things.'

My stomach tenses as my comfort levels drop. Breaker's story is turning out to be somewhat similar to my own. In the maze, that can't be a coincidence.

'He and his loved one married, and they had a daughter,' Keeper says, carrying on the story. 'His wife never recovered after the birth. We begged him to come home, but he had work in the Capitol, and he was proud of his position. Besides, the wife of one of his friends was willing to help with the raising of our granddaughter, Pure of Heart.'

'It wasn't until a few years later, once the doors were opened and things returned to normal, that the council got their revenge for being shown up by Princess Petunia's set,' Mender continued, his tone turning bitter. 'There was a backlash against the openness in her court after she was named heir.'

The mood in the room has turned sombre. The couple's pain is heavy in the air, causing me to feel a little awkward when I am forced to ask, 'Princess Petunia is Queen Ariana's sister, isn't she?'

Mender nods. 'When Queen Ariana's husband died, she vowed never to marry again. With Princess Petunia next in line for the throne, she declared her as successor. the council decided that was the time to exact retribution and issued the princess with an ultimatum—she could denounce her friends and remain heir or stand with them and be banished.'

Although I had heard about the heir's banishment, as we all did when we learned our history, this personal version of events brings the tale to life.

'Of course, the princess chose banishment to the World Above along with all of her friends who were married to creatures not of their race. We had hoped that because Breaker's wife was dead, he would be excused, but he was not.'

'So your family is stuck in the World Above?' I ask, tears forming in my eyes.

'Oh no,' Keeper says. 'Breaker wanted his daughter to grow up in the World Below. He had contacted us to see if we would take her in, but it all happened so quickly, and Pure of Heart was left with Breaker's friends. They formally fostered her, and she is part of their family now.'

It is like a blow to the stomach. I suddenly know who the girl in the portrait is and why she seems so familiar. Mender's next words confirm it.

'By the time we realised Breaker had been physically exiled, Pure had been living so long with the family, there was no thought of sending her back to us. We had never met her and, without our son to make the introductions, we would have been strangers to her. Some time later, she was fully adopted into the family, accepting a new name and a new identity.'

My heart is racing, and my hands are shaking so much, I need to place my cutlery on the table. Their metallic clatter fills the now silent room. The woman in the portrait is my mother—well, at least I think she is. These people I am eating dinner with are my great-grandparents. I keep my head down, processing everything I've just learnt about my family, wondering what to do about it.

'Fair, our grandchild, used to send us letters, but I from what I understand, she moved to the World Above herself to create a new life, and the letters stopped coming.'

I need to confirm my suspicions, and I want to find out if they invited me to dinner because they suspect who I am.

'Do you know anything more about her?' I ask.

Was that too obvious? Too late to take it back now.

Keeper sighs. 'We got the sense from her new family that she wanted to hide her true identity. Life was not easy for her—because of her true parents. We allowed her to slip away from us because we thought it was what she wanted… what she needed.'

'That is so sad,' I say, and I really mean it.

'It is, but we are not alone. Our daughter and her family live in the next hamlet. No doubt when we grow too old to run the shop anymore, we will move closer to her.' Keeper takes her husband's hand.

I have cousins. A smile tugs at my lips. I so want to tell them who I am and be welcomed into the family. I check myself. Is it fair to do that to them?

They let go of their son and granddaughter a long time ago and are content with their lives. Do I have a right to disturb their peace of mind, knowing their granddaughter is in disgrace and that I must leave tomorrow to try and save her? Would they appreciate that?

As these thoughts race through my mind and I attempt

to force them into some sort of action, I am conscious of Keeper standing and clearing the table. As if on automatic pilot, I rise to my feet. 'Please, let me help you with the dishes.'

'No, no young man, all is good.' She pats my hand. 'Perhaps Mender can show you to your room. You must be tired, and you set out on your quest again tomorrow. The maze waits for no one.'

I thank her for the meal before following Mender up the stairs and into a small bedroom with a single bed. A blue rag rug is the only floor covering, and a window in the ceiling frames the night sky, providing light.

'It isn't much,' he says as he pulls a comforter and sheets from the cupboard. 'It was our son's, and our grandson uses it when he comes to stay.

'It's perfect,' I assure him. And I mean it. I was going to spend the night sleeping in a field, and now I will be sleeping in my grandfather's old bedroom. 'Let me,' I say, taking the linen from him, and proceed to make the bed.

'Yes, well…'

I sense he wants to say something to me, and I will him to say the words I want to hear, making my decision for me.

'Well, goodnight, then.'

'Goodnight,' I say as the door shuts behind him.

I am left alone, wondering if I should have said something, and now it is too late.

··◡··

I snuggle under the down comforter, and even though my body is exhausted, I can't sleep. My thoughts chase each other in my head, not slowing for long enough for me to focus on anything.

Tonight I met my mother's family and found out that they're rather notorious compared to the straight-laced Fieth clan. When I think of my grandfather and everything he lost, I am hit by a sudden understanding. I know why my mother hid her roots all these years. I also know why Bernais treats her with such disdain—she's half elf, half gnome.

Her being charged with the crime of benefitting from her magic is not only to discredit the Fieth clan, it is also to reinforce the belief that any issue of a mixed union cannot help but be a vile, untrustworthy creature.

My journey through the maze took me to the Centre of Life all right—the centre of my own life. Pris was right to be wary about where this path would lead. It was never going to take me to the centre of the maze, but rather to a place where I could understand more about myself.

I sit up and lean back against the wall, all thoughts of sleep gone. I twist my newfound knowledge this way and that, probing my thoughts, wondering how this changes me.

My mother buried who she was so far inside, she never spoke of it, yet she carried feelings of inadequacy with her for her whole life. I now understand why she did not want to return below. In the World Above, people are more accepting of difference. Returning here would put her in the firing line of Bernais and other creatures who think like him.

Oh, and that is why Bernais is so against Pris and me being close. He's thinking, *like grandfather, like grandson*. Or is it that he doesn't want the royal line tainted with *my* mixed blood?

Funny thing—I'm more upset about my mother's treatment than the way Bernais and his friends have been treating me. It angers me beyond words that people think of her as an abomination.

I bite back a self-deprecating chuckle. This is a night of revelations. It is now clear to me why Pris insists on standing up to racism whenever she encounters it. If I accept other creature's views on Pris and me being together, then I am all but saying I agree with how they treat my mother.

I see my actions as Pris must, and shame eats at me. My stomach churns, and I worry I am about to lose my dinner. I want nothing more than to find her and tell her how sorry I am from the bottom of my heart. I can only hope I haven't lost her forever because of my own stupidity.

My mind is calming down. I crawl back under the covers as my eyelids close and sleep finally beckons. I'm just dozing off when footsteps on the stairs wake me. I roll over, but I cannot settle because of the voices coming from the room next door.

Mender and Keeper have lived so long alone, they mustn't realise how every word they say is booming its way through the thin walls. I try not to listen, but the conversation is too clear to block out. Besides, they're talking about me.

'If he did not recognise his own story in the telling of it, I am not sure we should tell him who he is to us. It would not be fair to him if his mother went to the trouble of concealing who she is, and we undo it all for nothing other than our selfish need to claim a great-grandson.'

'But Mender, we cannot let him leave without telling him.'

'Keeper, are you wanting to tell him for his benefit, or for ours? What good can it do for him to find out who we are when he is called to a quest in the maze? He cannot waste his energy, worrying about a new family when he will need all his wits about him if he is to succeed.'

'But it cannot be by chance that the maze brought him here. For some reason it wanted him to meet us. Perhaps we are meant to tell him who he is.'

'You know that is unlikely, Keeper. If the maze brought him here as part of his quest, then we can tell him nothing. He must find out for himself.'

'Ooh, you are such an infuriating gnome.'

They are silent for a while, then Keeper asks, 'Mender, do you think this is all still to do with Bernais Baarenson's campaign against his cousin, Petunia? He has never been the same since the Queen announced her as heir, then refused to retract it even when she left.'

'She is banished and can no longer take up the throne. Surely he cannot hold a grudge that long?'

'But husband, the Queen will not name another successor, and she is yet to produce any offspring.'

'True. Both the Crown cousins, Bernais and Elias, are high in her esteem. It will surely be one of them.'

'Which is why I think Snake's being here must be part of one of Bernais's schemes,' Keeper muses. 'Perhaps he wants to use Snake to remind everyone of how close Elias was to Petunia.'

'That is all so far away, Keeper, and knowing this will not help young Snake when he leaves here tomorrow.'

But it might help me when I get back to the Capitol.

My great-grandparents fall silent, and soon the sound of not-so-gentle snoring fills the air. Sleep now eludes me completely. I was given so many puzzle pieces to help me work out why I am here tonight, but they won't fit together. My head aches as I move them around, trying to make a coherent picture.

Eventually, I give up. All I can do is deal with what is in front of me and hope I will soon be able to gather enough pieces to make out the whole image.

As I doze, I'm still trying to decide whether or not I should introduce myself to my great-grandparents before I leave tomorrow. I mean, they know who I am, I know who they are—what can it hurt? Right?

CHAPTER 5

I Can Do This On My Own

The minute Snake disappears from sight, Pris picks up her pack and stalks off down Journey's End. I trail after her, not mentioning I do not think it a good idea to split up. I am pleased I kept my mouth shut when she spits, 'If he thinks I will follow him again, he is mistaken.'

A few minutes later she turns on her heel and heads in the opposite direction. She passes me, then moments later I hear her footsteps behind me.

'What the?'

She runs past me, then disappears only to be returned to her starting place once again. When her footsteps approach a third time, I put out a hand to restrain her.

'The maze does not work that way, Princess. You chose a path, and you must follow it to the end—there are no do overs.'

Her face crumples, but before I can reassure her it will be all right, she rearranges it into a look of fierce determination.

'We don't need him, do we, Percival?' she says, but there is a slight tremor in her voice.

I want to say we would be better off if he was here, but I sense that is not the right thing to say. 'We will be fine without him,' I tell her.

We walk in silence for some time, then the elf appears to recover herself and starts prattling. At first I try to block it out, but it becomes harder and harder. Finally, I can bear it no longer.

If I hear her say one more time that she doesn't need Snake and she has no idea what she ever saw in him, I am going to leave her to her own devices and join him. I would rather be with him than here with her anyway. She is an elf, after all, and elves are not my favourite creatures.

We started out all right. She was so certain she had chosen the right path. Then she decided to turn back and follow him because it would be better if they were together, but she found she could not.

'I mean, he is not really much use in a fight…'

I tune out her voice.

You had to go with her, I remind myself for perhaps the hundredth time. She is a princess, and of royal blood. If something happens to her because she understands so little about our ways, I will never be forgiven.

Something in the trees lining the path catches my eye. I pause for a moment but am unable to see anything. Mind you, if it was a sprite, they could easily hide from me. Especially as I can no longer sense them the way I used to.

I sigh. Being back here reminds me I am odd, fitting in nowhere. No longer a sprite, but not quite anything else either. And being in the forest reinforces that fact for me, especially as I am so close to my home. I cannot imagine how much more horrendous my life will be when I visit the

World Below if I let a princess down, and creatures have one more thing to vilify me for.

I do wish she would shut up though. It is difficult enough resisting the pull of the tree's song without her whinging in my ear as well. I mean, it is not as if I can do what the trees ask and join them—not anymore.

We are in a dense part of the forest, surrounded by woodlands as we follow a winding path. This is an ancient woodland, and the sage trees sense I want to be with them. If only they had taken away the song as well all those years ago, today would be much easier on me.

'He really should have waited. I mean, he needs me more than I need him…,' Princess Priscilla drones on.

My hackles begin to rise, not that I have hackles in this form. Really, this self-absorption is too much for me to bear. I stop walking, place my hands on my hips, and stamp my foot to gain the princess's attention.

'Oh for goodness sake, will you listen to yourself. Have some self-respect,' I hiss. 'So you got on well. So you came here together. So you are doing this partially for him. You chose not to go with him. Now own your decision, grow a backbone, and let us get moving.'

The princess stares at me, eyes widening in shock, and I brace myself for her reaction; she is known for her temper, after all. Then, after a moment's pause, she laughs. Not a small, ladylike giggle, but a loud burst of laughter. It's quite shocking. I stand tall and glare at her. Is she laughing at me? She carries on for a while. I spy some dust on my shirt and flick it off. She still hasn't stopped. Have I broken her?

She finally wipes the tears from her eyes and takes a couple of deep breaths.

'You're right, Percival. I'm acting like a lovesick teenager. I've never needed a boy before, and I don't need one now. Besides, you're with me, and you are much more valuable.'

Her brows draw together. 'Actually, I want to ask, why did you decide to come with me and not with him? I mean, I get the impression you don't even like me.'

I pause, wondering how much to tell her. In the end, I ignore the obvious invitation to deny that I dislike her and say, 'I came with you because you need me more, and saving you is more likely to gain me a better reward.'

Her head cocks to the side as she considers my answer. 'Self-interest is the only reason you came this way?' She nods. 'I can respect that. Well, I'm glad you are with me, whatever the reason.'

I resist the urge to preen. Elves are all silver-tongued, and they don't mean half of what they say. I will not fall for her words, as they are obviously intended to make me think kindlier of her. Instead, I say, 'If you are finished with your—what do human girls call it?—your pity party, there is a village not far up the road. I suggest we head there and get our bearings.'

Priscilla laughs again, and this time it's more controlled and a lot less alarming. 'It's a good thing you know where you are going, because I'm completely lost.'

Oops, I inadvertently took the lead. Perhaps not. I only made a suggestion. I must watch myself, as I do not mean to become part of this quest. What is done is done, but I will have to be more careful in the future.

'You know,' the princess is saying, 'I expected this to be a maze more like the one at Hampton Court. I expected hedgerows, twists and turns and dead ends, with the prize in the middle. All this open space leading to a forest feels more like an adventure.'

'Mazes can be different,' I say, not sure how much I can tell her in my role as observer.

'I get that, but once we were through the initial gates, it turned out to be more like a country stroll. Not that I'm complaining. Walking around the edge of the forest is lovely. The trees provide shade, and the bird song is so pleasant. Still… this can't be all there is. This is a quest, after all.'

Will the girl never cease talking? How I long to be able to return to Wimbledon and curl up by the fire in peace. All right, I will be in cat form when I do, but at least I will have some quiet.

The path wends its way through the forest. The trees now grow more tightly together, and we are deep in the shade. I could have sworn we were close to a village. The princess's chatter continues as my anxiety grows.

'I can almost imagine us walking through a forest in a fairy tale. You know, a path meandering through ancient trees… the deeper we go, the darker the path. I almost expect something to leap out at us.'

'Honestly, child, have you no common sense? Do you want to bring ill down on us?'

She stops walking and turns, her eyes growing wide with fear. Guilt pricks at my conscience. Just a little, mind you—she is still an elf, after all.

Her voice is uncertain when she speaks, and there is a tinge of fear mingled there. 'Can that actually happen?'

What do I say? Do I soothe her fears and tell her no. Or do I go with the truth, and say that of course it could, but it is unlikely.

She waits earnestly for my answer, and I realise I misread her. She is not angry at losing Snake. She is scared because she is in a strange world, and he is not here. *She should have thought about that before she decided to follow her own path*, I think rather uncharitably. Then I mentally kick myself. I remember what it is like being a stranger in a strange place. It is not her fault she is an elf, or that she knows nothing about her heritage.

'Come on. The sooner we are out of the woods, the better.' I am not confident it will be better for her, but it will be better for me because I will be further from my family, and the tree's song will no longer thrum through my veins.

···✌···

My mouth is running non-stop. It's irritating Percival, but I keep going, unable to control my tongue. If only I hadn't been so pigheaded about getting my own way, we would still be with Snake now. I'm sure Percival would rather be with him than me too, even if just to get a moment's peace.

Although my mouth has been telling the world how I don't need Snake, my head has been mentally shaking me. I am always so certain I am right. Why didn't I just listen to him?

Now I am stuck in a world full of magic, and I know virtually nothing about it, or what creatures I might encounter. I'm only just realising how much I relied on his knowledge of this strange world I only found out existed last week.

Funny, in spite of his wealth of knowledge, I was quick to pooh-pooh his concerns about how our being friends, more than friends, would be viewed. I decided I knew best.

Perhaps I was lulled by a false sense of security with the Fieth family and the dance at the ball last night. It all seemed so normal, I had almost forgotten this is a different world, and we were to sent out on a dangerous quest.

Then Percival asked me if I was tempting fate by

talking about things coming crashing out of the woods, and suddenly, I am now all too aware that I'm in a foreign land where I know none of the rules. For the first time in my life, I feel inadequate to face the challenge.

'Are you all right?' Percival asks me, his face contorted into what might pass for a worried frown.

I realise I have been silent, lost in my thoughts, and given my constant chatter up until now, he is worried.

'I'm okay,' I tell him, but I am not. Talking prevented me from thinking too much about... well, about every-thing. As we walk along in silence with only the rustle of the leaves and the twitter of birds punctuating our foot-steps, I am forced to confront the demons lurking in my head.

Will I be able to find the middle of the minotaur's maze without Snake? If I can't, then my parents will be convicted. The farcical trial at the ball last night was enough to tell me the charges were trumped up, but that does not make them any less real. It will not make the punishment any less real either—Bernais will see to that!

The very same Bernais who railroaded me into this quest with Snake—perhaps to get me out of the way. Or does he have something more sinister in mind? Is he hoping I won't return?

'Bring it on,' I say under my breath, checking Percival didn't hear me. He is oblivious. He appears to be having another of his 'moments.' Ever since we entered the forest, he has been zoning out every now and then. At first I thought he was just blocking me out, but I think it might be something more than that.

'Bring it on!' I say a little more strongly, drawing strength from the words. In the World Above, muggers targeted me all the time. Some of those attacks were quite violent, and I am still here. I will survive this too.

I instantly feel better, in control again. Okay, it was Snake who pointed out my muggings were unlikely to be random attacks, but I was the one who fought them off. Snake is not here to educate me on the World Below, but so what! I have Percival, and Percival seems to know more about this world than he does.

Ah, Percival is my guide in the World Below. I wonder if he could tell me more about who I am? After all, it might help me understand why I'm in this mess.

'Percival? Can I ask you something?'

There is no response.

I try again. 'Percival, are you able to tell me something more about my family, like how I'm related to Bernais and Elias?'

I may as well be talking to one of the trees.

While I am waiting for him to come out of his funk, I decide to go over what I already know. I am a Princess of Royal Blood—whatever that means. I also know that since arriving in the Seelie Court of the World Below, I'm the only elf I've seen with dark skin—apart from my father, that is. And I also know that many in the World Below believe my father is not part of the court.

Wind sweeps some strands of hair across my face, and I tuck them into my loose plait as I walk. I want to know about Bernais and Elias, but I also want to know why my father seems to be an outcast, and does that have anything to do with why my parents never told me about my heritage?

Percival is still lost in thought, but around midday we stop by a clear blue stream to get a drink and fill our water skins. He appears to be a little more aware, so now is as good a time as any to question him.

'Percival, you're here to help me understand this world, and I think it might be helpful for me to know a little more about my family, especially how I am related to Bernais and Elias in particular.'

Percival stretches in an almost feline way before pulling a comb from his pocket and tiding his already immaculate hair. When he is satisfied with his appearance, he answers.

'I am here to help with the quest only, but... as those two are part of why you are undertaking this particular folly, I think it might be all right to answer you. Can we walk as we talk? I would like to be out of these woods as soon as possible.'

He has not looked comfortable since we started walking under the trees. I would say he looks pale, but I am not sure whether that's his normal colour or not.

'Are you all right? You seem... um... unsettled. Is there something I can do to help?' I ask.

He pauses, his comb halfway back in his pocket, and regards me as if he is seeing me for the first time. I don't think he expected me to notice his unease. He slowly shakes his head. 'You cannot help me. It is just the woods. I will be better when I am out of here.'

He slips the comb fully into his pocket and we start out again.

'They are not your close relatives,' he starts. 'Bernais and Elias, I mean. Their mothers are cousins to Queen Ariana.'

He walks ahead a little. Is that all he is going to say? I catch him up.

'That still doesn't explain why Bernais appears so set against me, while Elias isn't,' I point out.

He humphs. I mean, literally humphs. Who does that?

'Elias was always sweet on Princess Petunia, the second daughter of Queen Althea. She chose to marry another, and he left the Capitol soon after. He was only recently recalled by Queen Ariana to take up the role of Chancellor. His absence from the political arena for all those years left him rusty. He is still finding his feet. If he remained at court, maybe he would have been better placed to keep you out of things.'

Well, that's an interesting tidbit, but it doesn't explain Bernais. 'And Bernais? Why does he hate me?'

Percival shrugs. 'I suspect he does not hate you personally, but rather, he is set against those of the old Queen's bloodline. You see, Queen Althea did not have Ariana until late in life, so her niece, Bernais's mother, was named heir.'

I can see a pattern here. 'So, when Althea had a child that changed?'

'Yes, and Bernais was not happy about his loss of status. Then, some years later, when Princess Petunia, Ariana's younger sister, was born, Bernais was no longer considered to be of Royal Blood. Bitterness at his loss of station has taken over his life since then.'

'I think I heard someone say Princess Petunia is the current heir, is that correct?' I ask.

'Not exactly. There was some… well… some horridness about who her friends were, and she was banished. Queen Ariana has no children, and did not remarry after her husband died, so….'

'So events created a power vacuum, and Bernais sees himself filling it?'

Percival nods. 'Precisely, although I am sure there is more to his machinations than that.'

'Of course there is,' I mutter. Percival has given me quite the history lesson, but at least listening to him is better than listening to the demons in my head. 'Carry on,' I urge as I almost trip over Percival.

He has stopped in his tracks, as if frozen in place. I step

forward to see what happened to him, only to be encased in some sticky substance that prevents me from moving. I can't even open my mouth to voice my frustration. My heart is pounding and fear washes through me. Give me an opponent to fight and I'm fine, but being trapped like this… it's mind-numbingly scary.

We stay locked in place for goodness knows how long. My fear builds and my mind imagines all kinds of bloody and murderous ends for us. The air is turning cold when a woman appears on the path.

Wrinkled beyond imagining, wearing a long skirt and blouse of good quality but well-worn fabric, she cackles like a witch as she moves closer. My heart pounds in my head. This is it. This is how it ends, and I can't even use my get-out-of-the-maze-free option.

'In a bit of a bind, are we?' She laughs at her own joke.

My fear turns to anger. I would say something smart back, but I can't move my mouth. I can't even clench my fists to release my frustration.

'Ah, Percival, it is a long time since you visited these parts.' She steps past him and stands in front of me. 'And this must be Princess Priscilla. Such a pleasure to meet you.'

The woman snaps her fingers, and my eyelids begin to droop. If my life is about to end, I want to face it front on. As I try to fight what is happening to me, my head starts to swim and my vision clouds. Try as I might, I cannot keep my eyes open, and I am soon sinking into an inky blackness.

My brain sends a message to my eyelids to open, but they are still heavy with sleep and magic and refuse the command. Listening to my surroundings, I try to sense whether or not I am in any immediate danger. I try to move my arms and legs, but they are heavy, like a weight is pressing down on them. I freeze in panic. Am I still bound by the spell?

Keeping my rising fear at bay, I force myself to concentrate to try and work out where I am. Apart from crackling, which I assume to be a fire, everything is quiet, I can't even hear birds singing. Wherever I am, I think I am alone.

I roll over and manage to half open one of my eyes to find I am lying on a bed in a simply furnished room. Opposite me, a fire warms the cosy space with comfy chairs sitting on either side of the hearth. In the centre of the room is a well-worn wooden table with a chair at each side. To my right is a door, and to my left is a bench under a window.

I wait for my head to clear before I open both eyes, swing my still heavy legs around, and place my feet on the ground. Pushing myself up, my legs are stiff but I'm able to stand. I'm not woozy, so I'm pretty sure the crone didn't drug me.

I make my way across the room, and then I fling open the door. Instead of the expected escape route, I find a wooden bench with a hole in it. I lean over and peer down. The depth of the hole and the smell tell me this is what passes for a toilet.

Back in the room with the door securely closed, I frantically search for another way out. I rush to the window, pulling and pushing against the frame, but it doesn't open. There's no other door to be seen. I am trapped unless I want to smash the window.

'Please do not break my window.' The voice comes

from all around me, and soon after, the woman from the forest appears in one of the chairs by the fire.

She waves her hand, and a pitcher of water appears on the bench, and a bowl of apples and pears materialises on the table. With a click of her fingers, a cast-iron pot places itself over the flames of the fire, filling the room with a juicy, meaty aroma.

'Come sit, child.' The woman gestures with a hand to the chair opposite her.

I eye her warily. What does she want with me? The tale of Hansel and Gretel floods my mind. I was terrified of that story as a child, and my knees tremble now. As I am trapped in this cottage in the centre of a strange wood. Has she brought me here to end my quest?

'I'm okay,' I say.

She smiles as if I amuse her. Perhaps she read my mind. 'Please, you will be more comfortable if you sit while we talk. Besides, if I meant to harm you, why would I go to the trouble of providing you with food?'

To fatten me up before eating me.

I consider the stew simmering over the fire. *Or maybe she intends to poison me.*

I sigh as I realise the true meaning of the food. I am going to be here for some time. I continue to stand as a sort of protest against the idea, then I reconsider. I want to leave here, and she is the only one who seems to be able to come and go, so I need her goodwill.

'Excellent,' she says when I lower myself into the seat. She folds her hands in her lap. 'Now, you can go no further in the maze until you access your powers and show you can use them. The minotaur's rules prohibit entry to the uninitiated.'

I grip the chair's arms as my wariness turns to alarm. 'What? Why didn't anyone tell me this before?'

'That is not my problem. My job is to check all those who come my way to ensure they meet the requirements of the quest and are able to proceed. You do not.'

I am frozen in place, my fuddled brain processing her words but coming up blank. The maddeningly calm creature sits in front of me, saying nothing. Is she waiting for me to speak?

'Where is Percival?' I ask, then mentally kick myself. I should be asking exactly what they need from me so I can get out of this goddamn prison.

She shrugs. 'He is free to go on.'

Is this woman purposefully trying to irritate me? I narrow my eyes and study her closely. No. I think she is answering my questions and no more. I decide to test my theory and try a different tactic. 'Are you going to train me to access my magic?'

She emits a tinkling laugh. 'Oh, my goodness, no. I am only the gatekeeper. All you need to do is complete the training you began in the World Above, access your full powers, and you will be able to move on.'

She can't be serious. I only just found out I had my magic. I can barely produce a flame, the simplest of spells. 'What training?'

'You can make a flame, can't you?' the old woman asks, a perplexed frown drawing her brows together. 'Of course you must be able to. You got here from the World Above. To do that, you must have discipline, focus, and be able to access your magic. Someone must have at least trained you to do the latter.'

Snake helped me form my flame—well, Snake and some random cat.

'You can access your magic. You just need to be able to figure out what the source of it is so you can learn to use it. Once you do that, you will be able to leave.'

She makes it sound so simple. I am not taken in. 'So I stay here until I learn that, even if I take a week? Or a month?'

'Oh no, my dear. I cannot let you stay in my home that long. You may stay two nights, then you must be gone.'

Surely it can't be that easy. 'What? So all I need to do is wait two nights, and then you will let me out?'

'No, dear. Either you use your magic to let yourself out before your time is up, or I use mine to expel you from the maze.'

I knew it had sounded too easy. So now, not only must I work out why members of my own family hate me, but I also have to learn how to use my magic and control it enough to get out of this prison. I curse my parents for keeping me apart from my true heritage. My life would be so much easier now if they had just fessed up. As it is, I don't even know where to start to figure out the origins of my power.

'Can you at least tell me what kinds of magic elves can use?' I ask, suddenly feeling very meek.

'Well, I do not normally do that... but I cannot see how that breaks the rules. It should be all right.'

My eyebrows raise. 'There are rules to this?'

The old woman frowns again, 'Of course. Rules govern everything in the World Below.'

'Sorry. Everything here is so... so alien to me.'

'Of course it is, my dear. In the World Below, we recognise four different types of magic: earth, air, physical, and particle.'

I am no better off knowing what they are. 'Can you tell me what each of those do?'

'No.'

'Sugarcoat it, why don't you?' My tone is harsh and sarcasm taints my words. The woman flinches, and a thread of remorse trickles through me. No, I will not feel sorry for her. She has trapped me here, and getting a straight answer from her is like wading through treacle.

'Can Percival help me?' I ask.

'He cannot come in. Whether he waits for you or not is up to him. He is free to wander the maze and can come and go as he wishes.'

My head is spinning. Is there anything else I need to ask to make sure I don't find myself unceremoniously kicked out of the maze? While I marshal my thoughts, the woman decides she has said all she is going to and blinks out of sight.

'What the…?' I jump to my feet. 'I can't believe this place.' I pace in front of the fire. 'I'm supposed to figure out how my magic works while stuck in a room with no one to help.' I spin on my heel and walk the other way. 'And if I don't, this is all over, and my parents will pay the price.'

I continue pacing for a bit longer, spiralling into my anger and muttering to myself. Pausing in front of the fire, I watch the flames for a moment. Being angry isn't helping, but I can't seem to calm down. I walk to the window and stare out at the trees.

'It is not going to help you, all that ranting,' a voice says from beside me. 'You need to be calm when you use your magic, or it will get out of control.'

I swivel my head, looking for the source of the advice. Glancing down, I strain to see. The angle isn't great, but I just make out Percival, who is sat leaning against the house, reading a book. In front of him is a blazing fire in a pit. Behind that is a tent erected with a camp stretcher set up inside.

'What *are* you doing?' I ask, speaking more loudly than

normal so he can hear me through the window. 'And where did all this… stuff come from?'

'I have made myself comfortable while I wait for you to find your magic and use it to release yourself,' he answers as he pushes himself to his feet, walks around the fire, and places the book on the bed. He returns and stands in front of the window so I can see him better. He doesn't explain the source of his comforts, but that is the least of my worries.

'How do I do that? Find my magic, I mean.' My voice sounds churlish even to my own ears, so I am not surprised when he glares at me.

'You will start with what you have and work hard to improve.'

My cheeks heat with shame, but I say defiantly, 'But two days is such a short time.'

Percival's gaze is unflinching. 'You had best get started, then.'

Panic bubbles up inside me. Until now I have been focussing my fear and transferring it into anger. Now Percival's call to action has stripped me bare. I cannot do this. I can barely make a flame. I will fail. And I hate to fail.

I hear my father's voice in my head. *Failure is a part of learning. And you can't learn if you don't even try.*

'Dammit, why do you have to be so inspiring,' I mumble. I take a deep breath, ignore the panic threatening to overwhelm me, and ask, 'Right, where do I start?'

Sighing, Percival moves closer to the window. 'You are an elf. Your magic is strong. You just have to learn how to use it. It should only take a small amount to release you from here.'

His gaze holds mine, and I am again reminded of the cat I met—was it only yesterday?—who showed me who I really was. Who convinced me I could make a flame.

'Percival, was that you—'

'We will start off using your flame to identify your magical abilities.'

He is deflecting, but why? If he is some sort of shapeshifter, then that is really cool. Still, if he doesn't want to talk about it. 'My flame? How?'

'We use your flame to identify the source of your magic. There are simple tests we can do that creatures have been doing for millennia.'

'All right.' What else can I say? It's not like I have many options.

'We will start with the easiest—earth magic allows you to pull the flame from heat found in the world around you.'

I take a deep breath to settle my nerves before saying, 'I understand. How will I tell if I form it using earth magic?'

He stands on tiptoe and looks into the room. 'Ah, how helpful—you have apples. Go stand close to the fruit bowl and make your flame.'

I walk to the table and take a deep breath. It takes a couple of attempts, but soon I have a small purple flame sitting over the palm of my hand. I only learnt how to do this yesterday, and I am still amazed I can draw power and make fire dance on my palm. I smile.

'Now, can you sense any heat in your flame?'

My smile disappears as I focus back on the task at hand. I stare at the licking fire, but I can't see any darker bits that might indicate heat. I pass my other hand over top. The flame is cold. I put my finger through it, waiting to feel the burn, but it is cool to the touch. I turn to Percival. 'It's cold.'

He shrugs. 'There is no point in the next step, then, which is sensing heat in the fruit, a part of its life-force, then drawing it out and using it to increase the volume of your flame.'

I try not to be disappointed. There are three other types of magic, after all. 'So I have no affinity with earth. What's next?'

'Air is the next easiest to master, but I think that is not your type of magic either.'

I frown. 'Why not?'

'Because there is no heat in your flame. Air magic moves an existing flame to you,' Percival explains.

I nod. 'You mean something like taking a flame from the fire and moving it to my hand?'

'Not quite. More like sucking the heat from the fire and using air to fan it into a flame on your palm,' he explains.

'And it would be hot because it comes from an actual fire,' I finish.

'Exactly.'

'Hold on, there was no fire nearby when I made a flame yesterday.'

Percival sneers. 'There is always heat around. What do you think is at the centre of our earth?'

I resist the urge to slap the palm of my hand to my forehead. Any pleasure I took from working out how air magic makes a flame disappears. All this talk of magic has me forgetting things I know to be true about the world. Now I see why Snake is so interested in physics and magic. My flame starts to flicker. I try to hold it, but it splutters out.

'You are tired,' Percival says. 'We shall test the other two options tomorrow.'

He turns to his tent, and I rush to the window. 'No, Percival, I am fine. I can keep going.'

He half turns back towards me. 'You need to make sure you rest. Magic takes something out of you, especially when you are learning.'

'But if I can figure out my magic, I can get out of here sooner.' I don't want to spend a night in here.

Percival shakes his head. 'You need to make sure you are well rested. Not just so you can find the source of your magic, but also so you are able to use it to get yourself out of there once you do.'

My stomach lurches. I had forgotten about that.

'Goodnight.' Percival picks up his book.

I lean my forehead against the windowpane and watch him as he lies on the camp bed and begins reading. For a few minutes, I watch the flames in his fire grow brighter as the sun sinks below the trees. I wonder where Snake is and if he is close by.

'Goodnight.' I am not sure whether I am speaking to Percival or to Snake.

I turn my back on the scene outside and begin to pull together a meal of stew and fruit. As the thick meat and gravy warms my belly, I stare forlornly around the room. I have never felt more alone.

CHAPTER 6

Maybe I Can't

Fixing my eyes to the page, I sense rather than see the elven princess staring at me. I want to tell her I think her affinity is with particle magic so we can move on to getting her out. I cannot. Not just because this is the same process all the greater creatures go through, but also because I am not meant to be helping her like that.

I worry I am exceeding the terms of my agreement with the council. Having the elf skip the air test is definitely close to overstepping my bounds. From now on I have to be careful to merely point her in the right direction.

The shadow she casts disappears. I rise and move to stand under the window. A chair scrapes and is followed by the familiar sounds of someone eating. Dishes clatter, and I suspect she is clearing up. Then there is quiet. I sit down, leaning my back against the cottage, listening to her movements, waiting impatiently for the sounds that will tell me she is sleeping.

My fire dies down, and I place some more logs in the

pit. Before retaking my seat, I dust down my clothes. There was a time when forest elements such as dirt would not have bothered me. Perhaps I have spent too long as a cat and now I cannot help but fuss about my appearance.

The princess tosses and turns. I count the minutes, trying not to become impatient, but she will not settle. I go to the tent and retrieve my book to pass the time until she falls asleep. When I am certain her breathing has become slow and regular, I bank the fire, close up my tent, and will myself to the maze entrance.

Eleanora is pacing when I appear.

'I only just called you,' I defend myself before she speaks.

My friend and mistress turns, hands resting on her hips. 'I have been waiting for your call to meet for hours,' she responds. 'You have no idea how worried I have been, imagining all sorts of dangerous tasks the minotaur might set for Snake and Princess Priscilla.'

'She prefers to be called Pris,' I say automatically, then clasp my hand over my mouth.

Eleanora's laugh rings in the night air. 'I thought she was "that elf", and now you are worried about what she prefers to be called,' she teases me.

I resist the urge to defend myself a second time. More worryingly, she might be right. Sometime in the course of a single day, my opinion of Princess Pricilla Crown shifted.

I humph, not ready to admit I might be warming to the elf, and change the subject by asking, 'So, do you want to know what happened today, or do you want to carry on teasing me?'

In a heartbeat, Eleanora transforms from amused to concerned. 'Percival, are you all right?'

'The minotaur decided to send us through the forests.'

No other words are needed; she will understand without elaboration.

She rests a hand on my shoulder. 'Oh, Percival, no. How are you holding up?'

Her touch undoes me, and tears form in my eyes. 'Not well,' I grudgingly whisper. I cannot say more for fear I will fall apart.

'I did not think this would be a test of you as well. If I had even an inkling….'

I shake my head. 'We both knew there was a possibility of my being drawn into the quest. For a number of years, I have been considering petitioning the Queen, but our trips to the World Below are always so short, there is never any time. The minotaur may have sensed my desire and made additional plans for me. Perhaps he thinks he is doing me a favour.'

Eleanora crouches down so her eyes are level with mine. 'Is that what you want, my old friend?'

I close my eyes to gather my thoughts. I have no idea what I want. I shrug.

'If you stick to the agreement we made with the minotaur, you will still be able to choose your own path,' she reassures me, then pauses. 'Hold on, you haven't been helping out already, have you?'

Time to change the subject. 'The elf and Snake split up this morning.'

A frown draws Eleanora's brows together. 'What do you mean, they split up?'

I knew that would distract her. 'Snake wanted to go one way and the princess another. They could not agree, so they each took their own path.'

Eleanora's mouth forms a perfect 'O.' She rises to her feet and begins pacing again. 'This is not good.' A few minutes later, she follows that statement with, 'Working as a team, they stood a chance. Apart? I just don't know. But our plan still might have a chance.'

Eventually, she stands still, staring at the gate, her lip with her index finger. 'Who did you go with?'

'The princess,' I respond.

She nods. 'And where is she now?'

'Trapped by a hag who will not let her go any further without learning to use her magic. If she cannot demonstrate her control, she will be expelled from the maze the day after tomorrow.'

Eleanor is silent for such a long time, I am not sure she heard me. 'Eleanora.'

'I am thinking. If she does not make it through, our plans might all be for nothing.'

'Snake might still make it to the centre without her,' I say, feeling the need to defend the boy.

'I am sure he will, and we will need him as well, but the princess is key.'

I am aware that the greater creatures Eleanora is friends with were up long into the night, plotting and planning. They are no novices in creature politics, but it has been a number of years since they have been forced to play the game at this level.

Although I am not part of their scheme, I understand that there is more at stake than I am privy to or want to be privy to, and I should give Eleanora time to move the pieces around to their new positions and see where that leaves us.

'It appears the minotaur is testing their strength of character before he allows them into the centre of the maze. It may have been his design that separated them. There is still a chance they may win through to face the final challenge together,' she muses.

'It is possible, but not a given,' I tell her. 'They are

quite annoyed at each other for some reason. I cannot see them working side by side again any time soon.'

'Perhaps this too is part of their testing,' she says.

Again, I have to disagree. 'I think this is… um… more personal.'

Eleanora's eyes crinkle with laughter. 'Ah, I understand. A lovers' tiff. I am sure they will get over it.'

'I am not so sure. Snake was very determined, and Pris…. She is quite conflicted."

'Love is a fickle thing, Percival, especially young love. They might come together again just when we fear they will always be apart.'

'And what would I know about love?' My tone is tart. My chance at love was scuttled before it was even afloat. No, I will not think on the past. I must focus on the task at hand. 'What do you want me to do, Mistress?'

A chuckle rolls from the Witch of Wimbledon's throat. 'It always comes back to that, doesn't it? You asking how you can be of help, and me being all too demanding. You can always refuse me. I will think none the less of you.'

Now I am embarrassed. I normally only refer to her as Mistress when I am teasing her. Or when I am annoyed that she has asked me to do something I dislike but will do it because I know it needs to be done. I like helping her because she stands up for all creatures like she and her sisters once stood up for me.

'Perhaps you could go and visit with your family one evening while the princess sleeps. Take some real time to figure out what you want for the future.'

I briefly consider her proposal. I would like to see my mother and brother… and Nisha too. However, I am not sure I am quite ready to decide my future. Besides, Eleanora really does need my help to see this through, even though she pretends otherwise.

'I am only suggesting you take the lead on this. I am a mere pawn in your plans,' I backtrack.

'Oh, Percival.' I sense she wants to say something more, but instead she asks, 'Are you all right to continue helping Priscilla—Pris? Being so close to the forest must be breaking your heart, and having to deal with an elf too....'

'I am fine, Eleanora,' I lie. 'I will do this for you and the others.'

'As always, my friend, our plots would not succeed without you.'

'Yes, we lesser creatures are often overlooked and therefore can do what you cannot.' It is difficult to admit that the only reason I can help is because greater creatures underestimate me.

'You had best go get some sleep, Percival. I believe tomorrow will be another long day for you.'

She hugs me briefly before disappearing into the night.

··◡··

I punch the pillow into shape and pull the blanket back up before rolling over and trying to go back to sleep. Exhaustion seeps through my bones, as I only dozed off and on all night. I flop over onto my back and stare at the ceiling. It's no use. I'm awake.

I throw off the covers and stretch before padding barefoot across to the window, wanting to check whether or not Percival is an early riser. His tent is firmly closed, and the fire in front of it is nothing but embers, so I am guessing not. My breath fogs the pane as I lean my head on the cool glass.

In the predawn light, I can just make out the trees at

the edge of the clearing in front of the cottage. They loom ominously, and my stomach does a little flip. Is Snake out in the woods? Is he all right? We should have stayed together. I wipe the fog away impatiently. Worrying about the past won't help me now.

I pour some water into a bowl and rinse the sleep from my eyes before washing myself as best as I can. After tidying the bed, I take my clean plate from the bench over to the table. I guess it is either apples or stew for breakfast.

When I take the lid off the pot, I am pleasantly surprised to find a porridge laced with dried fruit and nuts bubbling away. I load a good dollop into the bowl and turn to find honey and cream on the table. I do love magic, especially if it can do this. I pour a little of both over the top of my breakfast and hoe in.

The food is gone in moments, and it only takes a little longer before the living area is clean and tidy. Although the sun is not fully up, I head to the window, hoping Percival has appeared. It is still too early for him.

I pace around for a while, too restless to settle. Perhaps now would be a good time to do some exercise. Clearing a space, I start with some breathing exercises followed by a warmup before running through my kata. As always, the process centres me, and when I am finished, I am ready to face anything the World Below throws at me.

After returning the furniture to its original position, I pour myself a glass of water and gulp the liquid down. Then I make one last hopeful journey to the window. Percival has packed up his little camp and is patiently waiting for me. His face is drawn, almost as though he didn't sleep any better than I did last night.

'Good morning,' I smile. 'Have you eaten?'

He nods but says nothing.

'Are you ready to begin?' I ask.

'I awoke some time ago. I am merely waiting for you to finish whatever you were doing so we can begin.'

Someone got up on the wrong side of the bed this morning. 'I needed to clear my head before we start. I'm good to go now.'

I watch as Percival stands up and walks towards me. As he draws closer, I'm surprised to find his face is grey, and there are deep creases around glazed eyes. He has the look of someone ignoring a massive headache.

'Are you all right?' I ask. 'Perhaps you should go back to bed.' There isn't really time for him to take the morning off, but I worry he might collapse if he doesn't.

'I am fine. Nothing some tea won't fix.' The words are forced out through gritted teeth.

He clearly isn't anywhere near all right, but if he doesn't want my sympathy or help, so be it.

'Let us begin. Mind magic is what is tested for next. Magicians with this skill tend to be empathetic, and their magic allows them to heal, including healing the mind. I am pretty certain this is not where your abilities lie, but I could be wrong.'

Hold on, did he just call me unsympathetic? After I just asked him how he was?

'Are you paying attention?'

'Yes,' I answer, although I obviously wasn't.

'When those with physical magic, or mind magic as some call it, make a flame, they are actually forcing themselves and anyone close by to imagine the flame is there,' he explains.

'Like creating an illusion?' I ask.

'Exactly.'

I gnaw on my lip. 'So how do we test whether or not my flame is made this way?'

'First make your flame,' Percival instructs.

It is getting easier to create fire on my palm each time I do it. I hold up my hand and show it to Percival.

'Now, while you are holding the flame, imagine it is now a coin spinning in the air.'

'What? Are you serious?' My flame goes out as I lose concentration. 'How am I supposed to do that?'

Percival sighs, and I feel like the most incompetent creature ever. 'As I understand it, you imagine a coin near the flame. When you have control of it, you push it to where the flame is and make the fire disappear. It should convince you, and me, that the flame is now a coin if you do it quickly enough—if your magic is mind magic, that is.'

I look at him as if he is mad. He sighs again. 'Or I guess you could just try making the flame appear some-where else.' He holds out his hand. 'See if you can make one on my hand.'

I take a deep breath and go through the process I usually do when my flame appears, only this time I try to put it on Percival's outstretched hand. Nothing.

I try twice more, but I can't see anything. I try once more, and I imagine holding the flame there.

'Can you see anything?' I ask in desperation.

'Oh, you started? I was not sure,' Percival says inno-cently, and I want to punch him.

'Yes,' I growl.

He shrugs and drops his hand to his side. 'I guess that only leaves us with particle magic.'

'Are you sure?' I ask. 'I mean, from my perspective, this is an odd way to test for magic that deals with the physical being. Come to think of it, all these tests are rather odd.'

'No, I'm not sure,' he snaps. 'It is not like this is some-thing I do every day. I'm a sprite. We do not need to be tested because we all use earth magic.'

'Then how—'

'From watching greater creatures being tested,' he finishes. 'And none of them are as difficult about it as you!'

I ignore his bad temper. It's not my fault his headache is making him grumpy, and it isn't my fault I don't know much about magic. Still, he is trying to help me despite what is going on with him, so I try to keep my tone neutral as I ask, 'Is there something else we can try to test whether or not I use mind magic?'

He closes his eyes, and I wonder if I've pushed him too far. They fly open. 'Yes… perhaps. Eleanora has spoken of seeing colours around living things.'

'What, you mean like an aura?' I scoff.

He frowns. 'You asked, so no need to get snippy with me.'

'Sorry,' I say, and I am.

'I believe if you relax and attempt to absorb everything about a living object, the colour is just there,' he explains.

He isn't joking. I did ask him if there was another way, so I guess I will give it a try—even if it sounds like spiritualist mumbo jumbo.

Percival rubs his forehead. 'Perhaps you can have a go while I take my tea.'

Without waiting for an answer, he moves away and finds a tree stump close by to use as a seat. He reaches into his pocket, and a table appears, followed by steaming a teapot and a cup and saucer.

As he makes himself comfortable and pours some tea, I am dismissed. I may as well do what he said while I wait for him to finish. It's not like there is anything else to do.

I pick an apple from the bowl and drop cross-legged to the floor. Holding up the fruit, I try to take in every detail. When I peer at it more closely, I see that the skin is red, laced with flecks of a darker red. There is a slight bruise near the bottom that is turning a little brown. I smell its sweet, sharp scent before running my fingers over the silky-smooth surface. Nothing. I stare so hard at the apple, my vision blurs and the fruit shimmers. This is not working.

I rise and place the apple back in the bowl and then wander over to the window. Percival's tea things are gone, and he is cleaning his clothes with magic, then 'ironing' out the wrinkles. He pulls out a comb and tidies his hair. He is so fastidious. It makes me smile.

Glancing down at my rumpled outfit, I wonder if Percival will tidy me up when I escape from here. Or, better still, will I be able to do it for myself? Best I find my way out first.

'Ahem, Percy.'

He swings round and I feel the full force of his death stare. 'I am Percival, never Percy.'

'Um... okay.... Anyway, I don't think my magic is anything to do with nature and the physical.'

He raises and eyebrow. 'I am not surprised. You lack empathy.'

'Snippy,' I retort. I want to add, 'I don't,' but I am well aware that it is not one of my strengths.

We glare at each other. Time almost seems to stop as we face off. We can't go on wasting time like this—my deadline is looming. I break eye contact first. 'What now?'

He shrugs. 'Your magic must be particle magic.'

I almost sag to the ground with relief. We have finally moved a step closer to getting me out of this prison. 'Great. Can you teach me how to use it?'

'Hold on, let us not get ahead of ourselves. We should test it to make sure we are right.'

I tense a little, but force a smile. I mean, we tested all the other options, why are we wasting time on this?

Percival sighs. He does that a lot. 'We test to make sure

we are right. And we test because that is your first lesson on how to use your magic.'

That is so logical, I can't argue with it, but it slows things down. I clench and unclench my fists, trying to let go of my anger. If I am honest though, I am also trying to calm my nerves.

My mind circles back to my learning to make a flame, which was so difficult. Now that we have found my magic, I am worried I won't be able to use it before I am kicked out of the maze.

Oblivious to my misgivings, Percival carries on talking. 'Creatures with this sort of magic often describe seeing the individual parts that make up an object. Sometimes they can even see them moving.'

A light switches on in my head, 'Ah, like they see the particles that make things, like electrons and neutrons.'

'What?' Percival says, then simply ignores my comment. 'Start with the apple again. This time when you look at the fruit, you want to try and find all the tiny pieces that make it an apple.'

'Honestly, Percival, isn't any of your advice practical?'

Dropping his head into his hands, Percival moans, 'Must you always argue? Just once can you not do what I ask without complaining?'

I glare at him through the glass. 'Perhaps I wouldn't argue so much if you were a better teacher.'

He looks up, catches my eye, and calmly reaches into his pocket and pulls out a book. Opening it to the bookmarked place, he drops his eyes and starts reading.

My temper has got the better of me, and I have overstepped. Although my anger still has a hold of me, I say, 'I'm sorry, Percival. I didn't mean it. I wouldn't have been able to come this far without you.'

He continues reading as if I haven't spoken, although

maybe his posture isn't quite as rigid. I wait a moment, hoping he will relent.

'Grrrr.' Of course, he has no idea how infuriating his passive dismissal is. I have to try something else or resign myself to waiting until his mood changes. 'Tell me, do you shrink things to fit in your pocket?' I ask him.

He raises his eyes. 'Don't be ridiculous. I created a portal in my pocket that opens into the library at Eleanora's. Her daughter is home, and she is the one making sure I am fed and watered.'

My eyes go wide, and my mouth drops open. *What?*

'Get out of here! Really? That is so cool. What sort of magic allows you to do that? Will I be able to make a portal?'

He stares unblinkingly at me with his startling green eyes as if he is waiting for something.

The penny slowly drops. 'I know. I must find out what my magic is before I do anything more advanced.'

His eyes return to the words on the page in front of him. I am dismissed again.

Turning my back on the scene outside, I rake my gaze over the room. Percival is not going to help me until I try his stupid idea.

I pull out a chair and face the bowl of apples and pears. I take some deep breaths to relax, then I stare at an apple for forever. Well, at least for a couple of minutes. Nothing happens.

I resist the urge to leap to my feet and tell Percival he is wrong, that this is not my type of magic. I lean back in the chair and stare at the fire. I am so tired, all I want to do is sleep. I clear my mind and allow the flames to send me into a trance.

As I watch the fire flicker and dance in the fireplace,

something seems to shift within my vision. I'm able to pick out every tiny particle that makes up each curling tendril of fire. Percival was right, they do not sit still—they move around as if full of energy.

I turn my head towards the bowl. The room swirls about me and my head spins. I narrow my focus down to the bowl of fruit. I can identify all the bits that make up the apples and the pears and the bowl and the table, plus some stray pieces in the air.

'Percival,' I call. 'I can—' My vision returns to normal.

I turn and find the sprite peering in through the window. He is smiling.

'So particle magic is your forte. Can you do it again?'

I am grinning, and laughter bubbles up inside me. I resist the urge to clap my hands like an excited child. Instead, I return my gaze to the bowl and try again. I clear my mind and try to relax. Nothing happens. Frustration roils inside, but I press it down. Turning to the fire, I start the process of "seeing" the particles again.

I do this three or four times and then try breaking the fruit into pieces without using the fire. After a number of attempts, I am finally able to do it.

'One more time,' I tell myself. 'I did it,' I shout when I succeed.

'Now, can you make your flame and observe as the particles create the shape?' Percival asks.

I am shaking with excitement, but I do as he bids, and I'm amazed as all the stray pieces of stuff floating around in the air come together over my hand to form a flame. I rise to my feet, knocking over the chair, and punch the air. 'I rock!'

'Yes, indeed,' Percival responds drily.

My stomach rumbles, punctuating the celebration.

'You need to eat,' he tells me.

He's right, I'm hungry and exhausted. I finish off another large serving of porridge from the pot, and as I push the plate away, a portion of apple pie with cream appears.

So the crone is watching me.

I finish the desert. 'I wish I had some coffee,' I muse, wondering if the crone will oblige.

Nothing magically appears, and I chuckle out loud. I can't believe I actually expected coffee to appear. How this world has changed me. Percival disappears from the window, then reappears moments later. A cup of coffee materialises in front of me.

A smile curls the edge of Percival's mouth. 'With Eleanora's daughter's compliments.'

Could this day get any better? I sip the hot brew and relax in my chair. I am going to savour every mouthful of this because I have earned it.

I'm not quite done when Percival's voice shatters my peace. 'Well, if you have quite finished, you still have to find a way out of there.'

'You mean, like, make enough fire to burn the place down?' I ask cheekily.

'No.' The voice comes from nowhere, sounding very much like the crone.

'This is probably her home,' Percival tells me.

I glance around the room. 'If it's her home, then wouldn't there be other rooms and a way in and out?'

'Of course.' He nods. 'She is probably concealing the rest from you.'

'So if I can't burn it down—'

'You have to think of another way of getting out,' Percival finishes for me. 'And preferably one that causes as little damage as possible—you don't want to make an enemy of a crone.'

My slice of happiness has obviously ended. Damnation, must everything in this world be so difficult? I stand and study my prison, hoping for some divine inspiration.

CHAPTER 7

It's All About Family and Friends

Having tossed and turned for quite some time last night, I awake surprisingly refreshed as the rising sun bruises the sky a deep purple. Although I believed myself to be up early, my hosts were earlier still. When I arrive downstairs, the table is already set with a selection of fruit, breads, cheeses, and meats, and the bustle in the kitchen tells me more food is coming.

'Ah, good morning, my young friend. Are you ready to be on your way?' Mender asks, coming through the door, carrying a steaming pot of tea and some mugs.

'Yes, thank you.' I am suddenly awkward. While I dressed and tidied my room, I resolved not to tell Mender I worked out who I am. I find myself undecided again as I see him in the flesh.

Telling them I believe I am their great-grandson is the type of thing you do when you can spend a few days getting to know them better. Not when you're leaving a few minutes later.

'You didn't have to go to all this trouble for me,' I say a tad awkwardly.

'Nonsense. It isn't often guests grace our home nowadays.' He places the pot and mugs on the table.

As he settles himself, my eyes are drawn to the picture on the wall.

'An interesting pair, aren't they?' Keeper says as she enters the room.

'I think…. I am…. The girl in the portrait—I think she's my mother.' The words slip out before my mind is aware I'm saying them.

A hand gently squeezes my shoulder, and I turn to meet Keeper's eyes. 'Well, of course she is, lad. You look so very much like her.'

'And why else would the minotaur send you here to us if not to find your lost family?' Mender added.

Keeper's gentle pressure on my shoulder urges me towards the table. 'Come, eat. Then perhaps you might tell us what brings you to the minotaur's maze and how we might help you finish your quest.'

I take a seat, and Keeper loads my plate with food while Mender pours the tea. Meanwhile, I gnaw my lip, wondering how much to tell them about the pickle I find myself in.

In the end, it all comes tumbling out. Not just Mum being taken to face charges of benefitting illegally from her position in the World Above, but about Pris's and my search for the tokens to admit us to the Seelie Court, and how we were duped into taking on this quest. And I don't stop there. I also tell them about how I am sure I'm falling in love with Pris, and how we can never be together, and even if we could be, I messed everything up.

I clap my hand over my mouth, my cheeks heating. I

hadn't meant to say any of that last bit. Keeper and Mender chuckle, and Mender slaps me on the back.

'Ah, the path of young love never runs smooth. I am sure if she is the one for you, you will be able to make it up to her.' Mender smiles as he speaks and laughter lines crinkle around his eyes.

'Aren't you shocked that I... um... like an elf?' I ask, wondering why they decided to focus on this rather than my mother's situation.

'Son, things are a little less strict out here. There are almost as many mixed marriages as not. If you are happy, we are happy for you. I am more interested in spending our time finding out what we can do to help you help our granddaughter,' Mender says.

Keeper places her hand over mine. 'Snake, the heart wants what it wants. What I cannot understand is, why did you decide to go on this quest when you believe your mother would have been cleared?'

'It was because of something one of Bernais's supporters said to me. He told me that even if my mother got out of this, they would make sure she was charged with something even worse. I looked around me and saw that a large number of people in the court felt as he did. I needed to think of another way to rescue her from Bernais's clutches,' I tell them.

My great-grandparents nod their understanding.

I carry on. 'At the time I thought they hated her because she is not a creature of high standing, but after last night—'

'You think it is because she is half elf?' Keeper asks.

'Yes. Now, if I get through this quest, I will be able to request a boon from the Queen, but I'm not sure what to ask for. How will I keep my mother and myself safe from people with such hatred inside them?'

'Perhaps you should simply petition the Queen to keep you both safe,' Mender suggests.

Keeper places her hand over mine. 'You will always be welcome here—you and your mother. You will be far from the political intrigues of the Capitol, and they will likely forget you exist.'

'What about—'

'Your father would be welcome too,' Mender assures me, his eyes full of such love, it brings tears to my eyes.

'You have definitely given me something to think about,' I say. I wonder whether Mum and Dad would consider moving here after my quest is done—just for a while, until everything blows over.

As if sensing my concerns, Mender adds, 'Of course, you would need to discuss it with your parents first.'

'And whatever you decide, you must at the very least come back for a proper visit before you head back to the World Above.' Keeper smiles and releases my hand. 'We would love to spend more time with you, and I am sure everyone here would appreciate some more musical performances.'

There is a companionable silence while we finish our meal. Mender pours us each another cup of tea while Keeper shows me photos of the rest of the family. Through the window, I can see that the sun is well up in the sky, and I am forced to admit I can put my departure off no longer.

'I wish I could stay another night with you both and get to know you better…,' I start.

'We understand. You are on a quest, and you must be heading out, for we are not the end of the journey, just a stop on the way.' Mender's face wrinkles with his smile.

They help me adjust my pack to better carry the lute, and Keeper insists I take some home-cooked pies with me, saying, 'If you meet back up with your girl, these will surely help melt her heart.'

I kiss them both goodbye, promising to come visit properly once this is all over. I step away, then turn back and hug them both again.

'Whatever happens, I am so happy to have met you both.' I choke up as I speak.

Mender wipes a tear from his eye and gently pushes me towards the door. 'The sooner you leave, the sooner you can return,' he says gruffly, trying to hide his emotions.

Keeper follows me out, and they both stand by the doorway, watching as I head away. When I reach the edge of the forest, I turn and see that my great-grandparents are still following me with their gazes, arms around each other. I raise my hand in farewell before continuing on, and waves of love wash through me as I start out on the next part of my journey.

I stride along under the trees, more determined than ever to succeed in this quest. Perhaps I am more confident because I have more family in the World Below, and if I am forced to stay here at the end of this, it will not be such a bad place to be. Or perhaps it is because I have a better sense of who I am now.

This idea turns my thoughts to my mother. Why had she never mentioned her father's family, or who her parents were? Did she think I wouldn't understand, or did she not want me to be tainted by my mixed parentage?

Do I feel tainted? The creatures I know generally don't accept inter-creature relationships. Still, my father's family must know who I am, and probably Eleanora does too. They don't seem bothered by it. And, surprisingly, nor do I. I am still exactly the same person I was yesterday.

Ah! I palm my forehead. Pondering my parentage has

given me a different perspective on Pris's behaviour and why she doesn't give in to prejudice. I get it now.

My mother is the polar opposite. She spent her life hiding who she is, even from me. Would things be different now if she had stood up for herself and been counted?

To be honest, I don't know if my mother made the right choice. Or perhaps I'm thinking about this the wrong way. She chose what was right for her at the time, but it does not have to be my choice too. I swear, here and now, I will never be ashamed of who I am, or of any of my family.

One problem down, one to go. I still have no idea what I am going to ask for if we complete our quest. Then again, maybe I should wait and see if we are successful before worrying about that.

I move further into the heart of the woods, the air cooling my skin as I'm cut off from the sun's direct heat. My feet eat up the miles. My mood is so much lighter compared to yesterday, as if a weight has been lifted from my shoulders.

I have so much to tell Pris when we meet up again. I will see her again before this is over, won't I? Suddenly, I am uncertain.

'Hey, minotaur, am I going in the right direction to get back to Pris and Percival?' I laugh as my voice is muffled by the dense vegetation.

Of course, that is not how the maze works. It probably doesn't matter which way I go. The minotaur will place me where I need to be according to his grand plan, and I will only meet with them if he wants me to.

Besides, Pris might not be that happy to see me anyway. She is probably still angry with me for storming off like a child. No doubt there will be fences for me to mend. Then we might have a chance at making up.

My mind wanders, imagining an encounter similar to the one two nights ago in the conference centre when Pris fixed my hair and I leant down and brushed my lips to hers. When she didn't pull away, I pressed a little harder, and she responded, her mouth moving against mine.

Whoa, enough of that. Not that the thought of our reunion ending in a kiss isn't pleasant—it's that it is a little too pleasant. I slow my pace as the trees open up to a slow running brook, and I bend to splash water over my face to cool down.

Starting out again, my thoughts are still filled with images of Pris, her sparkling blue eyes, her flawless bronzed skin. I have to remind myself to keep my eyes on the prize. Only now, my treacherous mind is not sure precisely what the prize is—entering the centre of the maze, or winning Pris back.

Sometime later, I stop and eat a bite of trail bread for lunch before heading off again. The trees are less closely packed together, and the sun creeps through the canopy. I am unsure of where I am going, but I hope I am heading towards Pris… and Percival, of course.

As my mind once again fills with thoughts of Pris and our reunion, I spot a cottage through the trees. The white-washed one-story dwelling has a thatched roof and is very picturesque in the later afternoon sun. I hope this is the maze providing a place for me to sleep tonight.

As I draw closer to the clearing around the cottage, I spot Percival sitting on a tree stump, head in hand in a pose that screams despondence. My heart races as I scan the surrounding area. Where is Pris? Of their own accord, my feet start running towards Percival.

Cursing and footsteps drift out from the cottage again. I wriggle my bottom, finding a more comfortable position on the tree stump I am using as a seat, and try to concentrate on reading. It is my second book today.

I should not complain; it is quite pleasant sitting here in the shade. When I am in cat form, I do not read, and I am seldom home in the World Below long enough to indulge the habit.

At the end of the chapter, I reluctantly close the book and rest my head in my hand. The princess has made progress, but she is no closer to finding a way out of her prison than she was this morning. We will be here a while longer, so perhaps I had best set up camp. Standing up, I catch a shadow emerging from the tree line. Now alert, I peer into the distance, trying to discern if this figure poses any threat. My goodness, is that Snake?

My stomach unknots a little, and I allow myself a small smile of relief. At least if the elven princess is expelled because she cannot use her magic, there is someone to carry on the quest.

'Percival,' Snake says when he is almost at the clearing. He seems anxious. 'What are you doing here? And where is Pris?'

'It is good to see you, young man,' I respond. 'Unfortunately, we were caught in a crone trap. Pris is inside the cottage.'

Snake frowns as he takes in my words. I, in turn, am surprised to find the neck of a lute peeking over the gnome's shoulder. I am sure that is new.

Snake scratches the stubble on his chin and asks, 'Why

are you out here while she is in there? And where is the door?'

'I am out here rather than in there because this is your quest, not mine. I am waiting for the elf to use her magic to free herself. Once she does, we can be on our way.'

A frown draws the boy's brows together. 'What do you mean, she must use her magic to free herself? She only learnt to make a flame a couple of days ago. It would take months, if not years, of training to be able to make a door.'

I grin up at him. 'She can more than make a flame now—she can turn an apple into a pear.'

His eyes widen, I like to think in surprise, but I concede it might be disbelief he is displaying.

'But… but her magic hasn't been tested. She doesn't even know what type she has. It could be dangerous for her to use her gifts without knowing their nature.'

'Particle,' I inform him, unable to keep the pride from my voice that she and I identified her magic in less than a day.

'What?'

'Her gift is based on particle magic. She can manipulate her flame using traces of the things around her. I am unable to take her any further than that; sprite magic is very different.'

Snake's mouth forms an 'O.' I cannot tell if it is because he did not realise I am a sprite, or because he is impressed we made it so far into the princess's training.

Eventually, he shuts his mouth and slips his pack and the lute off his shoulders, leaning them against a nearby tree. He walks purposefully over to the window and stares inside. I follow him, standing on tiptoes to find out what the princess is up to. She is sitting cross-legged on the floor, making her flame change colour.

'I can hear you talking out there,' she says without missing a beat.

'Pretty flame,' Snake says with a touch of humour in his voice.

Does he not realise this is no joking matter? If she does not get out of here by tomorrow morning, her quest will be over. I open my mouth to tell him this, but I am stopped by the elf's laugh. It is a musical sound and is a big improvement on her ranting.

'Shouldn't you be working out how to get out of here rather than putting on magical displays?' Snake asks.

'I would. Only I can't find a way to use what little magic I know to manipulate the particles, make a door and leave this place. So I am passing time until the witch sends me out of the maze so I can start my quest again.'

'What do you mean, sends you out?' Snake turns and glares at me.

I shrug. 'She was only given a certain amount of time to free herself. If she does not succeed, she will be cast from the maze.'

Snake's glare turns to a growl. 'How can you be so calm about this? Why aren't you using every moment left to try and find a way out of here?'

This is directed at the elf. She does not answer, but her shoulders tense. She slowly turns her head, and her eyes glitter like ice. In spite of the warmth of the early evening sun, I shiver. When her gaze meets Snake's, she begins to speak in a tone meant to cut.

'It's easy for you to turn up out of the blue and criticise. I only learnt the nature of my magic today. Is it too much of a stretch for you to understand that I might be struggling with the next steps?'

In the silence that follows her words, I think I hear her whisper, 'Of all the things to fail at, why did it have to be this?' The words and her tone tell me she is tired and defeated. This does not bode well for her chances of escape.

Beside me, Snake clenches his fists in reaction to her anger. I wait for him to explode, but instead, I watch as he takes a deep breath and forces his fingers to relax one by one. When he finally speaks, it is with compassion.

'Of course it is difficult. Nothing in life worth having comes easily. I know you can do this.'

'How can you know? I haven't shown any natural talent with magic. And I have run out of ideas. Without magic I will be of no use to you on this stupid quest, so it's best I leave.'

I bristle at her self-indulgence. I open my mouth to tell her if that is how she feels, then she should call for Eleanora, but Snake speaks before I can get a word out.

'Using magic is like using any other tool. First you identify what you want to do, then think of ways the tool might be able to help you,' he explains patiently.

I turn and stare long and hard at the young gnome. My expression must have shown my astonishment, as he grins at me.

'I'm not just a pretty face,' he says and taps his head. 'My brain cells are in full working order.'

I am still staring in disbelief. Why did I not think of this simple first step? I mean, I am supposed to be helping the two of them understand this world, and Snake just talked me out of a job.

Pris's flame snaps out, and she shuffles round, half turning towards us. There is curiosity in her eyes, but her voice is still tart. 'What do you think I've been doing? I've spent hours trying to make a portal to get out of here, but I can't even start one.'

'Hmm, perhaps that's because making portals is some really advanced stuff. Think smaller,' Snake encourages.

Pris rises to her feet in one graceful movement, and her eyes dart over the room. She paces around the small area, a sign I now know means she is thinking. Snake is smirking, and I don't think that is helping her mood. She does a circuit of the room before she stops in front of the window and glares at us, hands on hips.

'Okay, smart arse—tell me what I am so obviously missing.'

Snake's grin widens until it is almost splitting his face. 'You need a door.'

· · ◡ · ·

My jaw drops. I don't move for a moment. I have been attempting to make a portal for hours. Snake turns up, and five minutes later, he points out the obvious. Frustrating does not cover my response, but I'm also a little annoyed at myself for not thinking of that. I force my hands from my hips and shove down a little of my frustration, 'So, Mr Know-It-All, just how do I make a door?'

Okay, so the comment is a bit snippy, especially as he came up with a great idea to help. What can I say? I'm tired and irritable, and at this point, I want nothing more to do with magic.

In spite of that, I am absurdly pleased to see he is all right. The moment I heard his voice, my heart started racing, and it is still fluttering—I'm just so relieved to see him. Even the smirk on his face doesn't bother me—well, not too much. When that cheeky smirk disappears, my heart sinks.

'Well… I….'

'Can you do it?' I ask, hoping the answer is yes, but sensing from the way his face changes, it will be a no.

Snake gnaws at his lip. 'Well… no. I mean, my talents stem from particle magic too. I open locks by moving the pieces inside to the open position with magic. I can also do small sleight-of-hand tricks, and I track artefacts from the World Below using the trail of magical dust they leave behind.' He runs his hands through his hair, and he looks so damn cute, my heart does a skip.

Then his words sink in, and my shoulders drop. 'Does that mean you can't help?'

'I can't outline the exact steps for you to make a door, but I can tell you that using particle magic is sort of like physics—you need to rearrange the pieces already there to be what you want them to be. Does that help?'

'You make it sound so easy,' I say, trying to keep the panic rising from my gut out of my voice.

'Percival told me you made a pear from an apple….' The hope in Snake's eyes almost breaks my heart. He is so sure I can do this.

'I did, and I wish I knew how I did.' I sigh. 'I was staring at the apple and wishing it was a pear because I ate the last one earlier and I really felt like another, and one appeared. I was so excited, and I tried to replicate the process, but….'

I am too embarrassed to tell him that I hadn't had the chance to enjoy eating the pear because I threw it against the wall in disgust. I relax my stance and try to shake the tension from my limbs. Most things come easy to me, and if they don't, I can work them out by studying and applying that knowledge.

Nothing magical I try works. For me, trying to use the power I can now sense inside me is like trying to grab hold of mercury. It moves and breaks and slithers away, leaving me angry and feeling useless. The fact that time is running out just adds to the pressure.

'You were doing it with the flame when you changed the colour. I'm sure you can change a small object.'

I raise my eyes to meet his, but he isn't laughing at me. He is serious.

'Why not try with the spoon there.' He nods at the bench beside me.

I pick it up and look at it. 'What now?'

'You have to visualise what you want to do with it,' Snake instructs.

'Like, turn it into a table?' I ask, raising an eyebrow.

He laughs. 'I applaud your ambition, but I can see why you're having problems. A spoon does not have enough molecules to do that because it is so much smaller than a table.'

I nod. That is so sensible and so glaringly obvious. I bite back a snarky comment, realising that I am annoyed at myself and shouldn't take it out on Snake.

Using my magic is still tied up with my parents not telling me who I am and feeling inadequate because I am just learning how to use my talents. Now the ever-present fear of failure is almost overwhelming. I take a breath, trying to rein my emotions in because they are clearly fogging my brain.

'So, maybe I should make a knife?' I suggest, and he nods.

I stare at the spoon until the moving pieces that make it up are visible. 'Okay, how would you change this into a knife?' I ask.

'The way I work is, I have a vision, then add intent and will—I guess that is the using the magic part. Have a picture in your mind, then see the particles in the shape of the new object. Once you have done that, tell them where you want them to go, but you need to do it forcefully because they will want to remain where they are.'

I nod, indicating I understand the concept. Turning around, I make sure my back is towards the window. I want to do this without an audience.

Closing my eyes, I envision a wooden knife the same length and colour as the spoon in my hand. When I have a clear picture, I open them and stare almost trancelike at the spoon until the surface appears to be moving. Focusing my mind, I will the molecules to move into the shape I want them to be in. The edges of the spoon start to move, wavering and softening. I am almost there. I mentally congratulate myself, and they spring back into place.

'Did it work?' Percival's rich tones break my concentration. I turn to find him and Snake trying to look over my shoulder.

I move backwards to block the window so they can't watch me work. I try again and again, pushing frustration and fear down between each attempt.

'I will do this,' I tell myself between gritted teeth.

Fifth time is a charm. Okay. Not a charm exactly, but it turns out sort of knife-shaped. I hold it up for inspection, expecting ridicule, and am surprised at the level of praise.

'That's great—better than I can do,' Snake says.

I grin, almost giddy with pride and relief, pleased I have achieved something today, however small.

'Good. Now it is time to make a door.' Percival's words evaporate my newfound happiness, and my stomach returns to its churning state.

Snake glares at the smaller creature. 'She should work her way up to something that big.'

'No,' I interrupt. 'I hear what you are saying, but Percival is right. I've spent one night here already, and sometime tomorrow morning, I'll be expelled if I am still inside this cottage. I don't want to leave this to the last minute.' I pull together what little confidence I have left and say, 'It's time to go big or go home.'

Snake's head tilts to the side and he studies me with intense green eyes. Finally, he sends me a soft smile. 'I know you can do this, Pris.'

The warmth in his eyes and the way he says my name draws me towards him like a magnet. His words calm me, and his confidence bolsters my spirits.

Breaking the spell, I shoo him and Percival away from the window. 'Promise me you won't look,' I tell them.

Percival tells me he won't, but Snake folds his arms across his chest. 'I can't promise that. What if you need our help?'

'That is kind of the point, I think.' Snake stares blankly at me and I feel the need to explain. 'This is some sort of test of the maze, and I believe I must pass it myself.'

What I don't say is that while I was playing with my flame before, I wondered if the minotaur somehow sensed that I have not fully accepted who I am in the World Below. This test is forcing me to face myself by making me learn to use magic. Snake must read something in my face, because his expression softens, and he offers me a sad smile.

'Funny sort of test,' Snake mutters.

You don't know the half of it, I think.

'But it is a test nonetheless,' I tell him. 'You're here, so I assume you passed your one alone. Please, Snake, let me do the same.'

Our eyes lock, and I can sense the struggle going on inside him.

'If you are thrown out—'

'If I don't succeed today, there will be time to try again in the morning,' I assure him.

He holds his hands out towards me. 'There are things I learnt… things I need to tell you… just in case….'

'You can tell me when I get out,' I say with more confidence than I'm feeling.

As if he senses my fear, he takes a step away from Percival towards me. When he is next to the window, his lips tug into an almost smile. 'Then I guess the only important thing to say now is, I'm sorry. I was an ass. I promise it won't happen again.'

I can't help the grin that splits my face. 'Yes, you were,' I tell him, then add, 'and you shouldn't make promises you can't keep.' His eyes twinkle, and I say, 'I was kind of an ass too, not as big a one as you, but still… it wasn't all on you.'

Our eyes lock, and I want nothing more than to walk through the wall and have Snake hold me and his arms. Then I want to find out what prompted his apology, but both will have to wait. Getting out of here is my only priority.

'Now, away with you.' I shoo him with my hands. 'If you ask nicely, Percival might organise you some tea or coffee from somewhere. I have work to do.'

He doesn't leave immediately, and if I'm honest, I enjoy his being there—albeit with a wall between us. Finally, he mouths, 'Good luck,' and walks over to Percival's rock, where the sprite is placing a pot of tea on a table. I watch as Snake sits beside him and accepts some of the steaming liquid.

Certain they will stay away, at least for a little while, I sit on the floor and face the wall beside the window, the obvious place for a door to be. I take a couple of deep breaths to calm my nerves before staring at the wall until the molecules move. With my will, I push them apart as if making a hole. When it is dinner-plate-sized, I can make out Snake and Percival chatting. I struggle to hold it for more than a moment, but the molecules press back in, closing the gap. I try again, but the same thing happens.

Okay, that won't work. The molecules clearly need to go somewhere. I try pushing the wall up far enough for me to slip under. It crashes back down with a *thunk*.

Of course—the wall has no support if I do that.

I attempt to make the wall into a wooden door, but nothing happens at all. I wonder if it is possible to turn something made of wattle and daub into wood. If it is, I conclude, it is probably more advanced than my basic skills can manage.

I lie back on the floor and stare at the ceiling. I am beyond exhausted—I'm completely drained. My stomach grumbles. Dragging myself to my feet, I head to the fire. I fill a bowl with stew, then I shovel a couple of spoonfuls into my mouth, and my body almost groans in pleasure. As I eat, I continue to stare at the wall.

So, I'm not strong enough to make the wall into a door. I can't make a hole large enough to get through because there is nowhere for the spare bits to go. Pushing the wall up makes the molecules denser and doesn't work because you can't defy the laws of gravity…. Perhaps Snake is right —this is too big a project for me.

No, think out of the box, Pris.

I glance down at the hard wooden table. Maybe I could turn the table into a door and move the wall particles around it. Just the thought of the mammoth effort it would take to achieve all that exhausts me.

I need to think small. Then it hits me—something small that can go up…. I place the half-empty bowl on the table and stare at the window. In my mind, I form a clear picture of how it would look if it were a sash window. Not much would need to change. I start rearranging the particles, pulling in a few extra ones to make two frames.

The window shimmers, then returns to its former shape. The steps are clear in my mind now: split the vertical frame in two between the four panes, create a horizontal break in the middle and push the top piece out a little, add some stray particles from the grooves for the sash to move up within in, and some stray particles to strengthen the two pieces. I am able to form the new window more quickly, pressing my will on the particles, forcing them to stay in place. Slowly, I let go. They hold their form, not wavering or changing from their new shape, and I breathe again.

My legs are like jelly, but there is no time to lose. I rush to the window. It is stiff and not particularly well-made, but I manage to force it open. Snake and Percival are still staring at the wall, waiting for a door, but they turn at the squeaking sound of the sash moving up, eyes wide.

I climb up and launch my body through the open window. I would have fallen to the ground, but Snake is there to catch me. I don't quite fall at his feet when he lets me go, but it's close.

'You did it! Not quite the way I expected, but well done, you!' Snake's face is warm with pride, and I take a moment to bask in my glory.

'Yes... um... well done,' Percival adds dryly.

I can't help myself. 'Go on, Percival—you didn't believe I could do it, did you?'

Colour rises from Percival's collar, and he glances at the ground before raising his eyes to meet my gaze. 'I had hoped, but no, I did not think this was possible. However, I find myself pleased you proved me wrong.'

My goodness, this is almost better than Snake's praise —almost.

I kind of expect the crone to appear and congratulate me, but she is nowhere to be seen. I am somewhat disappointed, but not enough to call her to me.

My purple pack appears at my feet, telling me my jailer is aware I am no longer inside. The cottage shimmers and expands, returning itself to its normal state. I guess that is all I will get from her.

By the time I hoist my possessions over my shoulder, Percival has cleared away his table and tea things. Snake has hauled his pack over his shoulder and is waiting for me.

'Let's get away from here,' I suggest.

The others do not need to be told twice. Although I am tired, I am floating on air as my fellow travellers continue to marvel at how I escaped from my prison using both my brains and my magic.

CHAPTER 8

Mending Fences

Falling into step beside Pris, I resist the urge to offer to take her pack. In spite of the fact that she can hardly walk in a straight line, she would not thank me for even hinting she can't carry it herself.

Her face is grey with exhaustion, which is only emphasised by the mass of white hair curling around her face. She turns to me, and her violet eyes are ringed with dark shadows. It is clear her first test in the maze was more physically and mentally demanding than mine.

She moves a little closer to me. 'I didn't get a chance to actually tell you I'm sorry too.' Her voice is pitched low so Percival, who is a few steps in front of us, can't hear.

'You have nothing to be sorry for,' I assure her. 'I was a selfish prat. I didn't even try to understand what you were telling me. When I thought things through later, I realised it hurt you when I put other people's opinions of us before your feelings. And, if I'm being completely honest, I never tried to understand your reasons for never accepting discrimination.'

I reach out to take her hand, but she pulls away so my

fingers only brush against hers. My heart stutters in my chest. I am too late. I pushed her away with my stupidity, and it's too far for her to come back.

She continues to walk beside me though, so perhaps all hope is not lost. After a few paces, she speaks again. 'I always believed we needed to work together to successfully navigate the maze. As soon as you left, I knew it was a bad decision. I tried to follow you, but the maze wouldn't let me.'

I don't know what to say to that. I deserted her, and still she tried to follow me. I am such an ass.

She laughs, which surprises me. 'I was so angry at you for not being prepared to fight for us, and I think I nearly drove Percival crazy with my ranting.'

My lips curve in a smile as I imagine the scene.

'Buuut… I had time to think last night, and two things occurred to me. The first was that maybe we both had some things we needed to face, and maybe the maze would always have separated us.'

I consider that for a moment. 'You may be right. What was the other thing?'

She reaches out and takes my hand. 'I have had to deal with being treated as if I'm different my whole life, and I'm used to it. I should have given you more time to come to terms with people treating you differently because you're with me.'

A little flame of hope flickers in my heart, but I am almost too scared to fan it. 'Does that mean you forgive me?' I ask, sending a sideways glance her way to assess the impact of my words.

She drops my hand. The corners of her mouth move to form a smile, but it doesn't quite get there.

'I am no longer angry at you,' she concedes. 'But if you ever run off like that again….'

'I won't. I promise.' There *is* hope. I suppress the stupid grin that threatens to plaster itself over my face. At least we're back to the stage of playful banter, even if there is a touch of acid in her comment.

'Did it take you long to find us once you realised what a prat you had been?' Pris asks.

'Not really. When I set out after breakfast—well, it was almost lunchtime I guess—I had some things to think over. I walked the rest of the morning and into the afternoon, going over what I now realise was my first trial. I had a bit to deal with. Then, I was thinking about how much I miss you.' Heat rises to my face as I remember exactly what I was thinking, and I hope Pris doesn't choose this moment to turn around.

I clear my throat. 'It was almost as if thinking about you brought me to where you were. I believe the maze is able to do things like that.'

'And you arrived just in time to rescue me,' she laughs.

'I didn't rescue you, I simply gave you some advice. You did the rest. I mean really, overachieve much? Even I can't change anything larger than a piece of fruit, and you changed a whole window.'

She stops and studies me. 'Is that true, or are you trying to make me feel better?'

'True story,' I tell her. 'I change mostly small things, imitating sleight-of-hand stuff.'

Her gaze still pins me in place. 'Have you ever tried anything bigger?'

'No, I mean we gnomes don't do higher magic. Besides, in the World Above, you don't want to stand out, so you only do small magic.'

'If you have no interest in higher magic, why are you going to study physics at uni, and why were you reading that book on magic and physics when we were on the train?'

'I like it,' I offer somewhat sheepishly.

Sometimes I hate that she is so smart. Of course I'm interested in higher magic. What gnome doesn't want their magic released and to be raised to elven status again? If only we could find a way to do that ourselves without waiting until the Creature Court deems a family has served their debt for a centuries-old rebellion.

Besides, I believe there is a different sort of magic in the World Above, or there once was, and I would like to be the one who rediscovers it.

Pris smirks, then carries on walking.

'What?' I ask as I catch her up.

'You really shouldn't lie. You're no good at it.'

Busted! We walk in silence for a while with Percival still a few steps ahead of us. This is more pleasant than travelling alone.

'Snake?' Pris's voice interrupts my musings.

'Mmm.'

'What was your first test?'

'Sorry?' I was so lost in the moment, her words don't actually register.

'You haven't said anything about what you did while we were apart. And there must be a story behind how you got that lute.'

'Yes.' Percival half turns as he speaks. 'Where did you get that lute from? It is a fine specimen—made by a master craftsman, I should think.'

I was so busy processing, I hadn't thought about what to tell Pris, let alone Percival, about the visit with my great-grandparents. I need some more time to think things through before I share.

'Let's find somewhere to camp for tonight, and I will

tell you everything,' I say, hoping they don't realise I'm putting them off.

They agree, and I relax a little, but just for a moment. How do you break it to people that you are a creature of mixed race when you only just found out yourself?

As the sun begins to sink below the tree line, there is a definite chill in the air. I am considering getting some warmer clothing from my pack when we find a clearing not far from a stream.

We set up camp, digging a firepit and lining it with stones before starting up a roaring blaze. I gather enough firewood to see us through the cool night, almost tripping over a fallen log in the process. Dumping the wood, I return for the log, thinking it might be useful as a seat. Meanwhile, Pris sorts through her pack, mumbling about finding some trail bread, when I stop her.

'My hosts gave me some pies for our meal tonight.' I pull them from my pack.

Pris's brows draw together. 'You had hosts who cooked for you?'

'Most thoughtful of them,' Percival says before I can answer her. 'Here, let me.'

He takes the package and mutters something under his breath. He hands the now warm pies back to me, and I share them out.

Pris continues to study me curiously as she greedily bites into a pie. 'Mmm, I think I am in love with your hosts.' She wipes some crumbs from around her mouth. 'This is the best meat pie ever, and I am not just saying that because I'm starving.'

She takes another huge bite and closes her eyes. I laugh as a look of bliss crosses her face. In the meantime, Percival has come through with a pot of tea and mugs. We place our sleeping bags around the fire and settle down to enjoy a cuppa. To be more precise, Pris and I settle down. Percival stands in front of the fire, staring into the flames, shuffling from one foot to another, his tea forgotten.

I raise my eyebrows to Pris, and she shrugs. 'Something about being in the forest bothers him,' she whispers. 'He won't talk about it.'

'Perci—'

'If you will excuse me, I have an errand.'

Before we can say anything, the sprite disappears.

'I wonder what that is about?' I ask.

Pris is frowning at the space where Percival had been seconds before. 'I've no idea, but I hope that where he is going, someone can help him with whatever is giving him the headache that is making him cranky.'

She leans back against the fallen log we dragged over earlier and sips on her tea. 'So,' she starts, 'are you going to tell me about your quest?'

I take a deep breath, wondering if there is any way I can put it off a little longer. She is so beautiful in the fire-light, and all I want is to spend an evening with her without all this stuff coming between us.

As if she can sense my reluctance, she turns, and her eyes bore into mine. 'Come on, Snake. Spill.'

I sigh. Nope, no way to put it off at all. I shuffle until I am close beside her, and then I lean back. She hands me my tea, then leans her head against my arm. I am stupidly happy she is so close, and for a moment I want to just enjoy the moment.

She nudges me. 'Your quest?'

Okay, so that moment has gone. I wish I had something stronger in my mug, then I wonder if I can use magic to make that happen. I am procrastinating again. I let out another sigh, and then I begin.

'Well… you know how my mum was adopted by my dad's family?'

I feel her head move against me, and I assume she is nodding.

'I always assumed the fact that she was not born into the Fieth clan, that she must have come from some sort of shady background, was at the root of why she felt she wasn't good enough for my father, and why we stayed in the World Above.'

Pris already knows this, but she listens patiently, as if she understands my need to lead in to what is coming. I take another sip of tea, gathering my thoughts. Then I tell her about my great-grandparents, and how I found out who my grandfather and grandmother were. When I am finished, I'm almost too scared to look at her.

'Ah, so the lute is from your great-grandfather. Ooh, and your great-grandmother made the pies. Fantastic, we can visit her after this and eat our fill of them.'

I freeze. Does she really not understand what I said? I wait for a moment to make sure before saying, 'My grandfather was a gnome and my grandmother an elf.' I say the words slowly so there can be no mistake. 'My mother and I are of mixed race.'

She leans forward and captures my eyes with hers, making sure I can see into the depth of her soul. 'I heard you the first time. I only care *who* you are, not *what* you are.'

'But—'

She leans in until all I can see is her eyes. Then closer still, and her lips press to mine, and all my objections about what people think about us being together fly out of my head. I pull her closer, and my body instantly responds to her soft form. I groan and force myself to pull away.

A frown draws her dark brows together, and her blue

eyes turn stormy grey. 'Tell me you aren't going to say we shouldn't do this because of what people will think.'

I shake my head ruefully. 'I'm not going to say that, but I still don't think this is a good idea. We are on a quest, and you are....' My body stirs again, responding to the smell of her hair and the warmth of her body so close to mine. I take a deep breath in an attempt to drown the parts of me protesting at what I am about to say. '... more than distracting. I don't want to be caught out with my pants down, so to speak.'

She blushes and lowers her eyes before leaning forward and placing a gentle kiss on my lips. My resolve wavers just as she pulls back and sits beside me, leaning her head on my shoulder again.

'You're right, of course, but just so long as you promise not to talk any more nonsense about races mixing and whether or not other people are happy with us being... um... friends.'

It takes a little while for my heart to stop pounding and for my body to settle enough to answer sensibly. 'I swear,' I tell her.

We sit together for a while, finishing our tea and staring into the flames. As the temperature drops, I put some more wood on the fire, and we snuggle into sleeping bags. I pull her closer, thinking two layers of bedding plus clothing makes us safe. It doesn't, and I lie very still, waiting for the deep breathing that tells me she is asleep before I am able to relax.

I watch the firelight flicker over her face until my eyelids begin to droop. A branch cracks behind me, and I am suddenly wide awake and alert. We are in a forest on a quest, for goodness sake. Why didn't we think to stand guard?

I sit bolt upright and turn my head to search for the

source of the sound, only to find myself face to face with a panther.

·· ❧ ··

I stand outside the entrance to my home, waiting patiently, unable to enter. I do not have to wait long. As the spiritual advisor in waiting, my brother Emrys is uniquely attuned to the nuances of the Wyld Woods.

'What took you so long, brother?' he asks, holding out his hands and bidding me to enter. He always insists on greeting me when I visit.

I step into the glade, and a sense of wellbeing falls over me as the trees' song stops for the first time since I entered the woods.

'I am part of a quest, brother. My time has not exactly been my own,' I explain.

'So the trees have told us.'

'I am—'

'Babysitting some young creatures. Yet you left them to come and visit?'

If sprites had eyebrows, Emrys's would have been raised questioningly.

'I planned to visit once my duties were fulfilled, but... the trees have been calling to me. I am afraid if I do not get some relief, I will not be of any use to my young charges.'

Emrys is the only creature I can be this open with. Perhaps it is because he is my brother, or maybe it is because of his ability to connect with me on a spiritual level. Not even Eleanora is privy to the true impact that no longer fully being a sprite has on me.

'I will guard your charges while you meet with Mother. She awaits you. Will you spend some time with Nisha?'

'I… I….'

My brother hugs me, fully aware of how my need to spend time with Nisha warred with my guilt at not being able to fully be with her and tore me apart.

'Until the next time,' Emrys says as he releases me and disappears back into the forest.

I stare at the tree guarding my home, remembering the night Emrys led me through—the night I left for the Capitol. That fateful night when I became less than I was, and I realised that Nisha and I could no longer truly be as one as our bond intended. When I knew staying here would bring danger to all I loved and cared for, and I made a decision to break my newly formed bond.

I offered my decision to Nisha, knowing she would be free to mate with another sprite, but would never be able to bond again. At least she would not have to be alone. My lips twisted into a wry smile as I remember the response of my new mate.

At that moment, I learned that Nisha had a mind of her own and would not be moved once she had made it up. I could not break the bond without her, and she had decided she was not interested in such a move. She would wait until I was whole again, however long it took.

I take a deep breath and head towards the centre of the glade where the elders commune. My home is silent as I avoid the family groupings of trees nurturing sleeping sprites. Some move restlessly as I pass, on some level aware that a creature who did not quite belong was in their midst.

Tears form in my eyes as I try to harden my heart against the pain my visit inflicts on it. This is why I return so infrequently. It hurts less to stay away than to be here.

I take a step into the elder circle, and immediately step

back into the shadows. My mother is not alone. My uncle, Nathanial, sits beside her amongst the roots of the Truth Tree, chatting animatedly.

'Do not hide from us, Percival.' My mother's voice rings in the thin night air. 'Emrys sensed that there is much you have to tell me, and I think it better another elder is here to listen and provide council.'

Steeling myself, I enter the moonlit clearing, then force myself to move closer, dropping to the ground to sit cross-legged, just out of the reach of the tree roots.

'Greetings, Mother, Uncle. I bring you news from the Capitol.' *And you are not going to like it,* my internal voice adds.

When I have finished my update, the clearing falls into silence. From experience I know that my mother and uncle are discussing the news, using the Truth Tree to speak mind-to-mind, and to give them clarity of vision.

'Thank you for your report, Percival. You have given the elders much to discuss,' Nathanial finally says. 'But now, I suspect you want to spend some time with your family.'

'I have to—'

'Surely you would not leave without at least saying hello,' a voice says from behind me.

I rise to my feet in a swift movement and turn, my heart thudding and a new song running through my body. My bond mate, the other half of my heart, stands less than a step away, and it is all I can do to stop myself launching myself at her.

'Nisha, I….'

'I know, my love.' She holds out her hand and leads me from the elders' clearing. 'You must leave soon, so let's make the most of what little time we have.'

As I follow her, my mother's voice rings out, 'Come

and see me before you leave. I have a tonic that will help you with the tree song as you complete your quest.'

Did she say complete *my* quest? I turn to say I have not decided whether or not to become a part of this folly, but Nisha tugs on my arm, and I forget why it was important to tell my mother anything at all.

. . ⌣ . .

Snake moves restlessly beside me, and cold air creeps inside my sleeping bag. I snuggle down, trying to warm up, then roll over onto my other side. As I start to drift off, my face is suddenly covered by something soft and filmy.

I am instantly awake and fighting to move the offending object away so I can breathe. I gasp in fresh air into my lungs and turn to abuse Snake for almost suffocating me with his sleeping bag, only to find myself face to face with a panther. It snarls and bares its teeth, giving the distinct impression it isn't happy.

Well, I'm not in such a good mood either. I'm never great when woken in the middle of the night. I glare at the panther, and it snarls again. My heart is pounding in my ears, and a sliver of fear runs down my spine. I reach out, searching for Snake. When my fingers find his, I lace them together. I do not have to face this threat alone.

'How may we help you?' Snake's voice rings clear in the night air.

I frown. Why is he talking to an animal? Wait, do animals speak in the World Below? Then I notice a slight shimmer around the edges of the beast. With my free hand, I rub my eyes, then really focus on the predator. The panther is made up of hundreds of sprites, like the one we encountered on Bodmin Moor, only the ones forming this animal appear to be vibrating with anger, and I can make out multiple sets of bared teeth. My grip on Snake's fingers tightens.

'You speak of help when you come here unbidden, threatening our home with fire.' The voice resonates through my body, raising my anxiety levels.

I glance behind me at the firepit, which has died down to a rich orange-red glow. It isn't a threat to anyone.

'We were just trying to stay warm.' Snake's tone is calm and soothing.

'You endanger us,' the sprite-panther insists. 'We demand you pay a tithe to our people for the damage you caused, then leave the area immediately.'

I bristle at the request. This is blatant extortion. I rise to my feet, I would like to say elegantly, but it actually takes me a couple of attempts to extricate myself from my sleeping bag. Stumbling, I'm forced to use Snake's shoulder to push myself upright.

'We were careful. We built a firepit and lined it with stones, and we made sure the fire stayed within the pit, well away from any trees,' I point out from my superior height.

The panther bares its teeth again. 'You did not ask permission to come here, nor did you ask leave to make a fire.' Although the voice is less menacing, it is clear the sprite-panther is not going to let us off the hook.

Snake joins me in front of the fire as I move into ready position. If the panther wants a fight, I'm game. Snake, ever the diplomat, has other ideas.

'We apologise most sincerely for not asking your permission,' he says, moving slightly in front of me.

'Even though we didn't know we needed to,' I add under my breath, earning a frown from Snake, who clearly does not want to fight with these creatures.

'Sprites have excellent hearing,' he tells me before turning back to the panther. 'We arrived with our friend Percival, and we followed his instructions, taking care to see our fire was well away from trees and would not harm anyone. He did not tell us we required permission to camp here.'

The glade falls into silence as we wait for a response. And of course, at that exact moment, there is a crash, and sparks flare behind us as wood shifts in the firepit. Fortunately, no embers spill on the ground, otherwise who knows what might have happened next.

The panther moves imperceptibly, its muscles bunching as if it is getting ready to spring into action. The clearing vibrates with tension, but ever so slowly, the beast relaxes.

'If you are friends with Percival, where is he?'

'He left us not long after we arrived here. We expect him back any time,' Snake assures them.

The sound of whispering fills the air as the panther figure shimmers. The whispering becomes more frantic, and I tense. Are the sprites arguing over what to do about us? It's kind of disturbing to watch.

Finally, the panther's head rises, and its yellow eyes sparkle in the firelight. 'If you truly are friends of Percival, we will forgive your trespass—this time, but there is a cost.'

'Of course there is,' I mutter, but Snake sidesteps to place himself directly between me and the sprites, I guess to ensure I don't do anything stupid.

I'm tired and annoyed, and I'm convinced the opportunistic sprites are taking advantage of us and our lack of knowledge on creature etiquette. Part of me is also angry at Snake for giving in to them so easily, until he speaks, and I realise he doesn't trust them either.

'What do you mean by price?' he asks warily. 'We do

not possess any gold. In fact, we have very little more than what you see here.'

The panther sneers. 'We do not want your gold or your possessions, gnome.'

'We will not tithe to you or offer our bodies for you to share—not even for a short time,' Snake insists, and I shudder as I remember the feeling of a sprite taking residence in my body as I walked on Bodmin Moor.

'We do not ask that either.' There was more whispering. 'I repeat, we do not ask that of you,' the panther says more firmly this time.

'In that case, how can we possibly repay your generous gift of letting us stay the night on your land?'

Do my ears deceive me, or is there a tinge of sarcasm in Snake's words?

The panther stares pointedly at Snake's lute.

'Ah,' Snake says, and his shoulders relax. As he half turns to me, I see laughter dancing in his green eyes. He raises a questioning eyebrow, and I shrug—a little music couldn't hurt.

He bends down and picks up the instrument before sitting on the log. Still weary, I move our sleeping bags out of the way while he tunes the lute, then sink down beside him.

As the first notes ring out clear and true, the panther dissolves, and the trees are decorated with hundreds of winged sprites. My lips curl into a smile as the sparkling beings light up the clearing. *Now this is truly magical.* I lean my head lightly on Snake's shoulder for a moment, and he drops his head to mine as we enjoy the moment until the sprites have made themselves comfortable on branches and leaves—anywhere, in fact, they can plant their bottoms, and the warm glow of the fire is the only light around.

I slip off the log and use it as a backrest as Snake starts

picking out a tune. He shifts slightly so he is half facing me, and his eyes capture mine as he starts to sing "More Than Words", and I know the Extreme song is all for me. I try not to swoon as he moves seamlessly into Tracy Chapman's "Baby Can I Hold You", but it's difficult, as his voice is rich as chocolate and is melting my insides in ways that should not happen in public.

As the last words of the song float into the night, the air in the clearing changes as the sprites twitter. I tear my eyes away from Snake and half turn to find Percival standing by the dying fire with two creatures about his size and two beings we have not come across before.

They have two arms and two legs, and a head with two almost black, liquid almond-shaped eyes in rather rounded faces. Although they are humanoid, they are not human. Their skin is the colour of trees once the bark has stripped. In fact, they resemble trees as much as they do humans.

Tree Sprites, I murmur, a smile forming on my lips.

Our audience reforms into a panther and confront the newcomers.

Here we go again, I think.

'What's happening here?' Percival demands. 'Emrys fetched me, saying the wood sprites were about to attack my friends. How is it these visitors, my guests, are not welcome in the Wyld Woods?'

I hear whispers about a spiritual leader as the panther drops its head and looks so much like a dog who has been told off that I snort back a laugh, earning a glare from Percival. No, Percival can't be their spiritual leader—one of the sprites with him must be. A rumbling voice pulls me from my musings.

'We saw the lute and just wanted some music,' the panther mumbled. 'The gnome was never in any danger, and besides, he had a warrior to protect him. We didn't think it would hurt if we encouraged the gnome to play for us.'

Percival shakes his head. 'That is not the way of our people. You embarrass us all with your thoughtless behaviour. Be gone.' He flings his hand out as if to shoo them away. 'Go ply your mischief elsewhere.'

'What the?' The words escape my lips as the panther slinks into the shadows at Percival's command.

I study Percival with new eyes as he watches the creatures leave. Who is the sprite who has been helping us? He has got to be more than Eleanora's lackey to be able to command others of his kind.

I turn to Snake and find him also contemplating Percival and the group he is with.

'Can you feel their power?' he asks, wonder lifting his tone.

I close my eyes, and to my amazement, I can.

···◕···

As the wood sprites slip into the shadows, I attempt to calm my anger. I had so little time to spend with my family as it was, and they robbed me of a great portion of it.

A hand gently rests on my shoulder, and I turn my head slightly to stare into Nisha's liquid black eyes, so beautiful in her sprite-form face.

'Do not let your anger overtake the joy of our reunion. Whatever time we had together would always be too short,' she tells me. 'Be happy and rejoice in the moments we had.'

As always, her ability to enjoy life no matter what it throws at her shames me. I close my eyes and allow her touch to flow through me, just for a moment. The mate bond urges me to embrace her as I force myself to step away.

I take another step and turn to face her. When I open my mouth to speak, she leans forward and places a finger over my lips, stopping my words before they can form.

'You will ask it again, and I will answer the same way, so let us save ourselves time and heartache. I am content as I am. We will be together again the next time you visit.'

She steps back and disappears into the tree behind her. My body jerks as if an essential piece has been wrenched from inside me, as indeed it has. Before I can react and follow her, Emrys drops an arm over my shoulder. 'We will take care of her, my brother, as we take care of all our family, until you are able to return fully to us.'

'How can you—?'

'Still believe this curse will be broken? I have to believe. To do otherwise would be to allow anger and disappointment into my life, and I refuse to do that.' He opens his arms and says, 'Come, let us say farewell.'

I move into his hug. For a moment I consider returning with him, at least for the rest of the night, but Nisha is right. No amount of time with my family is ever enough. Emrys follows Nisha, and I am left with the two elders: my mother, who did not have time to change into human form, and Nathaniel.

'It must be goodbye again, for now.' Nathanial clasps my hand in his. 'Thank you for bringing us the news of what is happening in the Capitol. Visit us again soon.'

My mother clasps my other hand and slips something into it, closing my fingers around the cool glass. 'This should help with the forest song, at least for a few days.' She touches her forehead to mine. 'Be well, my son. I will pray for your return.'

There is nothing else to say that has not already been said. What Nisha left of my heart when she departed breaks as my uncle Nathanial and my mother disappear.

I take a moment to compose myself before returning to the fire and facing the gnome and elf I must accompany to the centre of the maze. Their eyes question me, but the night's events are still too raw to be discussed with strangers.

'Why don't the two of you get some sleep? I will stand guard to make sure we are not disturbed by any other woodland creatures,' I tell them as I sit on a stone across the firepit.

The princess starts to say something, but Snake touches her arm and, when he has her attention, shakes his head. She glances back at me. I let out a breath of relief when she curbs her natural instincts and nods before following Snake back to where their sleeping bags are in disarray.

'Goodnight, Percival,' she says as she wriggles into her bed.

'Wake us if you need anything,' Snake adds.

'Of course.' It is difficult to even force those two words from my lips as I struggle with the whirl of emotions threatening to overwhelm me.

I place a couple of logs on the fire, barely holding myself together as I watch and wait for my two charges to fall sleep.

My hands clasp and unclasp as I try to manage my anger towards them. They are not my family, yet it is not their fault that I am with them and not the creatures I love. Yet to be with my family and my heart mate is always a painful reminder of all I lost through my own arrogance all those years ago. If it is anyone's fault, it is my own. It will do no one any good to dwell on the past though. What I must focus on is what I am going to do now.

Being so close to the forest, my forest, these last few days has been difficult—more than difficult. Today, watching the gnome and his elf reunite brought on a longing so strong, I could not bear it. I miss my bond mate. Although I told myself I was going to the glade to ask my mother for help, in reality I could no longer resist the urge to be with Nisha.

I have lost count of the times I asked Nisha if she had changed her mind about breaking our bond after that first night. When Eleanora took up the post of the Witch of Wimbledon in the World Above and asked me to go with her, I really thought she would accept. Nisha is always unshakable. Tonight was the first time my visit had not ended with the question, and if I am honest, that was not totally because our visit was cut short.

I had not returned to the Wyld Woods for some one hundred years when I went home tonight. As a cat in the World Above, my tortured soul was laid to rest, replaced with the constant focus on food, warmth, and hygiene. I was content for the first time in years. That contentment led me to ensure my visits to the World Below were not long enough to visit my family, and I fell into apathy.

Being in the woods these last few days, having the trees call me, but knowing I could no longer enter their embrace, has woken my soul. For the first time in years, I want to be who I was meant to be before I was cursed, ironically, by the father of the very man who sent us on this journey.

The only way left for me to reverse the curse is if the Queen agrees I have been punished enough and asks the magical flow to release me. If I join the quest, I could petition her to show leniency and free me. Nisha and I had been discussing the possibility when Emrys returned, and we never finished the conversation.

I am wracked with indecision. The longing to be whole again has returned. This half-life is no longer enough for me. But what if it doesn't work? To hope and then to have my hopes dashed a second time—will I survive that? Perhaps it would be better to remain a cat in the World Above than take the risk.

I jostle the embers in the fire with a stick in an attempt to raise a little heat to combat the predawn drop in temperature. As the sky begins to lighten, I am still no closer to an answer. All I know is, I must decide who I want to be soon, the cat familiar or the sprite I was born as, before there is no longer time to choose.

CHAPTER 9

Who's That Walking on My Bridge?

A s we pack up camp, taking special care to bury the fire so it can't spark a blaze, I worry about Percival. Surreptitiously observing him, it's obvious he didn't sleep last night. His pale complexion is grey, but more shockingly, his hair is ruffled. I'm sure he has been running his hands through it, and, worryingly, he's made no attempt to comb it.

Pris is chatting away, telling the sprite how we decided we will work together from now on. She leaves a gap for one of his acerbic remarks, but he doesn't stir. I doubt he even heard a word she said.

'We're ready,' Pris announces, and this brings Percival out of his daze.

The sprite reaches into his pocket to retrieve his comb and absent-mindedly neatens his hair. He then runs a hand down his clothes, using a spell to tidy himself up.

'All right, let us go.' He heads off down the path, not even checking to see if we're following.

Pris raises an eyebrow as she pulls on her pack. I shrug, as I've no idea what's up with Percival. Maybe it is something to do with the sprites he arrived with last night. By the time we catch Percival up, he is humming under his breath. He obviously does not want to talk.

Percival is completely off his game today as he deals with whatever is going on with him. I, on the other hand, have a spring in my step. After singing my heart out to Pris last night, albeit in front of hundreds of sprites, something has settled inside me. There is a promise of a future together, and I will not let anything get between us and that opportunity.

Pris slips past Percival and takes the lead. 'If anything attacks us, I think I'm better equipped to handle it,' she tells him, and Percival obligingly drops behind her, then allows me to pass him.

I wait for him to object, to say something along the lines of how he has forgotten more about these woods than she will ever learn, but he simply carries on humming. I hope he is at least aware enough to deal with anything that might sneak up on us from behind.

Fortunately, we travel most of the morning without encountering anything more dangerous than a hedgehog. I start to relax a little, but it would not pay to forget we are still in the maze and that the minotaur is still testing us.

My stomach begins to gurgle as the forest starts to thin out. Moments later we arrive in a clearing, and I am about to suggest we stop for lunch when Pris grabs my arm and points to the left. 'Snake, look.'

Raising my head, I find the path meanders through the open space for about another fifteen metres or so before turning into a rocky edge, then drops off completely. The other side of the gorge is far enough away for me to see it is deep—very deep—with the hint of a blue ribbon of a river running through it. We have somehow ended up in a mountain range.

To my left the cavernous mouth of a cave stands near a wooden swing bridge spanning the gorge. Surely that can't be the only way across? I peer more closely. There are slats missing, and those ropes holding it together look old and worn. I'm not usually bothered by heights, but the thought of crossing over on that bridge has me sweating as my anxiety level rises.

Something hits my pack from behind, causing me to stumble forward a step. I tense and swivel round, ready to take on whatever attacked me. Percival regains his feet and frowns at me, like the collision is my fault. At least walking in to my back has jolted him out of his daze. He rushes past me and looks around, distress written across his face.

'Why this?' I am pretty sure Percival isn't talking to us as he carries on asking what he did to deserve the bridge crossing. 'Why not the caves? Or the river?' He grabs at his hair again, as he tends to do when he's frustrated or stressed out. This time I'm pretty sure he's stressed. I know I am.

Pris glances questioningly at me.

'I've no idea what he's talking about,' I tell her.

Pris reaches out to the sprite, 'Percival—'

She stops as a huge, shambling creature covered in matted hair emerges from the cave by the bridge. 'Oh my goodness, is that a yeti?'

'No, how could you insult her like that? How can you be so....' Percival's shock at Pris's perceived rudeness causes him to momentarily lose his words. He recovers quickly though. 'This is a member of the ancient race of trolls.'

Pris grins like it's Christmas morning. 'For real? A troll? Like in *The Three Billy Goats Gruff*?'

Percival stares disdainfully at her. 'Please. Trolls are not only ancient, they are also noble creatures and are not to be confused with characters in some silly children's story.'

I bite back a grin. 'To be fair, Percival, *The Three Billy Goats Gruff* is based somewhat on truth. Trolls do guard bridges into magical areas.'

As I say these words out loud, I realise the troll is the next test the maze has for us. I hastily kick my brain into gear, trying to access what little troll lore I learnt as a child as a deep voice rumbles around the gorge.

'Who goes there? Who wishes to cross into the centre of the minotaur's maze?'

As she talks, the troll shuffles to stand in front of the mouth of the bridge, and the largest sword I have ever seen drags behind her, gouging a furrow in the earth. Taking a defensive position, she brings the sword up, crossing it over her chest. She cuts quite the daunting figure.

Pris stands with her jaw open, and Percival tucks himself in behind her. I sigh. I guess I'm up.

I step forward and announce with more authority than I feel, 'I, Sneak Thief, along with Princess Priscilla Crown and Percival the Wise, seek entrance to the minotaur's maze.'

'For what purpose?'

I do a double take. I don't remember that being one of the questions trolls ask. How much am I supposed to tell her? Should I spill everything? No, that wouldn't be right, as she only needs to know what we want to take from there. Well, at least I think that is all she needs.

'To retrieve what is held within.' I am rather proud of my quest-like response.

'Under whose authority?'

'What?' What is this, twenty questions?

I glance over to Pris and Percival for some help, but their postures scream 'We're leaving this up to you, mate.'

Pris does send me a smile of encouragement. I spread my hands in a beseeching 'a little help here' gesture, which she ignores. She nods towards the troll as if to indicate I should go ahead and answer her.

'Who gave you leave to enter?'

I widen my eyes at Pris, subliminally sending, 'Seriously, you're forcing me to do this?' She doesn't respond, which I guess is an answer in itself. I turn to the troll.

'Sorry, what was the question again?'

Did the troll actually sigh? 'Did the Queen invite you? Or the minotaur himself?' She annunciates each word clearly as if I am a total idiot.

I don't know how to answer because neither the Queen nor the minotaur invited us. The troll shuffles her feet, and I catch a glimpse of a thin face with a protruding nose through her matted, dirty hair.

Yep, there she goes, sighing again. I don't know what she expects. I mean, the council didn't issue us with a questing manual or anything. We're learning as we go.

'You can only enter the maze by one of three ways. You are either invited by the minotaur, or the Queen grants you entrance,' the troll repeats.

There is silence.

'You said three,' Pris prompts.

Finally, some help.

The troll crosses her arms over her chest. 'You defeat me.'

'What the…?' Okay, so most of my words have now left my brain. I glance over at Pris and do a double take. Is she honestly considering this?

Yep, she is assessing the troll, her gaze travelling over her like she is looking for any weaknesses. Percival is stepping away from her, as if he senses her madness and is distancing himself.

After a few moments, she turns to me and shrugs. 'I could probably waylay her long enough for you and Percival to cross, but it would likely result in myself and the troll getting badly hurt if she is intent on defending the bridge.'

'I will defend the bridge until my death,' the troll offers, standing taller, pride ringing through voice.

'Okay, let's leave that as our final option then,' I say, pleased my powers of speech have returned. 'What about you, Percival?

Panic crosses Percival's face before it returns to his usual blank expression. 'Me? You cannot ask me to do anything. I am only here to provide information about the realm, not help you overcome the obstacles.'

I smile. 'I meant have you any ideas from your knowledge of troll law that will help us get past her without anyone dying?' I clarify.

'Oh.' Then, 'Ooh, in my role as advisor, you mean.'

'Yes, Percival, that is what I mean,' I confirm, wondering what was going on in his head that had him thinking otherwise.

'Hmm, let me see. Trolls do not like direct sunlight. See how the bridge entrance is placed close to that cliff? I would think this side of the bridge is in shadow all day.'

'What happens if they are in the sun for too long?' Pris asks.

'Too long in direct sunlight and their body starts to close down, and they will die,' Percival says matter a factly.

Pris's eyes widen. 'We are absolutely not going to draw her out into the sunlight to kill her!'

'Thank you for that.' The troll's tone is sarcastic.

We three turn as one, suddenly aware the troll is listening to every word of our plans. Hustling everyone back to the edge of the woods, we form a close group out of her earshot and continue planning. As we chat, I observe the troll's eyes drifting to my lute.

'Can I bribe you with my lute? Or some music?' I ask.

She shakes her shaggy head, and an odour that reminds me of a rubbish dump wafts towards us. This troll could do with a bath.

'No, you cannot. However, the last troll gathering was moons ago. I don't suppose I could convince you to play a bit for me before we fight, can I?'

'I don't suppose you would let me cross in return for a song?' I counter.

'If it were up to me….' Her shoulders move in what could almost be a shrug.

Pris tugs at my arm, and I turn my attention back to our planning committee, although Percival seems more intent on glaring at the troll than helping us. For some reason he is taking this all very personally.

Pris taps her index finger on her lips. 'Have you noticed that in spite of water being close by, that troll is filthy and stinks to high heaven?'

What has that got to do with anything? 'Perhaps she can't leave her post for long enough to bathe.'

'I don't think that's the reason.' Pris frowns. 'Percival?'

The sprite continues to stare down the troll.

'Hey, Percy!' Pris tries again.

He turns around, raises himself to his full height, and glares at Pris. 'I told you never to call me—'

'Then you should be listening and not playing mind games with the troll,' Pris interrupts him. 'Is it possible trolls don't like water?'

Percival frowns at Pris, but slowly his anger leaves him, and he clasps his chin in his hand.

'You know, I do believe there are some trolls who

dislike water. It will not kill them, but it causes so much discomfort, they avoid it if they can.'

I nod, then a thought occurs to me. 'Pris, with your type of magic, you should be able to move water up here, perhaps even enough of it to distract the troll long enough for us to dash across the bridge.'

· · ◗ · ·

I freeze and a coil of panic rises from my belly. Snake must be mad. I reshape things, and only just. I can't move solid items, let alone slippery watery things.

'I haven't done anything like that with my magic,' I explain. 'I'm not sure I even can'

'Of course you can. You made a flame, which means you're able to draw particles together. Moving things around is the next step. You'll probably find pushing and pulling things easier than reforming them.'

Snake probably thinks he is being supportive and reassuring. Surely he can sense the blind panic rising inside me as he speaks. 'So, I just click my fingers and water will come to me.' Fear forces an extra dose of sarcasm into my words.

He grins a cheeky grin that would normally set my heart fluttering, but at the moment, it just adds fuel to the fire of my fear.

'No, of course not. It will take a bit of trial and error. Percival, can you help her?' he asks.

Percival's head drops to one side as he considers Snake's request. 'I can, but wouldn't you be of more help?'

'Perhaps, but I will be busy doing something else.'

Percival studies Snake, curiosity brightening his eyes.

'All right,' he finally agrees, 'but only if she promises to only ever call me Percival.'

'No can do,' I retort almost before I think.

'Pris,' Snake beseeches.

I sigh. 'All right. I promise to try to never call you Percy again.'

I shake my hands, trying to loosen up. What is wrong with me? All I want to do is needle Percival and aggravate Snake. All they are doing is staring at me like I have grown an extra head. Can't they tell I don't want to do this? *Can't* do this?

Worry and anger are clouding my mind until I have a thought that might get me out of this stupid plan. 'It might take me a while to learn how to move water. Won't the troll notice and think something is up?'

There, that will put a hole in his idea.

Snake grins again, and I have to resist the urge to slap that smile from his face.

'I've thought of that. I'll tell her you're going to fill our water skins because we've decided to eat lunch while we consider our options. I mean we can't fight on an empty stomach, can we? Then I'll play some music for her, and mention we hope it will mellow her when it comes to the fight. Hopefully that will distract her long enough for you to get some water up here.'

His smile and his posture tell me he is confident his plan will work. It isn't a bad plan, as far as plans go. If only it didn't rely on me doing the magic bit.

'I will distract her for as long as it takes for you to get control of enough water to drench her and move her out of the way of the bridge,' Snake finishes.

Percival taps his chin thoughtfully. 'It would help if you could move her closer to the stream below. Then the elf would use less energy to move the water.'

Apparently, we are doing this. When was that decided?

Snake nods approvingly. 'Good point. I'll try and do that.'

'Hold on, I didn't agree to this,' I snap. Some of my panic must have made it into my voice, because Snake stops and looks at me—I mean *really* looks at me.

'You were happy to fight the troll, but…. Ah… Pris, you can do this. I know you can.' Snake squeezes my arm.

I am disappointed that he is brushing over my concerns without truly considering them, without understanding my gut-wrenching fear that I will fail them both. At the same time, I want him to pull me into an embrace and tell me everything will be all right. How inconvenient being attracted to someone is.

I close my eyes, dig deep for the courage to be honest, then turn to Snake. 'I don't want to do this. The plan relies too much on my using magic—new magic which I can't even control yet. What if I let you down?' The last words come out almost as a whisper.

Then Snake does take me into his arms and says into my hair, 'Then at least we tried, and that is all we can ever do. No one will think any the less of you, whatever happens. I promise.'

For a moment I allow myself to lean into him, almost won over.

'But must we use magic?' I press, even though I know the answer.

'There must be a point to you learning how to use it,' he tells me, 'just as there is a reason the minotaur put me in touch with my musical heritage.'

I let out a weak laugh. 'You make it sound like he planned this.'

'Can you be so sure he didn't?'

I open my mouth to point out that he could not know

we would decide to use water and music to defeat the troll, then shut it. Perhaps this is exactly what he expected when he set our first task. 'I thought he was a beast,' I say, my comment sounding weak to my own ears.

'But clearly a very thoughtful beast if his tests so far are anything to go by,' Snake says wryly.

'You seem so sure this will work,' I say, my face still pressed against his shoulder.

He chuckles and his breath tickles my ear. 'I am nowhere near confident that this will work. If you have another idea, we can go with that. Otherwise…'

I'm still for a moment, trying to come up with any option that doesn't include my magic. Percival clears his throat, reminding me of why we are here.

'What if the point of telling you about your heritage was for you to explore what it means for your magic, rather than to make you sing more?' I ask.

'That's ridicu—' Snake stops mid word, and his breath tickles my ear. 'Mmm, that is a real possibility,' he concedes.

'But not one we have time to consider now.' Percival's tart tone breaks the spell.

Reluctantly, I pull away from Snake. I don't have a better plan, and this one is worth a shot.

'Okay, let's do this,' I say, grabbing Snake's water skin from the side of his pack.

He leans forward and plants a kiss on my cheek, 'This is better than luring her into the sunlight,' he tells me.

'That can be plan B,' Percival jokes as he starts down the path to the river below. Well, I *think* he is joking.

As I follow him, my eyes drift towards the river running below. How am I ever going to move water? Hold on. 'Percival, why don't we just cross over the river?'

Percival laughs. 'The other side is a sheer cliff. If you

balk at moving a little water, you would never be able to levitate all three of us to the top.'

My eyebrows rise up so high, I nearly strain a forehead muscle, 'Wait, I can levitate things?' Perhaps this magic thing will not be so bad after all.

As we walk, we hear Snake's voice drifting down, then the sounds of him tuning his lute. The lyrics of "Every Breath You Take" follow us as we make our way to the river.

When we reach the bank beside the fast-flowing water, I drop to the ground, cross my legs, and look expectantly at Percival. 'Teach me, oh master.'

Percival frowns. 'I really wish you would take this more seriously.'

I don't say anything. I mean, what should I say—'*I do take this seriously, but I am scared to death, and so I'm joking with you to relieve the tension*'?

Percival fidgets a little, and I realise he is also nervous. Finally, he says, 'Snake would be better at this than I, but I cannot sing as he does, or entertain the troll to buy us time.' He stares into space for a moment before taking a deep breath. 'Why don't you start by looking into the water and seeing if it is any different to other substances?'

I stare at the water, just like I did with the fire, allowing it to calm my mind until the particles are visible. There aren't as many as there are in solid objects, and they seem more loosely bound. I play a little with the water, practicing forming little waves and bubbles.

'Ah, that bubble thing might work. Can you make it bigger?'

I form the water into a small bubble, using my hand to tell my brain what shape to impose on the water, then add a little more liquid. It works. I clap my hands in excitement, and the bubble collapses, spraying water everywhere.

In spite of the last little lapse, I beam with pride, and even the usually dour Percival is smiling.

'You might actually be able to do this,' he says in wonder.

'Gee, thanks for the vote of confidence,' I retort, although there is no anger in my voice.

Buoyed by my success, I form another ball, making it bigger until it is the size of a giant beachball before the water drops back down into the river.

I think if I stick with beachball size and move it across the water before getting it to follow me, I might be able to make this work.

After a couple of attempts I manage to move the ball and we are halfway up the path when I stumble over a root and the water balloon bursts, drenching Percival.

'I will lead you so you can concentrate on carrying the water,' Percival suggests dourly.

That will help, but will one small sphere of water be enough to distract the troll? I need a backup.

Back down at the bank, I fill the water skins and leave them open just in case. Then I return to Percival. In my absence, he has dried himself off.

His right eyebrow rises. 'Where is the water bubble?'

'I want to try something,' I tell him.

I follow him a little further along the path until we come to an outlook about two-thirds of the way up. I lean out until I can see the river, and I stretch my magic out, calling the water into a ball. It takes a lot of energy and it's draining me, making me a little weaker, but I float it upwards, imagining a string attached to my hand. The water ball floats behind me like a balloon.

'The rest of the way is flat,' I say to Percival. 'I am less likely to drop it now.'

Percival grins. 'I do believe you are getting the hang of this, Priscilla.'

Percival just used my name for the first time. Okay, it's Priscilla, and I hate that, but it's better than elf girl, or princess said with a sneer. Perhaps today will not be such a train wreck after all.

By the time we reach the clearing, my head is like mush, and it takes all my energy to float the ball of water high above the troll. Snake launches into "The Script's Rain", and I almost lose control when I bark out a laugh. Trust Snake to make a joke at a time like this.

'I do not like this song of rain.' The troll scowls at Snake. 'The others are back. Will you eat, or will we fight?'

The troll is now a little away from the bridge, but not far enough for us to slip in behind her.

Snake raises a finger in the universal 'wait a minute' sign. 'Give me a moment, please, I don't want my instrument to be damaged.' He puts the lute into its case. 'Is there somewhere safe I can put it while we fight?'

Gleaming white teeth appear in the troll's face in what I suspect is her version of a smile. 'Put it inside my cave. It will be mine when we are done anyway.'

As she speaks, the troll moves towards the entrance of her home as if to make sure Snake knows where to go. Percival and my path to the bridge is clear, but Snake is still blocked by the troll. There is no way we will all make it to the bridge from these positions. I frown, worry starting to knot my stomach. My fights are usually one on one. I'm not used to worrying about others.

Snake is almost level with the bridge's defender when he says, 'Now.'

Even though I am worried Snake won't make it, I don't

hesitate. I drop the oversized water bomb and run. As I near the bridge, my ears are filled with a piercing howl of pain. Percival is ahead of me and almost at the bridge as I half turn to find the troll rolling on the ground. The vision reminds me of a dog rolling in something foul smelling. Snake is dodging her outstretched hand. Two steps later, he joins me.

'What are you waiting for?' he pants.

'Go ahead of me.' I move out of the way so he can pass.

The bridge swings and sways as the three of us move forward at a fast walk, testing each slatted wooden step as we go. A few steps in front of me, Snake grips the thick rope sides with both hands. I steady myself, holding tight to the rope with one hand as I clutch the open water skins in the other.

I almost slip a couple of times on my unsteady legs, straining to maintain my balance as the bridge swings to and fro. As I approach a gap in the slats, my mouth goes dry and my palms grow sweaty. I slow down to make sure I cross safely.

Glancing up, I see Percival is almost to the other side, and this gives me hope. Snake and I are about halfway across when the bridge undulates like a slinky, and my stomach clenches in fear—I had hoped we would be further across before the troll recovered.

'Run,' I yell at Snake.

He turns and glances over his shoulder, blanches, then increases his speed. I wouldn't quite call it running, but he pulls away from me. With the water bottles clutched to my chest, I can't match his speed, and I slip as the bridge moves under me.

Once I regain my balance, I twist my head to find the troll thundering after us, her huge body looming ever closer. One of the bridge slats cracks under her weight and I gulp, wondering if the ancient bridge will hold with all four of us on it. She may not have to fight us to prevent our getting to the other side.

I take a couple more uncertain steps and let out a relieved breath as Percival reaches solid ground. Then I concentrate on moving forward, but the bridge is less stable with the troll lumbering behind me. Silently I urge Snake to go faster, but he's finding it as difficult to move as I am as the planks ripple up and down, swaying with each movement. When he places his first foot the other side, the troll is so close behind me that her dank, musty smell fills my nostrils.

I turn, letting go of the side as I start to tip the water from the water bottles. The troll stops to watch what I am doing and bares her teeth.

'That tiny bit of water does not scare me.'

I'm grateful the lack of movement is slowing the swinging. I gather the water into another ball as the troll's eyes widen. She takes a step forward.

'It is over, little elf. Come with me now,' she coaxes, her eyes fixed on the water.

There is uncertainty in the troll's voice as I move back in time with her. Her steps are longer and surer than mine, and she is almost at arm's-length when I fling the gathered water at her and turn to run in a single movement.

The board bucks under my feet, forcing me off balance. I grab hold of one of the bridge's roped sides as something grasps my ankle. I swivel my upper body to find the troll lying flat, grinning triumphantly as she pulls at my leg. My heart is in my mouth, and I feel sick.

Pushing my fear down, I decide my quest will not end this way. My only weapon is the water skins. I am about to hit the troll's hand when, desperate and breathless, I tip the skins and dribble the last of the water out on her fingers. It isn't much, but it's enough to cause her to loosen her hold.

I pull free. The end of the bridge is still so far away, but I don't hesitate. Dropping the water skins, I grip the rope sides in both hands and half run, half pull myself forward.

The troll is crawling behind me as I try to move faster, but the bridge is moving so much, all I can do is hold on and stumble forward when the bridge swings flat. The troll doesn't seem to have the same problem. She is gaining on me. My heart is pounding so hard, the sound fills my ears.

Ahead of me Snake is calling for me to move faster. Fingers grasp at my boot and slip off. I'm not going to make it. In desperation I reach out with my magic. Gathering the last of my strength, I call the water from below.

A roar fills the air as a wall of water rises up over the bridge. Magic pulses through me, and for a moment, I am pure energy—then it overwhelms me, and I lose control. Water smashes down, and I hook my arms over the ropes, holding on for dear life until the water recedes.

Exhaustion flows through me in waves, but I can't stay here. My legs buckle beneath me as I try to move, and my wet boots slip on the soaked wood. Just as my body gives up, a hand clutches at my arm, and Snake literally drags me off the bridge to safety.

With my feet on solid ground, I turn to find the troll cowering a few steps away, clinging to the sides as if she might still fall off. A pang of guilt tugs at me. I try to tell myself we made it and the troll is uninjured, but she is shaking as if she is petrified.

Snake steadies me on my feet. 'Are you okay?'

I nod.

'You won fair and square.' The troll is so forlorn as she drags herself to her feet and shakes herself like a large hairy dog. As she returns to her side of the bridge, her shoulders are slumped in defeat.

Snake tugs at my arm, urging me away from the edge of the gorge. I am frozen in place, watching until the troll reaches the other side. Collapsing, she curls into a ball, and I can see her shaking from here. As I witness her distress, this no longer feels like a victory.

I stare down at my hands as if they are somehow responsible for what I have done to the troll. But it is not them. I have fought before and never caused this much damage to another being. It is my magic. The joy I felt using it to escape the witch's house is now replaced with horror at what it did to the troll.

Somewhere in the back of my mind, I sense Snake leading me away, but I am so wrapped up in my own thoughts that I pay no attention to where we are going. All I can do is focus on what an abomination my magic is.

CHAPTER 10

Another Decision

O ut of sight of the bridge, we find a clearing. We don't need to talk to agree we all need a break. I offer to make a fire to dry Pris out, but Percival steps forward and incants something. I stand aside as he points down the length of her body, and her dripping wet clothes dry instantly. My eyes widen.

Drying spells are commonplace for earth and air creatures, so it's not the spell that surprises me. It is more that Percival went out of his way to do something for Pris. Does this act of kindness mean he no longer dislikes her?

When he is done, Pris lets her pack slip from her shoulders, drops to the ground, and leans back against a tree trunk, her blank eyes fixating on some distant point. Her skin is pale, and she hasn't said a word since we left the bridge. I join her on the ground and start rummaging in my pack for some of the travel bread. We all need something to revive our flagging spirits.

With his head tilted slightly to one side, Percival stares thoughtfully at us both. 'I think this calls for some tea and cake,' he declares decisively.

The next moment he is pulling a collapsible table from his pocket, followed by a full tea set for three, and lastly, a two-tiered iced cake cut into eight slices.

My mouth waters and my stomach rumbles. 'Is that banana cake?' I ask as the sweet scent wafts past.

Percival smiles. 'It is. Eleanora's daughter makes them for the whole-food shop she runs. I am sure she will not miss this.'

I'm not so sure, but I'm not going to argue. I want a slice of that cake too much.

Pris still has not moved. Percival hands her a cup of milky tea and a slice of cake, and she takes them automatically. There is no cheeky remark about being civilised in the wild, or any comment about how delicious the cake is as she takes a bite.

As Pris eats and drinks, it is like watching a robot. I catch Percival's eye. 'Did she use too much magic, do you think?'

The sprite shakes his head as he dabs at the side of his mouth with a napkin. 'No. I mean there's no doubt she is tired because she is not used to using magic, but she did not deplete her reserves. The cake should restore her energy. I believe this is something more—something about *how* she used her magic.'

I finish my cake, and Percival offers me a second slice. I shouldn't, but the cake is amazing, and the cream-cheese icing is to die for. I wolf it down before taking a surreptitious sideways glance to see if the dessert has magically revived Pris. She ate every crumb, but her eyes still look haunted.

Percival begins to clear away our forest feast. We should move soon, but we can't go on with Pris like this. Reaching over, I take her hand in mine, lacing our fingers together.

'Are you all right?' I ask, then mentally kick myself. Is that the best I can come up with?

Her fingers move in my grasp as if she wants to pull away. I hold tighter.

'Tell me what's worrying you. We can work through it together,' I encourage.

She takes in a deep breath and expels the air slowly. 'There isn't really time for self-indulgence. I think maybe we should move.' She makes as if to stand, and I pull her back down.

I don't normally do the macho thing, and I know she could whip my ass if she put her mind to it, but I'm worried about her. Pris is normally so decisive. She makes a plan, enacts it, and moves on. Her almost catatonic state is out of character.

'Pris, I don't think we're going to get very far with you like this. Tell me what's wrong, and perhaps we can fix it together.'

She jerks her hand out of mine and turns to me, her face twisted in anger. 'We can't "fix" this.' Her fingers form air quotes around the word fix. 'The only way to fix it is to go back in time and change my decisions.'

There are tears in her eyes now, and as the anger drains from her body, she looks… lost… or maybe haunted. Her gaze that meets mine is full of hurt and fear and a little bit of hope.

'Or perhaps… magic can remove it?'

I want to ask her what she means, what she wants to remove, but she's in no state to answer questions, so I need to figure it out for myself. I am so not good at this emotional stuff. I don't know what she is talking about, and I don't know how to help her.

A hand drops onto my shoulder, and Percival leans in to whisper in my ear. 'I think she means her magic.' He steps away and takes a seat on a fallen log, pulls a book from his pocket, and begins to read.

Magic? She wants to lose her magic? Why? Then it hits me like the wall of water hit the bridge—she's afraid of what she can do with it.

I turn back to her and try to pull her into my arms. She resists for a moment, her frame rigid, but a little of the fight leaves her and she allows me to hug her, although her body remains stiff as a board, as if she thinks herself unworthy of comfort.

For a moment I don't know what to do other than hold her. I'm good at putting my emotions into songs, but not so great at putting them into words in this sort of situation. Still, if I don't try, how will Pris get through this? I take a deep breath and expel it slowly. Perhaps I should just start talking and the rest will come to me.

'We all go through something similar,' I say before rushing on. 'Every creature uses magic instinctively in a crisis at some point and does something that scares them. It's part of learning, or so my mother told me.'

I pause, checking Pris is listening. She shifts in my arms, and I take that as a sign to continue. 'For me, it was moving a knife through the air to chase off a bully.'

'Did you stab him?' Pris's voice is muffled by my clothes.

I shake my head at the memory. 'No, fortunately. I don't believe I intended to go that far. I did believe he was going to hurt me though, and I was scared. I only wanted to scare him away…. I'll never really know if I would have hurt him.'

'Why? What happened?'

I gulp. This is still difficult to talk about, even now. 'He stumbled backwards, tripped over a chair, and when he hit the ground, he landed on his arm.'

My heart is racing at the memory, and I take a moment before finishing the story. All these years later, the memory still makes me sick to the stomach.

'I can never forget the way his arm was twisted out of shape when a teacher helped him up. He was white as a sheet and howling in pain. I remember throwing up, and for months after, my dreams were haunted by those few minutes.'

Pris is still. I am not sure my story helped or made things worse. I'm about to offer something more, but she relaxes against me, then she shuffles around so she can speak.

'Over the years I've fought off quite a few attackers,' she starts, 'and I was scared each and every time. Those fights were different than today. When I use karate, I am in control, and my focus is on defence.'

She stops speaking, and I dare not say anything or even move. There is more to come, and she needs to get everything out.

'Even with the bubble of water today, we meant to frighten the troll, not hurt her, and I was in control. Then when I called the water…. I couldn't control…. I could have…. The fear in her eyes—that moment will haunt me forever.' She turns her face back into my body as if to hide from the sight.

I hug her to me, wanting to take away the pain—to make her feel better. But as my mother told me once, the pain and worry are there for a reason. I gently push Pris away so I can see her face—and so she knows my next words are said with love.

'Magic is a wonderful gift, but it must be respected. Next time you're scared, you will remember the face of the troll, and you will not lose control—the memory of her fear will stop you.'

Pris shakes her head, 'I will never use magic again.'

'To learn to control magic, you must practice, just like learning karate.' I want to explain that if she doesn't keep practicing, then she will then increase the chances of lashing out with her gift when she is emotional, but perhaps this isn't the time to point that out.

She shakes her head a second time. 'No, I won't use it again.'

I sigh, getting some insight into how my mother felt when we had the same conversation. 'That's a shame, because then you would be ignoring the purpose of the lesson. Magic is a tool like any other. You must learn to use it safely and not lash out. What happened today was one step in that learning.'

It feels weird hearing my mother's words come from my mouth, but I have never been more thankful for her advice than I am today.

Slowly Pris leans into me, and her lips brush my cheek with a kiss.

'Thank you for trying, and I hear your words....'

'But they will take a while to sink in. I know. I lived through this myself.' I offer her a small smile.

'If you two are finished, there is no time for canoodling. *We* must continue.'

If I had not seen the concern on Percival's face when he set up tea, I would take offence at his brusque tone. As it was, I simply laughed and said, 'The quest must go on whether we are ready or not.'

I stand up and hold out my hand to help Pris to her feet. Moments later we set out along a narrow trail leading us along the mountain ridge. As I walk behind her, I focus on the tense set of her shoulders. She is still quiet, but at least she answers direct questions now. Still, I hope we don't encounter any more challenges today, as I'm not sure she can cope with anything else.

No sooner does the thought jump into my head than we round the corner and come face to face with a stone wall across our path. The door in the centre is covered in black runes. Although I have learnt some of the language of our people, I cannot read these.

'Ah.' Percival smiles. 'Finally, the entrance to the maze.'

'I thought we were already in the maze,' Pris says, her voice still worryingly lifeless.

Percival shrugs. 'We are, sort of. Only the worthy can enter the maze proper. Everything you did over the last two days was to test your worthiness.'

Beside me, Pris tenses, and I worry that her temper is going to get the better of her. She surprises me by not ranting. Instead, she sighs and raises her eyes to the sky. 'Seriously, how many more hoops do we have to jump through before we actually meet the minotaur?'

I agree with her, but I want to lighten the mood, so I joke, 'At least we haven't had to face any fire-eating dragons.'

One of Pris's hands flies to her mouth, and her eyes widen. 'You mean, that's a possibility? Really? After all we've faced, there might be dragons?'

Lead balloons spring to mind, and my rapidly failing joke is not helped at all by Percival's next words. 'The maze isn't far from the dragon breeding grounds. I have no doubt they are called to play a part in the maze on occasion.'

Pris turns white. Time to change the subject.

'Well, this isn't a dragon,' I explain the obvious. 'It's a door. And if we don't find out how to get in, what's on the other side won't matter.'

I have seen doors like this before in creature houses in

the World Above. They are our form of safes. The runes are a distraction. The real trick is in the locks down the left-hand side. They are invisible to the naked eye, but when I place my hand on the wood and reach out with my magic, I can sense them hiding.

I smile, as this should be easy. As the locks appear, I realise I have spoken too soon. Five locks emerge. The most I have ever managed to hold and open before is three.

I try not to react, but my shoulders slump. I had thought that after all Pris had been through today, I could handle this one alone. Maybe Percival can help. I glance over my shoulder to ask him for advice, only to see him disappear into thin air.

···ᴗ···

The call to return home is so strong that I am pulled away so quickly, I do not even get the chance to explain to Snake and Priscilla. Guilt tugs at my stomach. After our troll fight and coming up just now to our next challenge, Snake and Pris will need me. However, I appear directly in the glade. This alone gives me pause to worry. Emrys rushes forward, and the fear on his face chases my guilt away.

My mind instantly conjures an image of a lifeless Nisha, and I almost collapse to the ground. 'What... what is... wrong?' I manage to stammer out.

Emrys slows down and waves me forward. 'Father. He hears The Spirits calling and asked for you to be brought to him.'

When I was home the night before, my father was working away from our glade, and I had not had a chance to speak with him. In truth, I had not missed catching up with him. For the last few hundred years, he has turned ignoring my existence into an art form. His disdain is based on his warning that my friendship with a witch would be my downfall, that I was reaching above my station.

When I was cursed, he felt vindicated. Even though an elf hexed me, and it was my decision that led to the action, my father focused on the fact that I only did what I did because of Eleanora.

'You called me back for this?' I ask, anger replacing my fear for Nisha.

'Apart from the fact that this might be your last chance to mend things with Father, he says he must see you,' Emrys admonishes me.

I draw in a deep breath and expel it slowly. 'Do you really believe there is any hope of his accepting me even now… at the end?'

Emrys's eyes darken with sadness. 'I truly do not know, Percival, but can you honestly say you would not regret trying to work things out with him?'

He is right, of course. I allow him to lead me to the Mother Tree. It sits at the centre of our glade, the heart and soul of our family and the only link with our ancestors. My father has been placed within the embrace of its roots.

When I am close enough to make out my father's form, I stop moving, shocked at how wasted the body of our once vital spiritual leader is. 'Is that really him?' I ask, unable to believe the change.

Emrys nods.

'Then it is truly his time,' I whisper.

'He has not got long in this world. We have called Mother back from tending the forest. Spirits grant us that she arrives before he passes.'

I find myself unable to move. Emrys prods me in the back. 'Father called for you. You should go to him.'

'What happened to him?' I ask, putting off sitting with him for as long as possible.

'He has been spending more and more time in the trees these last months. A few weeks ago, he began babbling about a big change that will eclipse the blight, and how we will need to protect the forest,' Emrys tells me. 'He came back this afternoon and announced that the time is come—the spirit world is calling him to help with the coming storm.' Emrys's voice catches, and he wipes a tear from his cheek. 'He walked himself to the Mother Tree, lay down, and asked for me to call you back. He gave me instructions about his passing and has not spoken a word since.'

'Why speak with me, then? Surely, as you are his apprentice, he needs to spend time with you.' As I try to process the fact that my father is leaving this plane of existence, my emotions battle for dominance. I am saddened by the state I find my father in. Angry because the last time he spoke to me was hundreds of years ago. Disappointed in myself because I never quite measured up to his standards. And, amongst it all, is the love for him I packed away so many years ago, but never really stamped out.

Emrys wipes away the last of his tears. 'You had best ask him.'

I square my shoulders and force my feet to take me closer. Stopping between the tree roots, I lower myself down to sit by the creature who once told me I would never amount to much and that perhaps it was justice that I was no longer a true sprite.

My jaw tightens as I push down the bitterness at being summoned by the sire who abandoned me. I take a moment before I speak. 'Father, I came as you requested,' I say, forcing my words into a neutral tone that hides my inner turmoil.

'But you are not pleased to be here,' my father croaks, rolling onto his side to face me.

Apparently, I was not as successful as I hoped at hiding my feelings. I study my father, taking in the translucent skin and hollow cheeks. His eyes, the sign of vitality in any sprite, are almost the same colour as his skin. There is very little life-force left inside him, and an unexpected wave of sadness passes through me.

He was always such a strong force in my life. Always determined we should set an example for the other sprites.

'Ah, you still hark back to that night.' My father barks out a laugh. 'You are still not happy about your punishment.'

He refers to my curse. Or not the curse as such, but to the fact that it was not able to be reversed.

'The magical flow only allowed Princess Petunia a partial reversal because you carried blight through our lands. Our great spirits tempered the process to punish you for your actions.'

Bitterness laces the words I spit out. 'And you fully supported them.'

'Ah, what a bad father I am, holding my son responsible for his actions.'

And so it begins—the arguments and the recriminations. I do not know why I bother. As if reading my thoughts, my father says, 'In spite of your misgivings and our... past, you still sit here beside me at my end. Why?'

Sick to my stomach, the urge to stop the snarking is strong, and I attempt to appease my father as I always do. 'More than anything, I guess it's because I am surprised you called for *me*.'

'And quite rightly too,' he says. 'And you are clearly still angry at me—and at the world. Well, at least your anger shows a bit of backbone. Good... good. If what I learned these last few days comes to pass, you will need the strength that anger brings.'

My brows draw together as I try to make sense of his words. 'I don't understand,' I say, trying not to snap. Must he talk in riddles? Why can't he just say his piece and let me be on my way?

With a sigh, my father rolls back and lays flat again. 'I am not sure I do either, not completely. There is something amiss with the flow of magic in the World Below—'

'Another blight?' I ask warily, leaning in closer. Did my father just show me weakness? Or is this another of his traps?

'If you keep interrupting me, I will never tell you all I must.' My father's voice is tart and disapproving.

There is the man I am used to talking to. I tense, thinking this time I might walk away. Or at least tell him I am no longer a child to be spoken to like that. I do neither though. I wait, like a good son, for him to impart his wisdom.

His body shifts slightly, and when he has found a more comfortable position, he speaks. 'I am sorry. Time is short, and that was rude.'

My eyebrows almost leap off my forehead. What that just an apology?

'I was hard on you, not appreciating that you had a larger role to play in the world than I envisioned. The Spirits set me straight, and I know you are somehow entangled in these events. Until I join them, I will not know any more, but it is enough for me to know that your life has not been a waste of time... that my son will be a part of world changing events.'

He closes his eyes, and the glade falls silent. His chest

rises and falls with uneven breaths. Has he finished with me, or has he fallen asleep? I am not sure whether I should leave, or if there more to come. I drum my fingers on the root of the tree while I wait.

'What I learned… I cannot tell you. The spirits say I must not… but I know I was wrong about you, and I wanted to tell you that.'

My fingers stop mid motion, and I am a statue beside my father. I cannot believe I am hearing words I long since gave up waiting for. He is not exactly offering an apology, but I believe this is as close as the shaman of our community will ever get to one.

'Soon you must choose between what you have and what you want, and the repercussions of that choice…. Ah… I should not speak of that either. What can I tell you?' He sighs, his brows draw together, and he sucks in a shallow breath before continuing. 'Perhaps all that is left is advice. Have faith in yourself. Trust your heart, my son.'

He reaches out a shaky hand and grasps mine. His skin is dry and almost lifeless already. He will not be with us for much longer.

'I am grateful for this farewell. Do not tarry now, for there is work for you to do.'

His eyes droop closed, and he drops my hand. I do not move. Having finally made a connection with my father after all these years, I want more. It is as though the years have been stripped away, and we are father and son again. I want to talk to him about my life, ask him whether or not I should join the quest and try to return to my natural state.

Instead, my mind keeps returning to the fact this is it. He has hours to live, and this is it for us. There are others he will want to speak with before his time comes, and I should make way for them. But I cannot leave the grove as he requests.

'I must stay for the mourning and the release,' I say, wondering how I will fit in the ten days of mourning before the body is burned to release the soul and still help Snake and Pris through the maze.

'No! You must go immediately.' His words come out with more strength than I believed he had left. 'Worry not, I am to be taken to the great Mother Tree and will live a life among the spirits. There will be no mourning and burning for me. Say your goodbyes now.' My father's voice is back to its usual commanding tone.

Every fibre of my being wants to rail against his command, but my heart knows it cannot disobey the request of a dying creature. I place my hand on top of his and say, 'Fare thee well, Father. May your spirit mingle with the Great Magic for eternity.'

The ritual words sound hollow. I have had so little time to process this awkward meeting, so to even begin to say goodbye to him is beyond me. Fortunately, we have a ritual for these types of farewells, and that must be enough.

'May you do great things and join with me one day long in the future,' my father finishes. He offers me a weak smile, the first I can recall since I was just a child. He closes his eyes, and as his face slackens, I understand his body is still here but his soul is already departing.

Emrys touches my arm and I look up. 'Come, I will send you back.'

I hesitate a moment, looking upon my father one last time, I stand up and follow my brother out of earshot. 'I cannot leave. I must stay, no matter what Father said.'

'He does not wish it, and he will not thank you.'

When I make no effort to move, Emrys says, 'Father told me the great Mother Tree will take his body when he joins our ancestors. He instructed the elders that there is to be no mourning because it is a great honour, and without a body, there is no need for release. We must respect his wishes.'

'But what if he is wrong? What if he is delusional? I cannot disrespect my father by not attending the rites, not when I am so close to home.'

My argument sounds hollow even to my own ears. My father would never disrespect the spirits by falsely declaring his heart's desire to be their wish, not even if he was losing his grip on reality. Emrys does not speak. He simply raises an eyebrow and waits. My body slumps as I give in to the reality of the situation. My brother places a hand on my shoulder.

'We will wait the full thirty days and hold the Celebration of Life meal. Perhaps by then you will be finished with this quest, and you can return for that.'

I am unable to judge whether this fits with protocol or is respectful, as the only shaman our people have had in my lifetime lies dying. Emrys is our new shaman, and I must abide by his decision.

'Have the spirits spoken to you? Do you know anything about the crisis he speaks of?' I ask, hoping for some clarity before I leave.

'The spirits will not speak of it to me, so I cannot tell you anything more.'

'Perhaps Father is overstating the importance of what is going on,' I suggest, unable to keep the relief from my words.

Emrys shakes his head. 'It might be nothing. Then again, it might just as well be something. Regardless, his words are wise. All we can do is trust in ourselves, whether we are everyday folk, or we are someone facing an extraordinary destiny.'

Sage advice, I think as I hug my brother and we share our sorrow for a moment. In thirty days, we will celebrate my father's life. Until that time, I must return to my quest.

'Spirits guide you.' My brother speeds me back to the maze before I can answer.

··◗··

'Damn, where's Percival gone?' Snake says.

'What?' I turn slowly to find the sprite has indeed disappeared. 'That shouldn't be a problem, should it? I thought lock picking was kinda your thing.'

'But—'

'Besides, Percy isn't allowed to help us—something about if he does, it becomes his quest too.'

Snake laughs. 'You're only brave enough to call him Percy because he isn't here.'

He's right, it does feel a little naughty, but honestly, the guy needs to loosen up. Snake, though, is changing the subject. What doesn't he want to tell me? I'm not fragile. I don't want his protection—I need his honesty.

'Can you pick this type of lock?' I ask.

He snorts. 'With my eyes closed.'

I'm unimpressed. 'That goes without saying, doesn't it, because isn't it all done by touch?'

He's silent. My brows draw together as I take in his slumped shoulders and the fact that he will still not meet my gaze. 'So, what *is* the problem?'

He releases the locks back into the door and turns to face me. 'I can't pull the locks out of the door, hold them in place, and pick all of them at the same time. There are too many.'

This is not good. Maybe fighting a dragon would be easier. Although my stomach is knotting, I school my face into what I hope is a look of bland curiosity. I can't let Snake know what I am thinking, as he clearly thought this would be his shining moment and is worried he will let us down.

'How would Percival help?' I ask.

'I hoped he would come up with some ideas on how I could open more locks at the same time—perhaps provide a way to boost my magic.'

I shift my focus to the locks. Did the minotaur know this would be beyond Snake's current abilities? Is he forcing Snake to dig deeper, to learn another lesson? If this is a test, then perhaps we need a different perspective.

'How many of the locks can you hold and open?' I ask.

'Three definitely, perhaps four,' Snake answers.

'Interesting that there are five locks, then.'

Snake's eyes widen as he catches my train of thought.

'Another test? Of course it is.' Snake blows out a sigh. 'We're both tired. We should take some time to think this through.'

He's right. With Percival gone and other problems facing us, now is the right time to rest and regroup.

'Let's make camp. When we've eaten and rested, you can show me how to pick the last lock.' I drop the lock picking into the plan casually, as if it is just something I should do to pass the time. Truth is, I have never picked a lock in my life. I don't know how to do it with my hands, let alone with using magic.

'Are you sure?' Snake asks. 'I mean, you defeated the troll, I sort of thought this was my thing to do. I mean, I must be on this quest for a reason.'

I was right, he wants to prove himself. Boys can be like that sometimes. I cross the couple of steps between us and force myself into his arms—a rather awkward manoeuvre with both of us wearing packs, but I hope it will take some of the sting from my words.

'You can't do this alone, and I don't think you are meant to. I might be wrong, but I think this is less about testing your lock picking abilities and more about forcing us to work together.'

Snake still holds me stiffly. I don't want to relive this morning, it's still too raw, but the one positive I have taken from it is that I would still be a quivering mess if Snake had not been there to support me. It is Snake's turn now. He must understand we're a team, and it is only as a team we will succeed.

'Look, if you hadn't distracted the troll with music, or if Percival hadn't helped me with the water thing, we would still be at the gorge. It took all three of us to get over the bridge.'

Snake does not relax his hold. I resist the urge to shake my head. Whether I want to or not, I am going to have to open up about my reaction to the water incident.

'And it was you who showed me how to deal with my… umm… angst over dousing and almost killing the troll.'

Snake's arms tighten, and this show of support warms me, but I can't let him shift the focus. 'You are not alone in this, but you do have to teach me how to pick a lock.'

It takes a moment, but Snake pulls me tight against his body. 'I'm being too macho, aren't I?' he murmurs into my hair, and there is a touch of laughter in his voice.

'Yep,' I say with a nod, then snuggle closer to him.

I want to stay where I am for a while longer. It's nice… more than nice. Unfortunately, my insides are beginning to melt, and my body is starting to get ideas that are best left until after this whole fiasco is over. I force myself to take a step back and say, 'Come on, let's find some wood and get a fire going.'

As I gather logs, I spot a stream not far from the clearing and return to gather our remaining water skin to refill. By the time we are settled round a blazing fire, Percival is still not back, and we decide to wait to eat until he has returned. Snake produces a padlock from his pack and passes it to me.

'Most locks, whether physical or magical, work the same way. The prongs from a key push pins back into a housing and keeps them there. The springs those pins lean on want to force them back into place.' He stops to make sure I am following.

'Got it,' I confirm.

He holds up two of the metal picks he has. 'This curved one is to push the pin into the housing, like a key would, and this flatter one is to hold it in place while you move on to the next pin.'

I nod.

'Okay, you have the theory, now comes time for the practice.' He hands me the picks.

At first I am all fingers and thumbs, but at least my fumbling makes Snake smile.

'Don't you have something better to do?' I snap.

He chuckles. 'No.'

Infuriated, I try to block him out and concentrate on the lock. Finally, after much practice and a few curses—okay quite a few curses—I get it.

'Yes!' I fist pump. 'I'm the master,' I crow, a grin splitting my face.

'Master?' Snake asks dryly, the twinkle in his eye taking the sting from his words.

I will not let his sarcasm ruin my triumph. Okay, this is

just the first step. I still need to learn to do this with magic, but I did it!

The sun is putting on a spectacular show of reds and purples behind the mountains, and the temperature is dropping fast. Percival still has not returned, and my stomach is protesting. I put on a billy of water and search for some leaves to make a warming tea while Snake rations out the trail bread. When we have finished and tidied up, Percival is still AWOL.

'We should get some sleep,' Snake says, reaching for his sleeping roll. 'We should be well rested when we tackle this lock.'

'Mmm,' I answer, laying my roll next to his.

I place a couple of extra logs on the fire before crawling in beside him, lock clutched firmly in my hand.

'I'm sure we can do this if we work together.' I wriggle back into him, searching for additional warmth.

He wraps himself around me and I settle into his embrace, allowing the heat of his body to relax me and all thoughts of lock picking disappear as I imagine rolling over and....

'I'll take first watch,' Snake says, abruptly sitting up, pulling me back into reality by reminding me we are not yet safe enough to be distracted by... things—no matter how much I'd like to be.

I drift off to sleep and am completely out cold when he wakes me for my turn to stand guard. I prop myself up on one elbow and find Percival must have returned sometime during the night and is now asleep across on the other side of the fire.

'What happened there?' I ask, pointing at the sleeping form.

'I don't know. He reappeared a little while ago,

produced a sleeping bag, and went to sleep without saying a word.'

A frown worries my brow as I consider the sprite for a while. *Nothing I can do now*, I tell myself. There will be plenty of time to sort Percival out in the morning.

I lean over and press my mouth to Snake's, losing myself for a moment in a long, lingering kiss. 'Go to sleep. We have a big day tomorrow.'

I watch the firelight flicker over his face until his breathing evens out and I'm sure he's asleep. Once I am certain, I pull the lock out and work at using my magic to open it. I easily hold the tension on the lock and push one or two pins into place, but it takes practice and a lot of concentration to force all six pins up and be able to twist the barrel to release the lock at the same time.

As the sun rises, I place the lock in my lap and take stock. I can now pick it relatively quickly, but I am certain I can only do one. If we want to make it through the door today, we might need something more. Perhaps I can help in another way.

Being careful not to disturb Snake, I make my way over to the door, press my palms to the wood, and try to sense the locks inside. I think I can make out their shapes but can't force them to come to the surface.

'It's a gnome specialty.' The voice comes from behind me, and I turn to find Snake watching me. 'Something about our magic draws the locks to the surface, like magnetic attraction.'

I run a hand over my hair and tug a little at my braid. No, there is nothing I can think of that will solve our problem. 'I can only open one lock,' I tell Snake. 'I thought I may be more help drawing the locks out, which would allow you to focus on picking them.'

Snake shakes his head. 'Not many gnomes can expose one, let alone five.'

A little bit down but not completely out, I return to the dying embers of the fire as Snake reaches into his pack and draws out some travel bread. What I wouldn't give for a full English breakfast about now. Still, the food is nourishing, and I'm hungry enough after my magical training to eat just about anything.

'So do all the locks need to be released at once for the door to open?' I ask as I chew the berry bread that is more like a muesli bar than actual bread.

Snake mumbles something, his mouth so full of food, I can't make out a single word.

'Sorry?'

He swallows and takes a sip of water. 'Yeah. The idea is to work one lock at a time, push all the pins up and hold them there until all the locks are ready. Then you turn the barrels all at once.' He makes it sound simple, but my nighttime antics have taught me it is anything but.

'Okay. That makes it a bit more difficult.' I wrack my brains for something that may give us an advantage, but I've got nothing.

'We can only give it a go,' Snake offers.

'What if we can't do it though?' The words slip out. 'I mean, our parents would then be at Bernais's mercy, and we both know that is not a good thing.'

Snake's green eyes darken as he holds my gaze. 'We have to try. We have come too far. I'm not prepared to give up. Are you?'

I am emotionally battered and bruised. My body screams with exhaustion, and I want nothing more than to soak in a hot bath and sleep in a warm bed. I allow my eyes to sweep down the length of Snake's body. Okay, there is *one* thing I want more.

My eyes return to his, and a sigh escapes from the depth of my soul.

'No,' I admit, 'I won't give up. If we are kicked out of the maze, then I want to go knowing we've given it our best shot.'

'Then let's not talk of failing before we've even tried.' Snake laughs as if he's trying to make light of everything. But the hard, stuttering sound does not come from his heart, and I think perhaps it comes from a place of fear. It dawns on me he is just as worried about our ability to enter the maze as I am.

Nibbling on my bread, I give myself a peptalk in an effort to lift my spirits and focus my energies in a positive way. I do not succeed, and my spirits fall as I finish my meal.

Snake starts clearing up and putting out the fire, taking care to cover it with earth. I sip on some water to wash the food down, then follow suit. Percival still has not moved, though I sense he is awake. I wonder what happened last night to make him more withdrawn than normal. When everything is tidy and packed up, Percival remains curled up in his bed.

I walk over to his sleeping form and announce, 'We are going to open the door.' My voice carries more conviction than I feel. 'If you want to come with us, you had better get up.'

He doesn't move, and Snake touches my arm. 'Leave him. He didn't look so great when he came back last night. I think he may have had some bad news.'

I reach out as if to comfort Percival, but I draw my hand back. The prickly sprite isn't big on physical contact, and I am not sure he would accept help from me.

'We can't just leave him,' I murmur. 'It feels wrong to

go on without him. And if he is hurting, then he may need us. I mean, he has been there for me....'

Snake drapes his arm around me and pulls me close, leaning his head against mine. We stand there for a moment, indecision holding us captive.

As the minutes draw out, and Percival doesn't move, my mind attempts to balance our need to get to the centre of the maze with my unexpected desire to help him.

'Perhaps he isn't meant to come with us into the maze proper,' Snake says.

The scales tip towards leaving.

'No.' The word slips out. 'We're a team.'

Snake shakes his head. 'No, we're not. Percival is not a part of this quest. He is an advisor, someone to help us learn about the World Below. Perhaps when we make it through the door, we will have shown we have outgrown our training wheels and can go on alone.'

I consider his words. Could this really be another part of the test?

I slip from Snake's embrace. 'Okay, shall we do this?' I keep my voice low but strong. Hoisting my pack onto my back, and with one last glance over my shoulder, I lead the way to the door before I change my mind.

Standing by the maze entrance, Snake runs a hand over the door. He squares his shoulders, then takes control. 'Once I expose the locks, you work on the one at the bottom. Hold the last pin until I tell you to go.'

I nod my understanding.

'Right, let's do this,' Snake says. Leaning his forehead against the wood, he takes a couple of calming breaths, then places his hands on the door.

Following suit, I kneel and put my hands close to the bottom lock. Allowing my magic to reach out, I study the mechanism. It is slightly different to the one I picked last night, but similar enough that I am able to work out how to open it. It takes me a little while until I am ready to hold the pins in place, and the effort causes beads of sweat to form on my forehead.

I concentrate on keeping the five pins open, waiting for Snake to tell me to finish the job. A headache is starting to form behind my eyes when he admits, 'I can't do it. I can move a couple of pins in the fourth lock, but can't quite get the last one…'

We can't do this alone. We need the whole team. 'Percival.' I reach out with my voice, reluctant to pull the sprite from whatever it is that has laid him so low.

There is no response. The quest is slipping away from us, and I can't let that happen. I let go of my empathy and make my voice as commanding as possible. 'Percival, we need your help. I'm sorry, but if you don't pitch in, we will fail here, Eleanora's plans will all be for nothing.'

The last words are a guess. I am sure something more than our quest is going on, and that Eleanora is involved in some way. What I can't work out is whether Percival is a party to it. I don't look over my shoulder, as it takes too much effort to hold the pins in place, but I sense his presence as he draws near.

'I am not sure…. It's not my area….' His voice holds an uncharacteristic uncertainty and a deep weariness I force myself to block out.

'You must be able to do something… anything,' I plead, the desperation coursing through me leaking into my words.

'My magic is relatively weak but… sometimes I boost my mistress.'

A shadow crosses over my face, and I see a small hand cover Snake's, the one closest to my face. Sweat drips into my eyes, and I long to brush it away, but both of my hands are on the door, holding my lock in place, and every ounce of my being is focused on that one task.

'I have one more.' Snake's voice is strained. 'Almost… there…. Now!'

Snick, snick, snick, snick, snick. With a loud thump, the locks release, and the door swings open. The momentum and wave of magical energy knocks me back onto my butt.

CHAPTER 11

Yet Another Big Decision

Air whooshes past me, and a thud reaches my ears as Pris hits the ground behind me.

'Ouch.'

'Are you okay?' I half turn to check she hasn't been injured and bite back a grin as she looks up with wide-eyed surprise.

'I'd help you up, but….' I jerk my head towards the door I'm holding open.

I'm so bone-crushingly tired, I want to join her, but I'm afraid the door will not stay open for long, and I'm not sure I can go through opening it again. If I'm exhausted, I can only imagine how Pris is feeling.

Sucking in a deep breath, I place my foot in between the door and the jamb and hold my hand out for Pris. Her fingers entwine with mine, and I pull, helping her to her feet. She lets go of my hand, and I hear the rustle of clothing as she dusts herself down.

I give her a moment before asking, 'Okay, guys, are we ready for this?'

I take the silence as a yes and push at the heavy door. It

slowly creaks open, the noise piercing the air. Percival ducks under my arm and is the first to enter. Pris and I allow him to take the lead, and we follow him into a dark corridor.

Holding out his hand, Percival creates a ball of light, revealing that we are not in a hallway, but a long, thin room. I jump as the door thumps back into place.

Waiting for my heartbeat to settle, I take in more of our surroundings. The sides to my left and right are walls. In front of me are three doors.

'Nooo,' I groan. 'Not another decision.'

'This is a maze, so I guess the decisions are in lieu of corners and turns,' Pris muses from beside me. 'How are we supposed to choose?' She takes a step closer to the doors. 'There's nothing to show us where they lead.'

'I don't know,' I tell her, finding it difficult to rouse my interest in solving yet another puzzle. Guilt prods at me as she continues to study the doors, and I add, 'Perhaps we can find some minor difference? There must be something about them to give us a clue.' I peer closely, but our options seem maddeningly identical. 'What do you think, Percival?'

The sprite doesn't speak. In fact, he doesn't move at all, and his face is still wearing the bewildered, hurt mask it wore last night.

I crouch down until I am at eye level with him and ask, 'What is it, Percival? Are you okay? Can I... we... do anything to help?'

His green catlike eyes focus on me. 'I... um... I have had some bad news. I shall be fine in a moment.' His voice cracks as he speaks, telling me he is unlikely to be okay any time soon. With that thought comes an understanding that getting through the next set of doors is not as important as helping Percival.

I place a hand on his shoulder. 'You take all the time you need.'

'But are you sure we have time to—'

I glare at Pris, and she stops midsentence. She glances down at the sprite, and understanding softens her gaze.

'Thank you for what you did, Percival. I hope that doesn't mean you joined our quest,' I say, wondering if that is adding to his worries.

He blinks a couple of times as if he is just waking up. 'What? Umm… no…I do not know. It makes no matter for the moment.' He shakes his head as if clearing his thoughts, then stares intently at the doors.

'These doors look familiar, like a test I saw once before. It's like… Mandor?'

Who or what is Mandor?

'Hello, old friend.'

I jump back up at the sound of a voice behind me and spin around.

A tall, gaunt male creature appears in front of us. 'It has been many years since we last met, Percival.'

Apart from his piercing grey-blue eyes, he is unremarkable looking, but there is something compelling about him. It takes me a moment to realise what it is; he literally throbs with power, which may explain how he is able to just appear in front of us.

The creature does not take his eyes off Percival when he speaks again. 'You managed to work out that these doors were made by me, so perhaps you can tell these children how to activate them.'

For a few seconds, Percival's eyes rake the man, and the idea that this might be some sort of trap is just wriggling its way into my mind when Percival says, 'You need to make the instructions written on the door appear by casting a reveal spell.'

It can't be that simple, surely. I slide a look at Pris, but she is watching Percival and the newcomer. I glance back at the sprite to find he has locked eyes with the stranger. It is as though the two of them have forgotten about us.

'How is she?' the man asks, his voice softening.

'You can always visit her and find out. It is easier down here. You must be aware she is close by.' Percival's tone is flat, uninviting.

I am surprised when tears form in the stranger's eyes. 'You understand better than anyone how it hurts us to be together while knowing we must soon part.'

'Perhaps you should have thought of that before you decided to ascend,' Percival snaps.

I frown down at the sprite. I have never seen him angry, but his hands are balled into fists. The appearance of the man and his doors have upset him, perhaps even more than the news he received last night.

'You act as though the decision was mine alone—like I had a real choice in the matter. Neither of us wanted to part, but it was for the best. Still, she asked this boon of me, and I came for her.'

'What is going on here?' Pris's voice breaks the tension, startling me.

I have to admit, the drama of the situation with Percival and the stranger had drawn me in so far that I had forgotten she was here.

Percival finally breaks eye contact with the stranger and turns to us.

'Princess Priscilla, Snake Fieth, meet the wizard, Mandor—Eleanora's mate.'

'Eleanora's mate?' Pris's eyes widen, and her eyebrows nearly fly off her forehead. 'I didn't know she was even—'

'Eleanora and I were parted by… have been apart for many years. Although my heart resides with her, we both moved on a long time ago,' Mandor's tone is neutral, though his hands shake a little as he utters the words, giving the impression he has not really moved on at all.

While Pris quizzes the Wizard, I am silenced into awe. Witches are only able to access their full power if they forsake their worldly ties and join the wizard council. Most wait until later in life to ascend, but Mandor is clearly still young.

Why would Mandor go through the heart-wrenching pain of breaking with his bond mate to do something he could have put off until the end years of his life? He clearly still has feelings for her. There must be more behind this story than a desire to devote the rest of his long life to the study of magic.

My musings are interrupted by Pris's demanding tones. 'And what is your role in this?' She gestures to the doors.

'I perhaps should not….' The wizard gnaws at his lips, then shrugs. 'I guess it does not matter now. Eleanora contacted me and asked if I would… um… offer myself… for the wizard's part in this quest.'

The frown draws Pris's brows together. 'She wanted you to help us?'

Mandor laughs. 'Eleanora is aware I would never betray my responsibilities to the Wizard Council, and she would never ask me to. It was more a case of making sure no one else tampers with the proceedings by offering myself to set the Wizard's Question.'

Pris's mouth forms an 'O' as I mull over the implications of the wizard's words.

'And why are you here in person?' I ask. 'I'm sure we can figure the doors out ourselves.'

Mandor chuckles. 'Go ahead.' He gestures to the doors. 'Try it.'

I step forward, reluctant now as I sense a trap. Reveal

spells are amongst the earliest learnt by creatures. I point at the doors and say, 'Noct.'

The wood glows orange as runes slowly appear. They swirl and dance, then finally fall into formation. I study each of them carefully, but they are unlike any runes I was taught. I turn a questioning gaze to Percival.

He shakes his head. 'Those are wizard runes. They are magical in themselves, and the options they offer depend on the creature asking them to appear. That is why Mandor is here, to translate for us.'

I turn to the wizard, not surprised to find the corners of his mouth tugging into a smile. 'Would you like me to read the script for you?' he offers.

I nod, not able to think of anything witty enough to recover my dignity.

'All right, then. Door number one leads to a true maze with twists and turns and traps, the type I believe everyone expects when they hear of the minotaur's maze. There is danger there, but it will take around a day or so to make it to the centre of the maze if you avoid the traps. If you succeed, you will bypass the minotaur.'

'What happens if we fall to one of the traps?' I ask, thinking it must be bad if we wouldn't have to face the minotaur. I am not disappointed.

'It depends on the trap. Consequences range from expulsion from the maze to... to...well....' He shrugs. 'Death.'

'I'm not liking the sound of that,' Pris mutters. 'Too much is left to chance.'

'Not to mention the potential death thing,' I add.

Mandor carries on as if we hadn't spoken. 'Door two opens to a garden maze. Think hedgerows and Hampton Court. It is less hazardous and normally takes about three days to traverse if you don't get lost along the way.'

'I am guessing the lost bit can go on infinitely?' Pris asks.

'Correct.'

'And the final door?' I ask before Pris can state her preference for the longer route even with the attendant risk.

'Ah, now, that takes you directly to a confrontation with the minotaur.'

Okay, I am not liking any of these options, but if I am forced to choose, I am thinking door one. We are exhausted from using our magic opening the door here, so at least if we choose that option, we only have one more day of this, and I'm confident we can overcome the traps.

'I will give you ten minutes to decide,' Mandor states before disappearing.

'First things first,' Pris says before I can put forward any suggestions. 'We must all agree to go the same way, no splitting up. We finish this together.'

'Yes,' I agree. I learnt my lesson last time.

'Percival?'

'What? Me?'

'Of course. You're part of this team,' I tell him.

'Um… I guess…. All right, I agree,' he says.

Then, before I can open my mouth to speak, Pris announces, 'I am tired of this whole game. I want to take the shortest route and head straight for the minotaur.'

· · ❧ · ·

Snake's eyes widen. He starts to speak, shuts his mouth, then rubs his hands through his hair. 'Are you mad? Do you honestly believe you can fight a minotaur and win?'

I laugh. 'Of course not.'

'Good, because for a moment there, I thought you had lost your freaking mind and were suggesting we head straight into the heart of the maze and fight the minotaur.'

'I did, and I am backing us to make it past him and into the centre to claim our prize,' I finish.

Snake stares at me as if he's only just met me. He begins pacing around the room, which is quite a feat, since it's so cramped. He's agitated, and he's trying really hard not to fly off the handle. After a couple of circuits, he stops in front of me.

'Please tell me you're joking. I mean, we want to finish this as quickly as possible to ensure our parents aren't harmed while we're gone, but this is madness. We can't beat a giant half-man, half beast warrior.'

'Mandor just said we had to fight him, not that we must win,' I point out.

Again, Snake opens his mouth to speak and closes it. He tilts his head to the side and considers me for a moment before asking, 'Do you have a plan?'

I smile. 'I think I do. What if the minotaur guards the entrance, and all we must do is pass him to get inside. We're smart and we're resourceful. I'm sure, with the three of us working together, we can do that.'

For the first time since we entered the maze, I feel confident. This is not about magic or learning about who I am—this is a battle against a larger foe. I am trained to fight, and mostly that involves outsmarting your opponent before they pummel you. Combined with Percival's knowledge of the World Below and Snake's ability to find options when there aren't any, I'm sure that with a little bit of planning, we can do this.

Snake runs a hand through his hair; this usually means

he is working something through. 'You're sure this is better than the one-day option and facing more traps?'

I nod. 'I am. We won't be able to predict what we will face there, so it will be next to impossible to prepare. If we choose the minotaur option, at least we know he'll be on the other side of the door, and we can make a plan.'

His hand goes to his hair again, and he pushes it out of his eyes. It's getting quite long and needs a cut. 'You make a fair point,' he admits.

'Besides,' I start. I'm not sure how to say this without sounding paranoid, so I just come out with it. 'While I'm sure Bernais and his cronies are plotting their next moves while we are out of their hair, Mandor's comment makes me wonder if Bernais has the power to ensure we don't come out of the maze—ever?'

Snake's eyes widen. 'I can't believe…. Percival, is that even possible?'

Our sprite friend has been strangely quiet since Mandor left, and I am not sure he has even been listening to us. However, he shrugs at Snake's question. 'Of course, there is always a chance someone could influence or bribe some being in the maze, but it would be a very brave creature who tampers with an official quest. They would have to answer to the minotaur, after all.'

'But he could, couldn't he?' Snake presses. 'I mean, Eleanora asked Mandor to come here, so she has sort of interfered.'

'Eleanora would never tamper with the quest. She only asked Mandor to come because she knows he will always do what is right, no matter what the cost to himself.'

Percival's words are bitter, hinting at their shared past. Although my curiosity is piqued, we don't have time to go into that now, so I say, 'I believe we can outsmart the minotaur—the three of us working together.'

Snake's eyes widen, telegraphing his surprise. 'But Percival is not a part of the quest. I'm sure the little boost of magic he gave to get us here would not be beyond the rules of helping….'

Snake looks at Percival for confirmation, but the sprite is silent. Instead, he rubs his chin thoughtfully and stares at the three doors.

'Yes, perhaps the three of us together could do this—defeat the minotaur,' he finally says.

Snake looks helplessly from Percival to me. 'Our only weapons are knives,' he points out. 'I mean, there is the bow and arrows, but I never got a chance to practice with them.'

'We are going to outsmart him, not face him head-on, just like we did with the troll,' I explain. 'What we have should be enough to distract him so we can get past him to the centre of the maze.'

Snake is quiet for a moment. I'm not sure he is convinced, but then he slips his pack from his shoulders. 'We'd best make sure our weapons are handy before we go through, then.'

I smile. I took the lead and made a decision. My team are supporting me. It feels good to be back to my old self.

Snake hands me some of his arrows. 'You might be able to do something with these—you know, change them with your magic.'

I nod and gaze at them. What could they be? I hold them together with my knife, and an image takes shape. I concentrate, and soon the wood and iron are re-formed into a sword. All right, it's not an amazing sword like magicians make in the movies, but it is sharp and serviceable and will suit my needs.

Snake hands me some travel bread, and I chew the

berry-flavoured grains to recharge my energy while we plan out the battle.

'When we go through, I will take the front position. Percival, you go to my right and Snake to my left. Our best chance is to split up, forcing him to battle on more than one front. If you see a chance to make it to the maze's centre, take it. At least one of us will win through to the end.'

Before the others get a chance to comment, Mandor reappears and stands by the doors. 'Have you decided?'

'Yes,' we all say together.

Mandor's right eyebrow rises as he regards Percival. 'So you decided to fight for your future?'

'That is my business.' Percival's tone is tart. 'Your only job now is to let us through the third door—allow us to face this minotaur.'

'So be it,' the wizard says, and my stomach clenches as he presses his hand to the wood.

As the door swings open, my mouth goes dry and the travel bread sits heavy in my stomach. I hope I haven't made a foolish mistake—I mean, this is a minotaur, not a karate instructor ready to teach us a lesson. He will be focused on stopping us from getting to the centre of the maze at any cost. I square my shoulders. Too late to back out now.

As I step through the entrance, Mandor says, 'Percival, when you see Ellie, please tell her my heart is still hers and hers alone, and I miss her every day.'

'I am not sure how that helps her or you, but yes, I will tell her.'

Percival's voice follows me as I walk into a cloying black void. Silence swamps me, and I can barely breathe. I am here alone with no idea whether or not the others have followed. This is not at all what I expected.

CHAPTER 12

Confronting the Minotaur

My feet slip from under me as the darkness around me changes. From within the void, I hear the wizard Mandor's voice echo. 'Use your head and your heart.' The words reverberate around me in the viscous air.

I try to walk forward, and I feel like I have walked face-first into a wet sheet. I gasp for air as I stumble. I am choking and falling and... then there is ground beneath my feet and I can breathe again.

As I struggle to stand, the pack on my back throws me a little off balance. Grasping my sword, I swing around, holding it in front of me. I raise my head, and my vision adjusts and shows me I am standing in the centre of a room about the size of my school gymnasium.

My gaze is drawn to burning red eyes inside a shadow-like bull's head. My eyes slide from the vision, as if they cannot quite believe what they are seeing. Behind him is a door—the door to the centre of the maze. I frantically search the room for my team, and my stomach clenches in fear. Has the minotaur decided to take me on in single combat?

The beast takes a step to the side, blocking my view, and I am forced to confront the beast that he is. Even though I try to stand straight and meet him front-on, my knees buckle, and I have to fight to stay on my feet. He must be seven, maybe even eight feet tall from his cloven feet to the tips of his horns. And that body is all bulky muscle and sinew lightly covered in brown fur. It would take both of my thighs to take up one of his biceps alone.

I fixate on his head, on the red glowing eyes and the snout that is twisted into a smile as if he has been waiting for this confrontation and is going to enjoy it. He dips his head in a parody of a welcome, allowing the light to catch the sharp points of his horns.

I shiver, then tear my gaze away and assess his other weapons. A sword hangs loosely in one of his large hands, and a mace swings hypnotically in the other. The spiked ball at the end of a chain is something I've never seen before. How do you combat that?

I am distracted by the sound of shuffling feet behind me. The minotaur's smile widens as Snake and Percival enter my peripheral vision. My heart rate calms a little at seeing them, at knowing I will not have to face our final test alone. They move into the positions I outlined before we entered the void. I'm relieved they're following the plan even though none of us could have imagined this entrance.

The minotaur roars, and my insides turn to liquid. Why did I choose to do this? Is there any way I can save us from our imminent defeat? Wait, can we refuse the challenge and choose another option? No, that is fear talking, and fear has no place in a fight.

This *is* the best option. Besides, Snake and I made it to the World Below, we have come this far through the maze, we have overcome every obstacle the minotaur placed in front of us, and the three of us will get to the centre. There must be a way around the behemoth guarding the door.

The room is slightly oval, with us at the apex and the door we need to reach at the furthest point. If the minotaur stretches out his arms with his weapons in place, there might almost be enough room for a piece of paper to slip past. The floor is flagstone, and the wall is stone. There really isn't much to work with.

As if he senses my brain working out a plan, the minotaur grasps his weapons and speaks. 'Ah, songsmith. Have you come to serenade me?' he asks Snake. His voice is mellow and cultured, which sounds odd coming from his beastlike face.

'Would it send you to sleep?' Snake quips in a rather jaunty tone. His voice is a little on the thin side, but I'm proud of him for not being cowed by our opponent.

The minotaur roars with laughter. 'No, young gentleman. You must know by now, nothing in my maze is that easy. I am here to test your mettle.'

Now that is just plain rude, I think. *Who does he think he is that he can boast of his right to test us?*

I straighten my spine and, ignoring my trembling legs, say, 'We wish entry to the centre of the maze.'

The minotaur laughs, a great rolling laugh that comes from deep in his belly. 'You two? Surely you jest. You come armed with a knife and a toothpick to fight me, the mightiest of the Queen's subjects?'

'How rude!' I say out loud this time. 'We came here on a quest. We earned the right to face you, so you could at least show us some respect.'

From the corner of my eye, I see Snake shuffle uneasily. 'Don't rile him up, Pris,' he tells me. 'He will be difficult enough to fight without you making him angry.'

To my surprise, the minotaur nods. 'You're right, of course—that *was* rude. I apologise. I don't get many visitors, and I do sometimes forget my manners. I guess the proper forms should be followed before I break you to smithereens.'

His apology does not reassure me. In fact he is so certain about the outcome of our contest, my resolve wavers a bit. I narrow my eyes at him. Perhaps this is just a tactic to put us off our guard, make us more fearful, as if his height and bulk are not intimidating enough. Or is this display of overconfidence something we can use to our advantage?

Ah, he still thinks Percival is only an observer in this dance. Is there something we can do with that? Even if he knew, he probably wouldn't see the sprite as a serious challenge.

If I have read the minotaur correctly, then Percival is our best chance of one of us getting to the centre. But how can I tell him of the change of plan without giving the game away?

'Percival,' I whisper without taking my eyes of the minotaur. 'Do you remember what I said about what we should all do if we get the chance?'

'I do.' His voice is soft, almost a whisper.

'How about you concentrate on doing just that.'

'Enough whispering,' the minotaur bellows as he leans his weapons on the ground and then relaxes. 'Who comes to challenge me for entry to the centre of the maze?'

This is it. This is the formal challenge before the fight begins.

'I, Princess Priscilla Crown,' I say.

'I, Sneak Thief,' Snake follows.

'And I, Percival of the Wyld Woods Tree Clan.'

The minotaur blinks twice, looks down at Percival, and

asks almost conversationally, 'Are you sure about this, Percival? I mean, you have not crossed the line yet. You can still claim the role of advisor and sit this one out.'

I start. Did he just offer Percival a way out? Will he take it?

Percival takes a step forward so he is in line with me before squaring his shoulders. 'I, Percival of the Wyld Woods Tree Clan, seek entry to the centre of the maze.'

The glow in the minotaur's eyes softens a little as he regards the sprite. 'That is a shame. You know I cannot treat you any differently to the others.'

Percival nods. 'I am aware of that, and I would be insulted if you did.'

The minotaur raises his weapons and crosses his arms. The friendly chat with his mate is obviously over, and we are back in quest mode.

'All right. Prepare to be obliterated.'

· · ✦ · ·

The minotaur's challenge fills the room, freezing me in place. Okay, so this is real now. I need to fight. Legs, move. Legs?

My legs are not listening. Taking a deep breath, I hold it together—just. Then the minotaur swings his mighty weapons. Finally, my legs get the message, but they move ever so slowly. I'm only saved from being crushed because the minotaur is so tall, I am able to step to one side and duck. Still, the wake of his swinging arm nearly causes me to lose my footing.

'Split up,' Pris yells, and I edge away from her sideways.

Actual sparks fly up from the stone as the sword strikes it at the end of its arc. The minotaur lifts his weapon for another attack. I don't move fast enough, and a burning slice of pain near my ankle causes me to stumble.

I glance down to find the blade cut right through my boot. I expect to see blood gushing from the gash, but there is barely a trickle. If a nick hurts like that, I hate to think what a full-blown strike will do.

I rejoin the fight to find the minotaur bearing down on Pris. He is totally ignoring Percival, which is allowing the sprite to slip in behind the beast and run for the door. Now I understand what Pris was whispering about before the fight.

When he reaches it, I expect him to slip through to safety. Instead, he turns to watch the battle. He can't be planning to help out in some way, can he?

A change in the air alerts me another swing is coming my way, and I dodge. For the second time, I am not quite quick enough. One of the mace spikes catches my arm and slices through both shirt and skin. At this rate my fight will be less of a battle and more a death by a thousand cuts.

I block out the pain and bite back my dismay as the minotaur raises the mace and prepares to take a swing at Pris. She is backed against a wall with nowhere to go. My eyes widen as the mace shimmers before my eyes.

'Duck,' Pris yells, and I do as she commands, shielding myself from splinters of wood and metal as the mace is blown apart.

I shake off shards of debris as I steal a quick glance at Pris. Apart from a couple of wounds on her face, she is okay. She wipes hair out of her eyes and looks up defiantly at the minotaur. Is she grinning? Yep. Then again, so would I be if I had come up with a move like that.

My relief turns to fear as the minotaur grips his sword,

preparing to retaliate. There is no thinking, just action. I reach over my shoulder and grasp one of the arrows sticking out of the top of my backpack. I rush at the creature, yelling at the top of my lungs. With all my might, I force the metal tip into a meaty part of the minotaur's calf and dodge away.

The minotaur turns as if in slow motion, sword raised above his head, and glares at me, I think less in anger, more in shock. He's already pegged Pris as the main threat, but now he can't ignore me. I may not be the warrior Pris is, but I will not let him hurt her if I can help it.

I'm dizzy from fear and the adrenaline rush as the minotaur reaches down and removes the arrow as if it were a minor irritation. He flings it behind him, narrowly missing Percival, and swings back around to face his prey —Pris.

I may not have injured him, but I did buy Pris enough time to slip further around past the minotaur and towards the door. When he sees this, he roars in anger, his red eyes blazing. He moves forward, swinging his gleaming blade at Pris. She ducks and dives, trying to turn the creature around, but even I can see she is slowing down. She will not be able to keep this up for much longer.

I only have my knife left, and I'm not sure what I can do with that. Whatever I decide to do, I must do it soon, or goodness knows what will happen to Pris.

I rake the room with my eyes, searching for something... anything that might help me. Pris is using her magic to pick up shards of the mace and is flinging them at the minotaur. He swats them away like flies, but they are distracting him. A sliver of metal finally hits home, and the minotaur ignores it. Pris's shoulders slump. Desperation and exhaustion shine in her eyes as they meet mine, but what can *I* do against the huge beast?

At the back of the room, Percival is jumping up and down, trying to get my attention. It is difficult to make out what he is saying over the minotaur's grunts and roars.

His voice finally breaches my ears. 'Snake, it is up to you now. Use your magic.'

Use my magic? What does he mean? What use is lock picking when the beast is bearing down on Pris?

In a last-ditch effort, I yell, 'Hey you, big and ugly— over here.'

The minotaur turns his head and grins. 'I'm saving you for dessert,' he says and turns back round to Pris.

Again, all I have done is gain her a moment to catch her breath and a slightly better position to make a run for the door. It is not enough.

Percival yells again. 'Remember who you are and what your magic is.'

What is he saying? Who I am? I'm a gnome? No, hold on, I'm only part gnome—I also have elf blood. Does that mean my bindings are not as strong as the other gnomes? Can I do some higher magic? Can I move or change something to save Pris?

I study my surroundings. It will have to be small, as I haven't done anything like this before. There's nothing in the room. It's bare except for... the pavers. I focus on the stone directly under the minotaur's foot as his big fist comes down towards Pris. I move a paver up, then quickly drop it again. The minotaur loses his footing, and the blow that would have certainly knocked her out only glances past her cheek.

While Pris shakes her head and tries to refocus on the fight, I move the paving stone under his other foot, and the minotaur stumbles to one knee. He turns his head to glare at me before launching back to his feet.

I might be your dessert, but I'm going to give you indigestion.

Pris runs a hand over her eyes and wobbles a little. That blow must have been harder than I thought. When she catches my eye, I direct her gaze to another paver and move it. Her wide eyes meet mine, showing me she's worked out my plan. She wobbles the stones in front of the beast as he turns and steps towards me. He trips and is forced to use his sword to stop from falling.

I glance towards Pris, and she slips closer towards Percival while shaking stones around the minotaur's feet. I do the same, concentrating on moving him away from the door when I can. One last effort and we raise the stones he stands on so the minotaur almost touches the roof, then drop them to the ground. As the beast falls, arms swinging, we rush to the doors.

Percival frantically reaches for the door handle, misses, then grabs it firmly and turns it. There is a thud behind us, and the sprite yells, 'Hurry, before he regains his feet.'

The minotaur's roar shakes the foundations almost as much as our magic did, and I slip, banging into Pris as footsteps thud from behind.

Percival wrenches open the door, and we pile over the threshold in a tangle of gnome, elf, and sprite limbs. The floor rocks and another roar sounds out, and I cover my ears as the sound almost bursts my ear drums. I grab for Pris, wanting to have her close by as death meets us. Then I realise the roar is not one of anger or a battle cry. Is that the sound of the minotaur laughing?

CHAPTER 13

Did We Win?

I disentangle my limbs and try to sit up. My body doesn't want to obey, so I sink back on the cold stone and try to get my bearings. Everything is fuzzy and the room is spinning. That blow to the head must have affected me more than I thought.

I need to take stock of the damage. Okay, a little at a time. I wiggle my fingers, then try to lift my arm. I push down panic as I realise I can't feel it. Snake groans, and suddenly my arm is free. I blow out a sigh of relief.

Concentrating, I move my toes inside my boots. Yep, they're working, but something pressing against my right ankle. I manage to raise my head enough to identify the problem. My foot is stuck between the door and the jamb. The minotaur swims into view as my vision clears, his sword slung casually over his shoulder. My ears are ringing, and everything sounds like someone has turned the volume down, but I'm pretty sure from the way he is baring his teeth that he is laughing.

Anger burns in my gut. He is laughing at us. We fought

against a mythical creature from legend, and although we didn't defeat him, we made it to the centre of the maze.

'I have not had this much fun in years. You have done well, my little friends. You almost made it,' he says, leering, or is that a grin?

'Wait. What do you mean we "almost" made it?' Snake asks before my brain is able to form the words.

The minotaur points at our feet, which slipped back into the room as we tumbled to the ground. 'You have not yet crossed the threshold.' He reaches down to the floor as he speaks.

Snake and I draw our legs back, but Percival is still trying to sit up and is unable to move quickly enough. The minotaur's massive hand closes around him, hauling him into a bear hug.

The creature stares down at us, and I notice his eyes no longer glow red, but are dark and liquid like a cow's, or a bull's, I suppose I should say.

The minotaur offers us a choice. 'So my friends, what say you now? Will you finish your quest and leave your friend to his fate? Or will you try and save him?'

I rise shakily to my feet and turn to Snake. His eyes plead with me, but I don't know what he is asking. I want to get away from this monster, but I won't leave Percival behind. All I want Snake to do is say we are a team, that we stand together, but a small part of me fears he might put saving his mother first, and no one would blame him if he did.

'Go,' Percival begs. 'I was not truly a part of this quest. I was only a helper. You can still retrieve the object and ask the Queen to save your parents.'

'No, we wouldn't be here if you hadn't helped us,' Snake says. My heart glows as he confirms he and I stand as one on this.

'We won't leave you behind,' I agree as Snake rises to his feet and tries to shake off his injuries.

He stands shoulder to shoulder with me, and together we face our common foe.

'Put Percival down, and we will finish our fight,' I say.

'No.' Percival wriggles in distress. 'You must not fail because of me.'

'But what about the boon you wish to ask from the Queen should we succeed?' I ask.

He shakes his head, and the sorrow his eyes pierces my soul. 'I am not sure that matters any more. I believe what you are doing here is part of something much bigger, something that affects us all.' The words are said so softly, I'm not sure I hear him correctly. Then he announces loudly and firmly, 'I waited this long. I can wait a little longer.'

Snake's fingers entwine through mine. I lean into him and whisper, 'Something happened to Percival last night. He seems both... well... broken and resolute. We can't leave him behind to be the minotaur's plaything. It wouldn't be right.'

'You can barely stand, my shoulder is killing me, and our weapons are gone. What can we do?' He sounds exhausted, defeated. Then he stands straighter and squares his shoulders. 'Can we try a distraction and hope he lets go of Percival?'

I consider the idea, but my head is still swimming, and I can't think of anything that might work. Finally, I admit defeat and tell him, 'I don't think so.'

'Then we must bargain for the minotaur to take me. If you free your parents, they are highborn enough they may be able to pull strings to help my mother. And you are more likely to succeed with Percival than with me because of his friendship with Eleanora.' I lean on his shoulder, and he squeezes my hand. 'You know this is the best option for everyone.'

I hear what he is saying, but I can't agree to this. I can't lose him just when we're… I am not sure what we are, but I am sure I am not going to let him go that easily again. 'What if the minotaur kills you?'

'I'm hoping he won't.' Snake releases my hand and steps over the threshold. I reach out to stop him, but I'm too late.

'I offer myself up instead of Percival,' he announces.

The minotaur bares his teeth, 'I knew there was nobility as well as music in you, boy. You have the heart of a true hero. And you will be a worthy opponent.'

He drops Percival to the ground and waits until the sprite scrambles back over the threshold before taking a battle stance, sword at the ready.

I can't do it. I can't let Snake face the minotaur alone. I glance down at Percival. He meets my gaze square-on, and in answer to the question he reads in my eyes, he moves to stand beside me. We step back into the room and join Snake, ready to fight as a team.

'Stop,' a voice rings out from behind the creature of legend. 'Surely this has gone far enough.'

··◡··

From the recesses of the room, someone asks the minotaur to stop. It takes a while to register, perhaps because my knees are knocking and my heart is pounding so loud, I can hear very little else. I have no idea where my attempt at bravery came from, but it disappeared pretty quickly.

I'm too scared to take my eyes off the minotaur, yet

someone is moving behind the beast. Part of me wants to check this isn't another threat, but quite honestly, I am too bone weary to care.

'Come on, Aeron. I like a good contest as much as the next person, but they won fair and square. You are only drawing this out because they are entertaining you.'

The voice sounds familiar, but I can't quite place it.

'Ah, but the boy stepped back over the line....'

'Only after you taunted them with the sprite. You had your fun. The rules of the maze have been met. You all acquitted yourselves with honour, but you were outsmarted by the children in the end.'

I wanted to argue that we are not children, but I bite back the words. Aggravating our rescuer with petty details will not help our cause. Pris is not so circumspect.

'We're not children,' she says, placing her hands on her hips.

The minotaur laughs, his belly shaking. 'I am hundreds of years old, little elfling, and my friend here is at least three hundred.... You have scarcely begun to breathe by comparison. Hush now, and let your elders talk.'

Pris's jaw is tightening, a sure sign she is annoyed, but even she must admit we *are* children when you consider how old the minotaur is.

'I must say, I am impressed by how the elf and the gnome stood up for the sprite.... They have spunk, I will give them that.' The minotaur strokes his chin with his free hand. 'And they fought with vigour.'

While Aeron is diverted, Percival grabs at mine and Pris's hands, taking the opportunity presented to urge us back into the hallway.

'Aeron, the rules state all the questers need to do is get past you to the door. They did that.'

Our champion is a little closer now, still hidden behind

the minotaur. The voice is *so* familiar. No, I still have no idea who it is.

'But how can I hold my head high and admit I was beaten in combat by two children and a wood sprite?' Aeron wails, carrying on as if his whole world is crumbling. 'The Queen might decide I can no longer be her champion.'

'Oh, really, that's what this is about? You don't want to admit to being beaten by us?' Pris steps forward, hands on hips. She glances at the ground, careful to check she did not inadvertently cross the threshold again. 'You can't admit we won, so you are making things up?'

'Pris!' I force through gritted teeth. 'Must you poke the bear? He may decide to decapitate us just for fun—quest be damned.'

'I take offence at that, young man. I will face anyone in combat, but I do not kill indiscriminately in a fit of pique.'

Honestly, what is going on here? Have I fallen down a rabbit hole into a bizarre new world where common-sense is absent? 'So she can call you a baby, but I can't say you might kill us?'

'I am an honourable creature—'

'It's all right, Aeron. Snake did not mean anything by what he said, did you, Snake?'

A figure moves out of the shadows to the minotaur's right. I stiffen with fright, then relax as I see Fairburn nodding, encouraging me to agree with him.

I guess needs must. 'Um, yes, I am sorry. I did not mean to call you dishonourable,' I tell Aeron, when what I really want to say is, 'What in the hell are you doing here, Fairburn?'

'Good.' The centaur smiles. 'Now, are we all agreed that the children made it to the door and so are allowed to proceed?'

'No, I will not admit defeat.' Aeron crosses his arms over his chest and refuses to budge.

Fairburn and Pris both sigh, but it is Percival who breaks the deadlock. The sprite steps around me so he can be both seen and heard. 'You were not defeated, Aeron. Not in battle, at least. I slipped behind you, and Pris and Snake used magic to outsmart you to get to the door.'

Aeron ponders his words for a moment, and I almost blurt, "You can't seriously be considering this?", but I wisely bite my tongue.

After a long while, the minotaur agrees. 'Yes, I can live with that. I am happy to tell people I was outwitted.'

I shake my head, unable to believe I am part of this madness. I'm too tired to argue that this is merely semantics and means nothing. Besides, it means we won, and we get to enter the centre of the maze—all three of us together.

·· ❤ ··

I turn on my heel, thinking it might be a good idea to move before Aeron changes his mind. I mean, he might throw another hissy fit and decide Snake and I should fight him again.

Striding down the darkened corridor, I head towards the light in the distance. I pull up short as the light is blocked out and a dark shadow moves towards us. I slump against the wall. I can't do it. I just can't deal with any more surprises today. The shadow can bleeding well have me.

The shape saunters closer, resolving itself into a dragon. It is a sign of how exhausted I am that it takes a moment for my mind to process that I am staring at an honest-to-god dragon.

My new nightmare towers at least two feet taller than I am and glows a deep purple in the half-light. I want to reach out and touch the pearly scales, but I'm pretty sure that's not the done thing. Especially not when it is smiling down at me like I'm its next meal.

My first thought is, did Percival know about this? I mean, he did mention dragons. When he pulls up beside me and exclaims, 'What now? A dragon? What more are they going to throw at us?' I am thinking perhaps not.

Some part of me is aware Snake is not with us, but by now my whole world is those dragon eyes. They are drawing me in. A part of me knows this is not a good thing, but I am powerless to do anything about it.

Little elf, what do you want here?

The voice in my head is deep and vibrates through my body. The dragon is talking to me in my mind. Cool! Deep in the recesses of my consciousness, someone is screaming, 'Wake up! You're caught in a dragon thrall.' I think it might be me, but I'm too blissed out to listen.

'Away with you, my young friend. I granted these three entry, and they are under my protection.' Aeron's voice comes from far away. It really is a very dreamy voice.

The dragon snorts, and the bliss disappears, but it doesn't release me. *What is it you want?* The dragon almost whispers the words, and I sense it is seeking an answer to the question rather than trying to frighten me away.

A way to free my parents, I tell it, trying not to appear cowed even though my knees have turned to jelly under his lizard-like gaze.

I am a female, and I think you want more than you are admitting to even yourself. The dragon snorts again. *You seek your place in the world—in both worlds. I hope you find what you are looking for.*

She blinks, and it is like there was an elastic band holding me in place, and as she releases it, I stumble backwards into Snake, and he wraps his arms around me.

'Are you okay.'

'I'm not sure,' I tell him, and he pulls me closer.

'What are we waiting for?' Aeron grumbles.

He must have pushed Snake in the back, because he throws himself forward and I move with him, landing face-first in the belly of the dragon.

I freeze. The sensation is not unpleasant. Her skin is soft and cool, and I imagine this is what faceplanting into a very large snake would feel like. I turn my head to breathe, and one of the sharper scales surrounding her belly cuts into my forehead, and my blood trickles down her skin. Instinctively, I try to reach up, but I find I can't move.

The dragon steps back, and I'm frozen in place by a blanket of warm air. The air gently pushes me upright until I am on my feet, then it simply dissolves.

'Th-thank you,' I stutter.

The dragon bares her teeth, and I wonder if she's decided to eat me after all. She snorts. 'You would not even make an entree. We princesses must look out for each other, so it is written.'

She turns away, sweeping her long tail in close so she doesn't bowl us over, before dropping onto all fours and leading the way into the room at the end of the corridor.

Amazement tinges Snake's next words. 'So, that was a smile?'

I don't respond. I sense something portentous in the dragon's words, and her tone suggests I should understand what she means. Her words distract me as I head towards our goal—the centre of the maze.

'Does Snow White spring to mind?' Snake asks as

Percival drops to a knee, mumbling something about Queen Ariana.

'What?' I drag my gaze back from the undulating form of the dragon as Snake's words sink through the haze in my brain.

Snake is right. Directly in front of us, in the centre of the room, is a woman asleep in a glass coffin. Her red-gold hair frames a delicate, fine-boned face. The lines are too sharp for her to be considered beautiful, but she could be described as regal. She has been dressed as if for a funeral in an emerald-green gown piped with gold, and her hands had been laid across her stomach. Apart from her pallor and the fact that her chest does not rise or fall, she could be just sleeping.

Curled up in front of the coffin's plinth is a huge emerald dragon. It opens a yellow eye and glares balefully at us before turning its attention to Aeron and Fairborn. The flicker of its snake-like pupil tells me it is probably communicating with the elder creatures.

I allow myself to relax a little and be dazzled by the fairy-tale display of magic. In my dreams, this was what the World Below was like until I stepped through the gateway a few days before and saw the reality. Then it hits me like a sledgehammer—the dragon and the woman are the only things in the centre of the maze except for us. Are they what we were sent to retrieve?

Snake must have arrived at this conclusion at exactly the same time. His eyes widen before his face settles into a mask of dismay.

Leaning in towards Snake, I whisper, 'Who is she?'

Snake half turns, but can't take his eyes off the woman. 'I have no idea.'

I shift my focus to Percival, but his face is blank and he

is lost to us again. Before I can ask Fairburn, Snake's voice fills the chamber.

'Are we here for the woman or the dragon? And just how do you expect us to take either of them out of here?'

⁂

My voice echoes around the room, and I try not to start at the sound. I really hope someone will step forward and tell me I'm wrong. I want them to tell me it is the ring the woman wears, or perhaps a dragon scale, that we are to take back to prove we made it to the centre of the maze.

The room is silent, and the longer it stays that way, the more I'm sure that my first guess was right.

The smaller dragon curls up by the larger one—her mother, I assume, because dragons are generally solitary creatures—as Fairburn and Aeron take up positions behind the glass case.

Percival has dropped to his knees and is muttering something about the poor Queen and us of all being doomed. Is that Queen Ariana in there? No wonder people haven't seen her for a while.

I raise my gaze and stare directly at Fairburn. 'What's going on here?' I ask. 'Did the council send us on a false quest?'

The centaur does not answer. His head drops and his face softens as he looks at the Queen.

I do not get annoyed often, but I am angry now. I risked everything to try and save my mother, and they played me for a fool. The Queen is dead. How will I ever save Mum now?

'It is time for the truth, Fairburn,' a voice rumbles through the cavernous space.

I sweep the chamber with my gaze, but no one else has entered. I can't make out who spoke. The larger dragon raises her head and stares straight at the three of us. A sigh from Fairburn draws my attention back to him.

'No, Snake, it was not in vain, but nor were we completely honest with you either,' the centaur admits.

Pris moves beside me and takes my hand before saying, 'I think it is well past time for the truth, don't you?'

I don't know if it is because she is such a force to be reckoned with, or whether it's because she is a princess, but people listen when she speaks. And I'm beyond grateful they're listening now.

'I think it is the least you owe Snake, Percival, and me after what we went through the last few days,' Pris finishes.

The younger dragon snorts, in approval I think, and Fairburn colours. He glances at Percival, who is still on a knee.

'Percival, I am so sorry to find out about your father. His end is quite close now, but I know he asked you to come back and finish what you started with Princess Priscilla and Snake. I want to thank you for your sacrifice,' Fairburn says.

What? Something happened to Percival's father? That must have been where he was last night.

I place a hand on his shoulder. 'Percival, you should have said. I'm so sorry.'

Pris helps him to his feet and bends down to hug him. Percival bristles at her touch but does not move away from her. He doesn't speak, but then again, he is a very private creature.

We place Percival between us and turn back to Fairburn. 'Percival's sacrifice makes it even more important that you come clean with us,' Pris says, her arm still draped over the sprite's shoulder. As she faces Fairburn, she looks fiercer than I have ever seen her, like a momma bear protecting her offspring.

Aeron smiles. 'Yeah, Fairburn. Time for the truth.'

I think he is enjoying the fact that Fairburn is now the one being brought to task.

Fairburn sighs. 'I am a guard, a soldier. Words are not my tools, and I did not want to be the one to tell you this… but… as Queen Ariana's protector, I am the only one allowed to come here.'

'Is she still alive?' Pris demands.

'In a way,' Fairburn responds. 'Magic is holding her on the precipice between life and death.'

So, it *is* the Queen in the glass box. She is alive, but she is definitely not in a position to help us.

'Where do I start?' Fairburn speaks as if to himself. 'Do I explain the magic or the politics or….'

'For goodness sakes, centaur.' The larger dragon's voice rumbles in my head. 'Let me. Children, I am Am'rena, Queen of the Dragons and soul sister of Queen Ariana. Together we have tended the magical core of our world for over three hundred years.'

'You were there…,' Percival whispers, awe in his voice. 'I remember… not quite… but….'

The dragon continues over him. 'The magical flow has been slowing for some time, and the work we are doing to keep it moving made the Queen sick. Fairburn brought her here a month or so ago, placed her in stasis, and we have been trying to cure her since then.'

Everyone knows the Queen, or King, in rare instances, of the World Below is the only creature able to access the magical flow, but this is the first I have heard of a dragon partnership. I am still processing this while Pris kneels to

225

better converse with the dragon. I guess not having learnt about magical history means she is more able to just accept this and feels able to talk to a dragon without being invited.

Pris's head drops to one side as if she is trying to make some sort of connection with Am'rena. 'Do you know what the problem is with the flow of magic?' Pris asks out loud.

'In the past, the Queen of the Seelie Court and the King of the Unseelie Court would work with their dragon sister and brother, and everything flowed smoothly. When the World Below sealed itself off, something happened to the river, and it was never quite right again, not even after the barrier was partially opened.'

'I'm not surprised,' I blurt, immediately identifying the problem. I falter when all eyes in the room turn to me.

'Why not enlighten us, then.' Fairburn's words drip with sarcasm. 'I mean, it took our scholars almost a hundred years to come up with a solution.'

Am'rena snorted. 'Don't be so quick to dismiss him, centaur. Your scholars are hampered by politics and a limited view of the world. This elf-gnome has the benefit of a different education, and I see he knows the answer.'

I raise an eyebrow. *Are you reading my mind?* I ask in my head.

Snorting again, which I now believe might be a dragon laugh 'Yes.' There is no apology. 'Tell them.'

If the Queen of Dragons has faith in me, I won't doubt myself. 'Once you block a river, dam it, so to speak, the water changes course. If you unblock it again, it might flow as swiftly, but will probably take a different path. If you only unblock some of it, it will never run the same again. I imagine the magical flow to be the same.'

Fairburn nods curtly, confirming my assessment. 'Although it is much worse. Magic flows like an infinity sign. We blocked the flow at the crossover point, which left magic stagnating in the World Above and the World Below. This caused a blight in our world, and the Dark Ages in the World Above. When we opened some of the gates and allowed some of our people to go back and forth, the blight was eradicated, but magic was never the same.'

'While I work with The King of Dragons in the World Above to do our bit, your King and Queen have not worked together to do theirs,' Am'rena added.

'You're telling me a dragon lives in my world?' Pris laughs out loud.

This is what she finds astonishing? Sometimes I have no idea how her mind works, but I guess that's part of her charm.

'No,' Am'rena rumbles. 'He does not live there. We all live in the Dragon Realm, in the World Between. He does visit through the portal at Loch Ness though.'

'The Loch Ness Monster,' Pris and I say together, then lock eyes, laughing.

This story is too bizarre, and amusing though it is, it does not explain why we are here. I decide to take a leaf from Pris's book and go the direct route.

'I appreciate your need to sort out magic and wake the Queen, but why involve us?'

'Yes,' Pris says, rising to her feet so she can better face Fairburn. 'I think it's about time you tell us why you brought us here.'

. . ◡ . .

I am filthy, tired, wounded, and a little unsteady on my feet. I want a soak in a bath and sleep a comfy bed, but even more, I want to know why we are here in the centre of the maze when we cannot remove anything to finish our quest.

Fairburn clears his throat, and his hooves shuffle. 'Right, the Queen has been sick for a while, something her closest advisors and I kept from the rest of the realm. Unfortunately, Bernais's network of spies found out about it.'

'He has always been a snake in the grass, putting his own interests before the realm. I banned him from the maze. I will not allow him near me,' Aeron states, banging his sword on the floor for emphasis.

I don't need convincing. I already knew Bernais had something to do with what is going on. Even so, I'm not sure he would harm the Queen, as that would not serve his purpose. He would, however, try to save her so he could claim the glory.

'You're not telling us anything they aren't talking about in every village market,' Snake says, earning a dour look from Fairburn.

I flash Snake a "let him finish" look before encouraging the centaur. 'Go on,' I urge.

'Hoping for the Queen's imminent demise, Bernais began jockeying for position, hoping to counter anyone she nominated as heir. You, Snake, are here because the Queen indicated your clan's punishment was at an end and that you all should be raised to elven status. Bernais could not permit this because the balance of power would change so much, and it might shift out of his—'

'He accused my mother, hoping he could delay proceedings,' Snake interrupts, bitterness in his voice. 'My family already worked that out.'

Fairburn nods. 'I am afraid this is just his first move—'

'Because he will raise the fact that my father married a person of mixed race,' Snake finishes again. Then he stands straighter, as if he has just thought of something. 'Bernais wanted me to do this to get me out of the way and to further sully the name of my family. Wouldn't it be useful for him to leak that the reason I failed was because I was not of pure blood?'

Percival stirs beside me. 'That would be just like him, to use that against you. He despises anyone who is not an elf, but, if it is at all possible, he despises those of impure blood even more.'

Snake takes a step forward. I can see he is excited about something. 'You, or perhaps the council and you, wanted me to come on this quest, didn't you?'

Fairburn nods encouragingly. 'Can you see why?'

'You want me to help the Queen because by helping her return to full health, she will not only counter Bernais, but it will give her even more reason to raise my family to their proper status.' Snake finishes, then stops, a frown creasing his brow. 'What made you think I would be of any help?'

Fairburn smiles and my heart literally flutters. 'Because you are the son of your father and grandfather.'

Snake seems to accept that answer, and I can see he is about to ask what Fairburn wants him to do, but the centaur is still speaking. I am sure I know what he is going to say, but I want to hear it.

'And you, Priscilla—you are here because your mother is the Queen's closest relative but chose a life in the World Above. When she did, she relinquished her claim to the throne—'

'But she didn't relinquish mine,' I finish. 'Bernais wanted to bring me to the World Below to get rid of me so no one could stand against him.'

All the pieces click together. I know who I am and why I am both listened to and hated so much, and why I was attacked in the World Above, and why my parents kept me away from their home. They were protecting me from this.

'And now you want me to help the Queen so Bernais does not rule in the World Below,' I finish.

Although I am pleased I finally have some answers, I'm not sure how I feel about this. Okay, Bernais can never be King, that is clear, but I don't want to be Queen of the World Below—ever.

Am'rena snorts. 'You get ahead of yourself, girl. Your Queen can still live for a few hundred more years if we save her in time, and there are others who might be pardoned with a stronger claim to the throne than you.'

'Oh.' I hadn't thought about where my mother might sit in the order of succession. And perhaps I have other cousins and such.

'The most important thing is to save the Queen and bring stability back to our realm,' Fairburn tells us.

Snake cuts straight to the point. 'So, what do you want us to do?'

'We want you to finish your quest. You were tasked with bringing what is in the middle of the maze out, and that is Queen Ariana. Only she can't be moved until she is cured and the magical flow is restored,' Fairburn says.

I close my eyes. My brain is sluggish, but it is putting together the puzzle in front of me, and I am sure I know what Fairburn will ask.

'You must all go to the Unseelie Court and convince the King to return here to at least help heal the Queen, and preferably to work with her to heal the magical flow.'

I knew it. Something else occurs to me. Although I do not want to leave Snake behind, perhaps he can go back to the Capitol and keep an eye on our families. And Percival will want to return to his family so he can say a proper goodbye to his father.

'I know that I must go to the Unseelie Court to petition on behalf of my—is she my great-aunt?—but why must Snake and Percival go with me?' I ask.

Percival takes my hands, and I force myself not to start in surprise, but my eyes are instantly drawn to him.

'My father told me something bigger than us was happening and that I had a role to play. He would not tell me what it was, but I see what it is now. I am to be the one to introduce you at the Unseelie Court,' he tells me.

'You are?' I ask.

'Of course. I knew many people there before they were sent to the World Above. I must go and help you.'

I want Percival to come with me, but it would be selfish to pull him away from his family at a time like this. 'But, Percival, what about your father?'

He shrugs. 'We have said our goodbyes. I will celebrate his life at the thirty days gathering. I am at your disposal until then.' He gives my hand a small squeeze and warmth fills me. While I could do this alone, I don't really want to. Percival being there will definitely make things easier for me.

'None of you have to go,' Fairburn interrupts, 'but I believe you are more likely to succeed if you all go together. We will give you some privacy so you can discuss what you want to do.'

CHAPTER 14

Saving The World

I am angry at Eleanora for not telling me everything about the quest and what the council had been up to, yet I'm also grateful. I have cut myself off from my true self while I have been her familiar in the World Above, allowing her to direct my actions rather than making choices about my life.

I now realise that she wanted me to be a part of this quest because she understands me. She knew if Pris and Snake were going to fail, I would help them and become a part of the quest, and therefore be able to petition the Queen to see her way clear to returning me to a full sprite. This is what Princess Petunia had always intended once her sister took the throne, but she was never able to do it because she was banished.

Now I see Eleanora wants more for me. She wants me to believe I am more than her eyes and ears. She wants to show me my own value so that when I face a Queen and ask for my reward, I know exactly what I am asking for and that I deserve it.

I will go to the Unseelie Court. I do not need to listen

in on Pris and Snake arguing about who should go. I leave them to withdraw into the hallway for some privacy and join Fairburn and Aeron, who seems much more friendly now that he is not trying to cut me down with his sword.

What I need to do before we leave the centre of the maze is have Fairburn tell Pris the one piece of information he is holding back. It is only fair she knows exactly what she is getting herself into. As I approach, I try not to look at the Queen. It disturbs me to see her so lifeless. I clear my throat.

'You need to tell Pris *everything* before we leave,' I say, and Fairburn turns in surprise.

He crosses his arms over an impossibly muscled chest. 'Why, Percival? What good will it do?'

I stare at him in wonder. I know a centaur's heart beats differently to the hearts of other creatures. They run in herds and do not mate for life. But Fairburn cannot be this insensitive to how finding this out from someone else will affect the princess.

'Coming to the World Below and trying to save her parents is unsettling for Pris. She is trying to get a sense of who she is, and that changes almost every day. Surely it would be better if we told her everything,' I argue. 'Having her whole history would give her confidence in the court.'

'It is her family's job to tell her about this. I have been given no leave to pass on that information, and I expect you to keep it to yourself as well,' Fairburn instructs me.

He is very scary when he uses that commanding tone. I also sense he will not be swayed from his position.

'As you wish. But do not complain to me when things fall apart later,' I sniff and turn on my heel.

Pausing before going through the door, I turn back. 'Out of interest, who ordered you not to tell the princess?'

There are only a few creatures who Fairburn would

consider able to command him, and I am curious about who is pulling his strings.

Fairburn strokes his chin. For a moment I think he isn't going to answer. Then he says, 'Her father asked me not to say anything.'

From Fairburn's smirk, I have not succeeded in keeping my surprise from showing on my face.

'There is nothing sinister in this,' the centaur adds. 'You know more than anyone does that Princess Pricilla's family situation is rather… um… complex. Malachi simply requested that she be told about her heritage by her family. I believe that request should be respected.'

His dark eyes pin me, and I glare back at him. I can see Pris's father's point, but he would have no way of knowing how much Pris craves that knowledge, or how this could impact her emotionally to have it withheld.

I turn and watch her as she argues with Snake, and I hope that Snake refuses to be left behind because I sense she is going to need him when we get to the Unseelie Court.

.·◡·.

The determined set of Pris's jaw tells me her mind is made up. I would bet my entire instrument collection that she believes I will go along with whatever she says too. Clearly, the knock to the head scrambled her brains.

'You aren't Queen yet, so don't even try and command me.' I'm aiming for levity, hoping to charm her.

'But someone needs to be looking after our parents,' she presses.

She knows my weak points, but I can come up with

something better. 'I think Fairburn can handle their security more effectively than I can.'

As I mention the centaur, her eyes take on this funny, googly, glazed look. Hold on, does she fancy that muscle-bound oaf? After all his double-dealing? Jealousy gnaws at my stomach. 'Pris, is this because you don't want me around?'

Her eyes clear and she frowns at me. 'What? No!'

The green-eyed monster then gets hold of my mouth and says, 'Would you prefer Fairburn escorts you?'

'Oh my god, you're jealous. Just because I admire his muscles—'

'I'm not—really, I'm not. That was just….'

I'm not sure what it is. I am tired, and I thought this would all be over when we made it to the centre of the maze. Now here I am, arguing with Pris when all I want to do is pull her into my arms and tell her I am going with her, and no argument she can come up with will change my mind.

What a great idea!

I wrap my arms around her and pull her to me. I draw her in closer. She leans into me, and just for a moment, I simply enjoy the feel of holding her.

'I am going with you,' I say gently but firmly. 'Not because I don't want to let you out of my sight, although that is part of it. I am going because I need to, if only to prove to Bernais that I am every bit as good as he and his elf friends are.'

She sighs and her body finally relaxes in my arms. 'I know you are better than him.' Her voice is muffled as she speaks into my neck.

'Thank you, but I think I want to prove it to myself. I want to stand up and be counted. Besides, I believe Fairburn is holding something back, not only about you, but about me as well. Something is going on at the Unseelie Court, something I can help with, and I want to find out what it is.'

Pris snuggles closer into my neck. 'I like this new you, and I love how you haven't told me that you shouldn't be with a potential heir to the crown.'

I laugh. 'You know, I hadn't even thought about that. Anyway, Am'rena told you not to get too ahead of yourself.'

Pris's laughter tickles my neck, and I smile. I step back, bend my neck, and touch my lips to hers. She tilts her head and slightly parts her lips, and I accept her invitation. Closing my eyes as the kiss deepens, I lose myself in the feel of her body against mine.

'Have you decided?' Fairburn's voice booms from the other room.

I groan. For a moment I had forgotten where we were and that we weren't alone. 'I hope we get a good night's sleep in a real bed before we head out,' I whisper.

Pris's lips twitch into a smile. 'Sleep?' she jokes, and I groan again.

· · ·◡· ·

We walk hand in hand back into the centre of the maze. The cool air brushes against my hot cheeks, and I am sure my lips are swollen from the kiss. Fairburn takes one look at us and smirks knowingly. My face is burning, and this is one of the times my darker complexion comes in handy, hopefully hiding my embarrassment.

Beside me, Snake glares defiantly at the centaur, daring him to say something. My lips curl into a smile—my hero. I slide an arm around his waist so we present a united front, and Snake responds by slipping his arm around me. Percival moves to take the place on my other side, and I drop a hand onto his shoulder. My team is here.

'We will all go to petition the King of The Unseelie Court,' I say.

'Excellent,' Fairburn says as if he expected nothing less. 'Am'ratha will fly you, and her brother Ed'rathe is waiting outside to transport Percival and Snake.'

What did he just say? 'You want us to fly there? On dragons?'

He must be joking. I mean, this is like something out of a fantasy book, not something I ever expected to happen in my actual life.

'How else did you think you would travel from here to there?' Am'rena rumbles. 'My children will transport you in the blink of an eye. There is no time for dilly-dallying.'

Besides, it will give us a little time to bond, Am'ratha says.

I do a double take. *Bond?*

I look at Snake to get his take on this, but he is still engaged in a staring contest with Fairburn. Males!

Am'rena raises her head, and her golden eyes capture mine. *This is just between us,* she tells me, confirming my suspicion that no one else can hear our conversations. *Am'ratha is one of my potential heirs. She has been paired with you, and your travelling together will give her an opportunity to assess whether or not she can work with you in the future.*

My first instinct is to object. Tell them I am not an heir and never will be.

Unaware of what is going on with the dragons, Snake asks, 'You want us to go now? What about our packs and things?'

'And you can't expect them to turn up at the Unseelie Court looking like this.' Percival indicates our outfits. He, of course, looks like he has showered and changed, which he might well have done while we were… um… talking. 'And they smell,' he adds, his nose wrinkling in distaste.

Fairburn shrugs and his muscles ripple. I try to contain myself, as I don't want Snake getting the wrong idea again. A sigh escapes me. Snake and the promise of that kiss pop into my mind, and I realise that if we are to travel now, it will have to remain a promise. I lean against Snake, and I can't help thinking this is more like a punishment than a reward for making it to the maze's centre.

Snake leans his head against mine and whispers in my ear, his tone teasing, 'While you were fixated on his muscles, he said we can leave our packs behind.'

I smile and squeeze his hand. No need to tell him it was the memory of our kiss that distracted me.

'I am sure those at the Unseelie Court will take care of your needs when you arrive, including providing bathing facilities and… beds….' His eyes sparkle. 'For sleeping.'

I'm not sure I like his innuendo. It is too close to where my own thoughts were for comfort.

'So, if you are ready.' Fairburn gestures to a door that miraculously appears to his right. It swings open, giving us a glimpse of the sun setting over the top of the Wyld Woods. Have we only been in here for a few hours? It feels like days.

I step outside to find myself face to face with the most magnificent golden dragon. *Wow.*

Why, thank you, he says into my mind, and my cheeks heat.

'Em'rethe, it's not polite to read the thoughts of other creatures without their knowledge,' his sister admonishes as she exits behind me.

'I know, but she does think I'm beautiful.' Em'rethe preens.

'She thinks you're showy and conceited.' Am'ratha sticks her nose in the air, exuding superiority as she joins her brother. They both lower themselves to the ground before looking expectantly at us.

'Time to mount up,' Fairburn orders.

I want to argue, but everything in this moment is so surreal. There are two dragons behaving like human siblings, and I still can't believe I am supposed to ride a dragon like something out of some fantasy tale. With all the things I have been through in this maze, it is this one thing that has me frozen to the spot, unable to even twitch a muscle.

It's easy. Place your foot on my leg, grip a scale, and pull yourself up. Your legs go around my neck. Hold on to any scale, and I will keep you in place with my magic. We are not flying far, just a hop through the portal, then on to the castle. You'll be fine, Princess. I will keep you safe.

That's easy for you to say.

Am'ratha snorts and Fairburn pushes me gently in the back. 'It is said to be one of life's most exhilarating experiences,' he encourages.

Snake and Percival are already around the other side of their mount. *If Snake can do this, I can*, I tell myself, although I would really rather it was me riding with him than Percival.

No, you do not. I am by far the better flyer, Am'ratha chuckles.

It's Am'ratha's snipe at her brother that finally moves me. Their interplay is so… normal. It allows me to relax a little.

I follow the dragon's instructions and am soon in place. The ground is so far away even though she is still sitting. I sense her muscles bunching, and I am thrown forward. I grip one of the hard scales protecting her neck. It is cool and silky beneath my fingers.

Sorry, you are my first ever rider.

I smile. *Then we are well suited because you're the first dragon I've ever ridden.*

I sense her relax beneath me before she pushes herself onto her hind legs. The evening sun reflects on her skin, colouring it in swirling purple hues. My grip on her scales tightens as my body rocks forward with her movement, and my stomach lurches as she leaps upwards.

'Safe journey and good luck,' Fairburn yells as Am'ratha's powerful wings unfurl and we take to the sky.

Acknowledgments

It takes a team to produce a book, and I am very lucky to have a great support team.

To my arc readers Sandy and Tracey. Thanks for reading this before it looked lovely and all your amazing feedback really made me think about how to make this story better.

Also, thank you to the team at Creating Ink, especially Sali Benbow-Powers, and the team at Hot Tree Editing and McKinley Hellennes Krantz for improving my story telling and making it more readable.

As always, my love and thanks to my moral support Jim, and my son Sam for putting up with me when I hide away to finish a book. Without them I wouldn't eat and I would miss every deadline.

I also want to thank the awesome team of authors who joined me in releasing The realm of Darkness Boxset where the digital copy of the first World Below series published. It was a great ride. We made the USA Today Bestseller's list, and it was a blast.

Finally, thank you for reading my musings. If you get a chance please let me know what you think of the book by leaving a review on your favourite site.

About the Author

Vivienne has been writing books since she was fifteen years old, but only friends and family were allowed to read them. Forced to give up work because of family commitments she was encouraged by friends and family to finally put some of her writing out there for others to read.

Born in Invercargill (New Zealand), she has lived in; Dunedin (New Zealand), London (England), Petersfield (England) and currently lives with her husband and son, their dog Trouble and cat Lola in North Sydney (Australia).

When not reading or writing she can be found walking, crocheting, knitting and watching movies.

For future releases and current news you can find Vivienne at www.viviennelfraser.com.au where you can also join my newsletter.

More by Vivienne Lee Fraser

If you enjoyed The World Below, why not try The Guardians of Time Series Time Travel Adventures?

Swagman

What if the Swagman did not die when he jumped into the billabong?

What if he ended up in medieval England embroiled in a plot to set a new king on the throne?

For once in his life Swagman John is lost for words. Accused of stealing the lamb he rescued fears being thrown in jail. But instead of protesting his innocence he backs into the waters of the billabong and falls. Certain he is dead, John cannot believe the lamb when he tells him he has been brought through a time and space portal to Medieval England. When Mistress Barabal and Squire Stanislaus stumble upon John in the New Forest he is taken back to Winchester Castle where he actually finds the King has been killed and his brother Prince Henry is about preparing to take his place and his new friends are assisting him.

Suddenly talking lambs are the least of his worries.

Caught up in political intrigues he does not fully understand, John finds dungeons and magic are not just for fairy tales, and that there are people prepared to go to great lengths to see William the Conquerer's other son crowned king—even as far as murder. Just as John wonders if going to prison for stealing sheep was not a better option all along, he finds there is an even more sinister foe meddling in with history.

Against such odds how can John set history straight so he can return home to his family?

Alchemist

Would you Travel 900 years into the future to save the lives of some dogs?

Alain, Apprentice Apothecary and sometime Alchemist, is on a high after saving the life of his king. After all the excitement he is not content to slip back into everyday life. So when he is offered the chance to travel with his Master to the future and investigate a strange disease in dogs he leaps at the chance.

Taken through a portal to The New Forest in 2017, Alain finds life in Medieval England had not prepared him for a world full of machines where everyone lives in manor houses and there is no real magic. Uncomfortable and homesick he regrets leaving the comforts of home until his new friends decide to help with his investigation. Just when returning home is a real option, they uncover a sinister plot behind the animal illness that threatened more than just family pets.

Will Alain risk everything he holds dear to stop those who threaten the future of mankind?

https://viviennelfraser.com.au/time-guardians
*

Or if you enjoy Fantasy Adventure why not try
The Wizard and The Warrior

Centuries ago prophets predicted the rise of a great wizard and a formidable warrior who would save the people of their land. Now an invasion fleet is heading for Aria, is it time for the Wizard and the Warrior to arise and save them all?

Runaway bride Aliah wants to be more than someone's wife. Fleeing his destiny, Seamus has no idea what he wants from his future. Thrown together by fate, the two journey to the nation's capital; one to warn the king of an impending invasion, the other to do the unthinkable— train to be a wizard.

Their chance encounter takes them on a wild adventure where they must face their pasts and decide their future, all while helping Aria prepare to defend itself.

However, fate has not finished with Seamus and Aliah. In an unexpected twist, they are placed at the very centre of the conflict facing their home, and must decide whether or not to take up the challenge.

With the gods on their side, it should be easy for Aliah and Seamus to identify and locate the real power behind the invasion and find a way to defeat him; all while pulling together a support team and having mid-night lessons to learn how to use their newly acquired magical tokens. Well, it would be if the gods weren't hiding more than they shared.

Aria's future hangs in the balance, can two runaways tip the scales?

What one reader on Amazon said: Great book - it might be targeted at youth readers, but even as an adult, I was hooked on the storyline. Can't wait for the next one!

https://viviennelfraser.com.au/wizard-and-warrior-one